*M*ay I have this dance?"

"You most certainly may." Taking his hand, Rachel rose and stood next to him. He drew her near as she put her hand on his shoulder and swayed with him to the music. The horses continued chewing wild grasses and looked over at them with bored expressions.

But Dirk was not bored. His entire being seemed to be drawn to this woman. She felt right in his arms... She spoke to him in such a forthright, honest manner... She even looked at him right, all alluring eyes and mystery and playfulness. They stared at each other as they turned in their own intimate little world, communicating without words. Instinctively both fought fear as they recognized something neither had felt in some time. Rachel broke away first and sat down on the blanket again. Dirk joined her in silence. They watched the moon rise soon after the sunset, following the same path as its predecessor.

"This is the most beautiful place I've ever visited, Dirk," Rachel whispered. "And I'm scared to death."

"Is it the valley," Dirk asked, gently turning her face toward his, "or me?" He kissed her softly before she could answer, drawing her close, then allowing her to slip back out of their embrace. They sat for a moment, dazed by the whirlwind of emotions, by the romantic setting, but most of all by the kiss.

"It's you," she finally answered.

LISA TAWN BERGREN

Refuge

WATERBROOK
PRESS

REFUGE

PUBLISHED BY WATERBROOK PRESS

2375 Telstar Drive, Suite 160

Colorado Springs, Colorado 80920

A division of Random House, Inc.

ISBN 1-57856-468-9; formerly 0-88070-875-1

Library of Congress Cataloging-in-Publication Data
Bergren, Lisa Tawn.
    Refuge / Lisa Tawn Bergren.—1st WaterBrook ed.
        p. cm. — (The full circle series ; #1)
    ISBN 1-57856-468-9
        1. Ranch life—Fiction. 2. Montana—Fiction. I. Title.

PS3552.E71938 R43 2001
813'.54—dc21

                                                                        2001023378

Printed in the United States of America
2001—

10 9 8 7 6 5 4 3 2

To my grandmother, Marion,
who unfailingly believes in me,
my mentor in faith, humor, loyalty,
strength and unconditional love.
No one could ever replace you, Mukki.

I will sing of your strength,
in the morning I will sing of your love;
for you are my fortress,
my refuge in times of trouble.
Psalm 59:16

Rachel

CHAPTER ONE

"…and if you weren't heading off to some crazy mountain town, you would be here helping me."

"Sorry, Susan. If I wasn't on my way to Elk Horn—not that I want you to remember the name—I'd be on my way to the Bahamas. I'm on vacation, remember? No phone calls."

Her boss sighed over the cell line from San Francisco. "Right. No phone calls. So vacate! Vamoose! I'll talk to you in a couple of weeks."

"Talk to you then," Rachel agreed. She hung up and stared out the tiny plane window at her right. She and Beth were supposed to be hitting Club Med this year, but instead Rachel found herself on a minuscule plane bouncing over air pockets formed by the soaring Rocky Mountains below.

She closed her eyes and envisioned herself vacationing on a tropical island, sipping iced tea served by handsome, single men. Her stomach rose as the tiny puddle-jumper dropped five hundred feet.

The pilot leaned around the tiny curtain that had been placed there in a vain attempt to conceal the cockpit's blinking lights and array of instruments. "Quite a ride, huh?" he asked loudly of Rachel, giving her a cocky wink and a grin. He leaned back into his seat before he could see her grimace and turn what she knew must be a pale green as they sailed upward and then down again.

"Might as well be on a roller coaster," Rachel mumbled. She closed her eyes and turned her thoughts to warm ocean breezes, hoping to settle her stomach. Maybe she could get away to the tropics this spring, alone if necessary. The startling mountainous beauty below was lost on her. In Rachel's eyes, this was the end of the world, and she wasn't pleased to be arriving at its edge.

"Fifteen minutes till we reach Elk Horn International Airport," the pilot yelled over the din of the engines.

"Elk Horn *International?*" Rachel wondered in amusement. She surmised that the term could refer only to their proximity to the Canadian border. Rachel forced herself to look at the majestic sight outside her window, but her thoughts were elsewhere. *I just want to get off this horrible little plane and see Beth.* The trip from San Francisco had frazzled her nerves, especially the last three hours she'd spent on the small aircraft. She laughed at a brochure in front of her detailing the mileage program. *I'm taking the train home,* she thought.

The plane glided into the huge mountain valley and slid onto the tiny runway. In spite of herself, Rachel was impressed with the pilot's ability. She looked eagerly out the window for her oldest and dearest friend, finally spotting Beth beside a huge red Ford, waving excitedly.

"Oh my." Rachel grinned at the sight of the four-wheel-drive truck. "I hope she doesn't have any guns mounted in the back window."

The plane reached the small terminal and lurched to a stop. Moments later the pilot left the cockpit and released the locks that held the door in place while ground personnel pulled the door outward, letting in a wave of clear mountain air.

Rachel inhaled deeply, noting scents of pine and manure and dry dust.

"Thank you for flying with us, ladies and gentlemen," the pilot announced with practiced care. "Enjoy your stay in Elk Horn, and please call us again for your Rocky Mountain travel needs." Concluding his speech, he ducked out the door and stood at the bottom of the three steps to assist anyone who needed help deplaning. He was gruffly ignored by the other five passengers, men on their way to hunt or fish in one of the last great American wildernesses. Rachel reluctantly accepted his hand, more for his sake than hers.

Seeing her friend, she let out a cry. Grinning widely, Beth ran forward and threw her arms around Rachel. The two women gave each other a long hug, both talking excitedly at once. They drew several admiring stares from men around them but were too absorbed in their reunion to pay much attention to them.

"Welcome to Montana!" Beth said with a huge smile of pride, as if she personally had created the land. "Looks like you had your share of single men on board," she said more quietly. "Anyone interesting?"

"No," Rachel responded firmly but with a laugh. "All that testosterone in a compressed compartment could be dangerous. I didn't want to stir anyone up."

"No big deal. This place is swimming with men. You'll be happier here for the next two weeks than you would have been on some island crawling with men just lookin' for a good time."

"Yeah, right. You'll have to prove that one to me," Rachel responded as they moved toward the baggage claim area.

"I mean it, Rachel," Beth said. "I've even found the perfect man for you."

Rachel stared at her. "You're not serious."

"I am."

"You've got to be kidding! I've only been on the ground three minutes, and you're already trying to settle me down in this god-forsaken valley of yours."

"I knew you'd never forgive me if I didn't provide at least a little romance for you during your vacation."

"I don't recall asking for any assistance." Rachel smiled.

"Who better than Madame Morgan to assist zee mademoiselle in zee arena of love?" she asked, using their quasi-French accent from college. "Dirk Tanner is a wonderful guy. Besides," she said, reverting to her normal accent, "he's Matt's best friend."

"I don't know, Beth. I really just want to hang out—"

"Trust me. You're gonna like him." They collected Rachel's luggage from the baggage shed and walked toward the parking lot, each carrying a suitcase.

Beth smiled affectionately at her best friend. "I'm so happy to see you! It's been too long."

"Tell me about it," Rachel scowled. "You had to go off and get married."

"Hey, you're the one who dared me to place the ad in *Rancher's Journal*," Beth protested.

"Yeah, but I never thought you'd *respond* to anyone who wrote you, let alone *marry* one of them!"

"You're going to have to get used to the idea."

"I'm trying. I guess it's just going to take time to get it into my head that you're an old married lady and not footloose and fancy-free like me." Rachel gave her a teasing smile as Beth put an arm around her shoulders.

The two tossed Rachel's bags in the back of the Ford. "Good grief, woman!" Beth exclaimed, grimacing at the weight. "All you need is a pair of jeans, a few shirts, and maybe your swimsuit. This is not the fashion capital of the world."

"Maybe I'll help change that," Rachel grinned.

They drove north on the highway for about twenty miles before turning off on a long dirt road. Rachel grudgingly acknowledged that the valley was spectacular, with lush green grasses and underbrush giving way to thick forests and towering mountains. Swift rivers flowed downward to the call of a distant ocean, fed from underground springs and the late spring thaw of glaciers high above. But Rachel soon focused on questioning her friend before they reached the house.

"How do you like being an old married woman—and a ranch hand? I want the dirt." Beth had to have some gripes that might ease her feelings of loss. It couldn't be as idyllic as she—

"Oh, Rachel. I'm the happiest I've ever been in my life! To be surrounded by all this"—Beth gestured out the windows—"and to have found someone to share the rest of my life with. I couldn't be happier!" As Beth talked, Rachel noticed how good her friend looked. Her brown hair was bobbed stylishly and her eyes sparkled when she talked. Her peach skin had a healthy blush to it.

"Couldn't be happier, huh? Your life is obviously unique, and I'm sure it has its perks. But don't you get desperately lonely for people?"

Beth gave her a puzzled look and pointed out the approaching gates. "Home. The Double M. You'll see it's pretty tough to get lonely here." They drove through an entrance made of huge logs and a hewn sign that echoed the ranch's cattle brand. Rachel spotted a tractor plowing in the fields. "That's Matt," Beth informed her. "He's hoping to cultivate some rich meadow grass that can supplement the feed."

Cultivate the meadow grass? Supplement the feed? Rachel almost laughed at the terms coming from her city friend's mouth, but she managed to hold her tongue as Beth showed no signs of amusement. Her friend seemed to be speaking a whole new language. *This is going to take some getting used to.*

As they drove up, Rachel admired the new log home Beth had written her about. It had a gigantic porch, and its two-story windows reflected the breathtaking valley behind them. Beth pulled the Ford to a halt in front and hopped out to greet two muddy Labradors. The dogs ran to see who their mistress had brought home, jumping on Rachel's immaculate stone-washed jeans and splattering her with paw prints.

"Chad! Wellington! Off!" Beth yelled at the hounds. "Sorry, Rachel. You're better off with darker jeans around here." But Rachel was too busy laughing at the dogs' names to be too concerned about her clothes.

"You couldn't think of anything less pretentious than Chad and Wellington?" she asked.

"Matt and I tossed a hundred names around and, in the end, decided on those for fun," Beth explained. "But it didn't help them much. As you can see, Chad and Wellington don't carry themselves in a very gentlemanly manner. Come on in. You can change and help me get ready for supper."

"Cooking? I'm on vacation," Rachel said with mock indignation.

"Yes, you are. And you'll never work harder on zee holiday, I guarantee you. Think of it as"—she looked her up and down in silent challenge—"as an experience."

"Beth Morgan, are you really going to make me sorry for missing Club Med this year?"

"Not at all," she said with a mischievous smile. "But you won't be sitting around drinking anything with a little umbrella in it. This is a meat and potatoes and milk kind of vacation, girl, and you're gonna love it."

Rachel followed Beth inside and upstairs to a cozy bedroom tastefully decorated in rich red, blue, and green plaids that complemented the log walls. It was rustic, but Rachel immediately felt at home.

"I really could use your help," Beth sheepishly admitted. "The hands come in for supper in about thirty minutes, and I've got to get it together."

"Leaving hungry men waiting could get ugly," Rachel agreed. "How many we talkin' about?"

"Fifteen," Beth said, dropping the number casually as she walked out the door.

Rachel merely raised her eyebrows at the number. She hurriedly changed clothes, leaving her dirty jeans on the floor in the corner and her bags unpacked. "I guess I'll put my feet up and relax later," Rachel mumbled to herself. She left her room and followed the grand staircase to the bottom floor, pausing on the last step to take in the view of the living room. It was huge, with the biggest stone fireplace she had ever seen and enough chairs and couches to accommodate twenty people. The shape of the room blended well with the staircase behind her and the towering windows along the front wall. Rachel had to admit that the tall white pines and blue mountains beyond offered one of the most spectacular views she'd ever seen.

The sound of clanking pots and pans drew her attention toward the kitchen where her friend was already working ove huge cast-iron stove. Beth threw her guest an apron. "You want to flip steaks or tear up lettuce for a salad?"

Rachel looked at the eighteen huge, Montana-grown steaks sizzling on a gigantic grill. Beside them boiled a giant pot. Beth caught her gaze. "Fresh red potatoes. Forty-five of 'em from our garden, which I'll introduce to you tomorrow. Lettuce or steaks?" she repeated, a little harried as she glanced at the clock.

Rachel looked at the splattering grease and said, "I'll do the salad." Beth pointed her to the refrigerator for several heads of lettuce, four bunches of carrots, an armful of tomatoes and green onions, and one red pepper.

Rachel threw the vegetables together in short order. "Can I help with anything else?" she asked.

Beth turned from the stove and grinned at the beautiful bowl of greens. "Leave it to a Californian to present the prettiest salad ever to grace the Double M's table. The guys get excited when I throw in a radish with a leaf of iceberg."

"Only the best for your ranch hands," Rachel said with a smile.

Matthew Morgan, Beth's husband, overheard her statement as he pulled open the screen door. "I hope you can give your best hug to this ranch hand," he bellowed to Rachel. She laughed as the huge bear of a man pulled her into his arms, smelling of dirt and sweat.

His wife protested. "Matt! She just changed her clothes after the dogs got to her. You'll get her all dirty again. But you could come give your wife a kiss." Matthew smiled broadly at Rachel over Beth's head as he kissed and hugged his wife, despite her protests. "Welcome to the Double M, Rachel."

"Thanks, Matt."

Matthew Morgan was a blond, blue-eyed, six-foot-tall Montanan, muscular from years of hard labor on the ranch. Rachel grinned at the couple as they embraced, noticing how tiny Beth appeared beside her husband.

The rest of the men rumbled in after their boss, stomping their boots outside to free them of caked mud before entering the house. They laughed and talked loudly as they filed in one by one, placing soiled caps and cowboy hats on pegs by the door. Each ranch hand washed up in the huge hallway basin before entering the dining room. As they caught sight of Rachel, most seemed embarrassed by the presence of a strange woman and mumbled greetings of "Ma'am" or "Evenin'" with a nod or shy smile.

They all seemed like a boisterous but gentle lot, and they quieted as they gathered around the table. Rachel caught one boldly staring at her and met his eye until he looked away.

One of the other men, Jake Rierdon, was a friend of Rachel and Beth from San Francisco. The twenty-eight-year-old son of one of Rachel's wealthiest clients, Jake had made it through architectural school before admitting that his true passion had always been the earth, not what was built upon it. Recently he had accepted Beth and Matt's offer to work at the Double M. Rachel was about to greet him when Matt cleared his throat to introduce her.

"Boys, this is Rachel Johanssen, a friend of Beth's from California. She'll be visiting with us for a couple of weeks. Introduce yourselves when you get a chance, and do your best not to scare her off or Beth will have your hide."

The men laughed and then bowed their heads for Matt's blessing over the food. Rachel was not used to saying grace before a meal, and she was surprised to observe the custom among the rough ranch hands. Matt's prayer was simple but well spoken. When he was done, the men joined in a robust *amen* and noisily moved to sit down while Matthew helped Beth and Rachel serve. In minutes, the whole crew was eating and sharing lively conversation about the day.

Rachel felt like a foreigner, and the talk around her might as well have been another language. The men discussed the north fields, the spring runoff, and a stillborn calf. *Where am I, the Old West? I wonder if these guys have ever even heard of the Internet.* Yet despite feeling slightly displaced, Rachel found their earthiness and casual manner somehow alluring, a refreshing reminder of how simple life really could be. Wanting to be a part of their easy camaraderie, Rachel turned to her tall friend sitting on her right.

"Well, Jake, how are you settling in?"

"Great!" He nodded. "After six months here, I'm happier than I ever would've been as an architect."

"Your family must have been shocked to see you leave San Francisco."

Jake shrugged. "I love my parents, but I've chosen a different life than they would have picked for me. This is my home now, and they'll have to accept it someday."

Rachel lowered her voice so only he could hear. "I have to ask, Jake. Why *would* you turn down a dream job at one of the best architectural firms in the country to come here?"

Jake sat back and stared at her thoughtfully as he chewed a bite of steak. "I bet it won't take more than three days for you to figure it out."

"I know that as soon as I get back, Eleanor will call me up at the office to grill me. She'll say something like, 'Rachel, darling, let's get together and do lunch. I heard you *just* got back from Montana, and I'm *dying* to hear what you think of my eldest son living there.'"

Rachel's voice was affected and phony, an obvious imitation of Eleanor Rierdon.

Beth giggled, and Rachel turned to see that she and Matt had overheard her. "You're pretty good at that," Matt said.

"Now I *know* that's not a compliment."

"We hear from dear Eleanor quite a bit," Beth said with a heavy sigh. "She simply cannot understand how Jake could have chosen to stay here."

Matt added, "We're trying to keep Dirk Tanner from stealing him away. His foreman, Frank, is thinking about retirement, and Dirk has his eye on Jake here."

Foreman? Rachel knew Jake had always been a natural around horses, working summers in Wyoming and Idaho through college, but foreman? In spite of herself, she was impressed. "How would it be to work on another ranch, Jake?" Rachel asked.

"I like Timberline. Dirk's a good man."

"Told ya," Beth whispered in Rachel's ear.

"I bet Dirk will be coming around even more now," Matt pretended to grumble. "He'll be after Jake for work and Rachel for a date as soon as he gets a good look at her."

"Sounds like a womanizer," Rachel whispered back to Beth.

"Not really. He just knows a good thing when he sees it."

Rachel turned away and said to Jake, "I think I'd like to focus on my horseback riding this trip. Since you're Joe Cowboy now, maybe you could give me a few pointers."

"Sure, Rachel," the younger man returned.

"Now wait a minute," Matt said. "Jake doesn't have a lot of time on his hands. I'd rather you take up my neighbor's time instead. At the rate Timberline's growing, it won't be long till Dirk's ranch gets to be twice the size of mine."

"You want to use me to distract him?" Rachel pretended to be appalled.

"Basically," Matt grinned.

The conversation eventually turned to other topics, but she could still feel the interest most of the men had in her arrival. Several of them eyed her off and on until their big bowls of ice cream and peaches disappeared. Then they rambled off to relax for the evening.

After she and Beth had finished the dishes, Rachel set her towel down and said, "I think I'll get some fresh air." She walked out onto the wide porch, and a tall figure stepped out from the evening shadows, joining her at the rail. The man was big and strong from years of ranch work, and his proximity vaguely intimidated her. She edged sideways and smiled, pretending to be at ease.

"Good evenin', Ms. Johanssen. My name's Alex Jordan."

"I'm pleased to meet you, Alex. Enjoying your evening?"

"Hard not to on a night like this," he said. But he didn't look out toward the valley as she did then. She could still feel his gaze upon her.

He was handsome, but Rachel felt an uneasiness she couldn't explain. She fought the desire to turn and go back into the house. *It's his eyes,* she thought, *something about his eyes.* "Well"—Rachel shivered and rubbed her hands over her arms—"it's cooling down now. I think I'll go and get a sweater."

"I'll be right here." He edged closer, making her pause.

Rachel's smile was thin lipped as she tried to cordially get rid of the man. "It was nice to meet you, Alex, but I don't know if I'll be back out tonight. Now, if you'll excuse me…"

"Come for a ride with me," Alex persisted with a grin. "I can give you pointers that city boy inside and Dirk Tanner don't know."

"Thank you, but I don't think so."

Matt apparently had overheard their conversation and casually walked out onto the porch to join them. "Everything all right out here?" he asked Rachel, but stared at Alex. He brought a mug of coffee to his lips, sizing up the man. Matt was an inch or so shorter than Alex, and the hired hand stubbornly met his boss's gaze without backing down. Matt stood firm.

"I'd appreciate it if you'd give Ms. Johanssen the respect she deserves, Jordan. She's a guest here at the Double M. Don't want her going home with anything but the best memories, or the missus will be on my tail." He smiled, but challenge was plain in his eyes. "Now head out and check on that pregnant sow in the barn," he directed sharply.

Alex gave him a hard look and turned on his heel, stalking toward the barn in obvious anger and kicking up dust.

Matthew turned to his guest. "Sorry about that, Rachel. Most of my men are solid, but the need for manpower on a ranch this size forces me to hire a few on the edge. He pushes me, but I keep hoping he'll fall in line one of these days. Let me know if he gives you any more trouble."

"Thanks, Matt," she said.

He smiled and headed off toward the stables.

Beth came out and joined Rachel. Her eyes followed her husband. "We have fourteen ranch hands, but Matt still loves to be the one to check on the horses every night." She paused and looked at her friend. "I heard that exchange from inside. Are you okay?"

Feeling foolish for her shakiness, Rachel replied brightly, "I'm fine, really. I just feel like I survived an episode of *Gunsmoke* as the little lady between two cowboys."

"I'm sorry about that. It was bound to happen. When I first came here, even as Matt's wife, there were some pretty serious lines that had to be drawn between Matt and the men. They get a little starved for female attention, but most of 'em are harmless."

"Thanks for the warning."

"Hey, if I'd warned you, you might not have come. Look, you go grab that sweater, I'll go grab some tea, and we can sit out here and catch up."

The women were still sitting on the porch two hours later when the last wisps of the northwestern sunset subsided into pitch-black skies with radiant stars. Glancing at her watch, Rachel realized with surprise that it was very late. She was not used to the sun's schedule so far north, and her inner clock had been thrown off. When Beth caught Rachel yawning in the middle of another ranch story, she cut it short.

"That's it. To bed with you. Tomorrow is your only day to sleep in, and then I'm puttin' you on ranchers' hours, so enjoy it while you can."

Rachel gladly succumbed to Beth's orders and, after placing her china teacup on the kitchen counter by the sink, climbed the stairs to her handsome guest room. Shivering in the cold, she undressed quickly, threw on a flannel nightshirt, and climbed into a big bed that was loaded with covers. In moments she was warm and cozy. She snuggled under the bulky comforter and tried to think back on the day's events but was asleep before she'd even left the airport terminal.

CHAPTER TWO

*I*n the morning neither the rumbling of the men eating breakfast nor the noise of Beth's kitchen cleanup awakened Rachel. She groggily opened her eyes around ten and stretched as languidly as a cat before sitting up to gaze outside. It was a fantastic summer morning, clear and warm. She slipped on a pair of jeans and a white cotton shirt. Grinning, she dug her brand-new cowboy boots out of her suitcase and struggled with them until the unwieldy things were on and neatly placed under her jeans. Then, slightly unsteady because of the boots' heel height, she clomped downstairs to seek out her friend.

Beth was nestled in a big living room chair, drinking a cup of coffee and reading *Rancher's Journal*.

"Looking for *my* husband this time?" Rachel asked her.

Beth laughed. "No," she said, looking down to her boots. She hooted with glee. "Look at you! I don't even have a pair of Tony Lamas yet, and here you are! Matt's gonna give me the hardest time after he sees those. He's been after me for months to get some, but I've avoided it."

"People have told me they're the most comfortable shoes in the world, once they're broken in," Rachel said. "We'll see. How about a cup of java for this slow-rising cowgirl?"

17

"On the stove," Beth directed. "I just brewed a fresh pot."

Rachel entered the kitchen, a cold room in the absence of Beth, the men, and cooking food. As she poured herself a generous cup of Beth's dark brew, she heard heavy footsteps on the porch.

A loud voice called, "Beth, I can smell your coffee for miles. I'd pay a dollar for—" The man stopped in midsentence as he came through the porch door and realized he was speaking to a stranger. He hastily took off his hat and walked toward her hesitatingly.

Before her stood the most captivatingly handsome man she had ever seen. He was six feet, four inches tall with broad shoulders, brown hair, and a layer of stubble over a strong mouth and jaw line. His eyes were dark, almost black, and they sparkled when he smiled, complementing the laugh lines around them. Rachel was breathless.

She managed to meet his extended hand with her own as he said, "Excuse me. You must be Rachel Johanssen. Matt and Beth let me stop in and share a cup of coffee with them when I can. I forgot they had company."

"Company?" Beth said from the kitchen doorway. "This woman is my best friend, and from now on, she's part of the ranch help. You can join us both. Rachel, this is Matt's closest friend and quickly becoming one of my own, Dirk Tanner. Dirk, this is Rachel Johanssen. I've already told you all about her." She casually moved off to pour Dirk his coffee.

"Where's Matt?" Dirk asked.

"He left early to run into town with Jake."

As they sat down, Rachel realized how messy she must look. *I haven't even combed my hair!*

Dirk watched her quietly, drinking in her beauty. He observed her long, sable hair, mussed as if she had just jumped out of bed. It made her look enticing, and he turned his head away, embarrassed by his train of thought. He forced himself to pay attention to Beth's chatter, but sneaked a look at Rachel once in a while. She had a straight, long nose, giving her face an aristocratic twist. But it was her eyes, large and green, that softened her face and made her striking. Her figure was slim, and he liked how she filled out her jeans, T-shirt, and boots, which were all obviously new purchases.

He finished his coffee quickly and, sensing that Rachel still was not at ease, excused himself. "I'll be by later after supper," he said. "I apologize for barging in on you two."

"No, no. You're welcome anytime, Dirk," Beth said. "Why don't you come back tonight in time for dessert?"

Rachel smiled in seeming agreement. Was that encouragement in her mesmerizing green eyes? Dirk smiled back and rose. "That'd be great," he said, forcing his eyes back to Beth.

"Well, all right," Beth said. "I'll save you some dessert tonight. We'll expect you around seven."

"See you then." Dirk paused in front of Rachel, looking down at her. "Pleasure to meet you, Rachel. I'll see you later." He walked out the front door and back to his Jeep.

As soon as he was driving away and definitely out of earshot, Rachel jumped up and ran to Beth, pretending to strangle her. "I'm going to murder you! Why didn't you tell me he was coming? Why didn't you tell me he was so drop-dead handsome? Aargh!"

Beth grinned. "So you liked him, h'm?"

"Liked him? He's gorgeous! And his eyes! They're so intense they make me want to stare. I found myself constantly turning away so I wouldn't look obvious." She released Beth and sat down again. "Why didn't you warn me he was coming?" she repeated. "I look horrendous!"

"Oh, you do not. If I were a man looking at this tall woman in tight jeans and boots, I'd think, 'Yes, she looks mighty fine.' Definitely not horrendous. I can tell Dirk was smitten, so quit worrying. He'll be back tonight, and you can make yourself up like you want."

Rachel just moaned.

"I'm telling you, it went fine! Dirk likes a low-maintenance woman."

"Yeah, right," she said, leaning her head back against the chair. "But it would've been nice if I looked maintained at all!"

Dirk drove through the gates of his ranch still thinking about Rachel. Beth had told him that she was smart and successful, but he had expected a diminutive woman with New York–type, tiny glasses and San Francisco chic, not the down-to-earth, striking beauty he had just met. *Rachel is not a woman who needs help in finding dates.*

He parked the Jeep in front of the house and paused for a moment before getting out. *I can't believe I forgot she was coming today.* He shook his head. *Smooth move, Dirk, barging in on them like that.* Shaking off his mood, Dirk headed into the house to take care of some paperwork before joining his ranch hands in the fields.

His housekeeper, Mary, greeted him as he walked in the door.

"Dirk. I was just getting myself a cup of coffee. Would you care for some?"

"Oh no, Mary. I just had some at Beth and Matt's."

Mary tried to hold back, but she could not contain her motherly curiosity for long. Following Dirk into his library, she casually asked, "I suppose you got a chance to meet Beth's good friend from California?"

Dirk picked up a pile of mail and pretended to study a letter. "Good friend?" he said with a purposeful blank stare. "I guess you mean Rachel. Yes, I met her briefly." He was in no mood for an interrogation from Mary.

But it was too late. Mary knew he was bluffing. She had known him since childhood. She had seen his parents, good friends of her own, die in a terrible accident on the high mountain roads. She had watched him grieve their loss and, later, the loss of a woman he loved. She knew that his reluctance to talk about women was a means of protection. But she believed that one day he would have to give in and trust once more. They'd been over it, time and again. He could repeat her lectures verbatim, finishing her sentences for her, but refrained because deep down he recognized the wisdom behind her words.

It wasn't that there was a shortage of women around Dirk. He attracted the largest following of women in the valley, and Beth teased him about being the most eligible bachelor. But none had touched his heart.

"From what Beth tells me," Mary said, "Rachel has a lot to give the right man." Dirk cast her a sharp look that he hoped would tell her to mind her own business.

She quickly added, "But then, I haven't met her yet myself."

"No, you haven't, Mary. But knowing you, I'm sure you'll find some excuse to go over to the Double M to check her out."

Mary walked toward the door, smiling. "I do plan to bake bread after services tomorrow. Maybe I'll drop by with an extra loaf." She turned back toward Dirk. "Let me know if you need anything."

"Thanks, Mary. The best thing you could do for me right now is not push this woman on me. I liked what I saw of her. Now let it rest."

"Okay, okay. But you just open your mind, Dirk Tanner. You've spent a lot of lonely years on this ranch. And even my company's no substitute for true love." Satisfied that she'd had the last word, Mary bustled off to prepare the ranch hands' noon meal.

Dirk sat down in a leather chair at his big oak desk. There were piles of bills and a stack of letters to be answered, but to his dismay his mind kept turning to Rachel. He stared out his library window, lost in the memories, old and new.

There had been no one in his life since Debra left him. He'd dated a few women but had never been swept away into a mad current of love as he had been with her. Gorgeous and ultrafeminine, his ex-fiancée had given him a reason for living after his parents' unexpected death. He had cared for her, trusted her, and loved her deeply.

It had been seven years since he had confronted his fiancée after finding her kissing his foreman in the stables. Dirk's brow furrowed at the memory. Debra had stood defiant and unwilling to change, even as he pleaded with her.

"You have betrayed me," he had said. "But...I still love you. Please. Walk away from him, Debra. Come back to me, and I'll forget this ever happened."

She had laughed in his face. "*You've* been betrayed? No, I'm the one who's been betrayed. It's always your ranch, your men, your church. When do I come first? I don't want to live this way anymore. You won't ever be ready to get married, and I don't think I'd want you even if you were. I'm tired, Dirk. Tired of you and of trying to live up to your high-and-mighty standards."

It hurt even now. The humiliation of being left for another still sounded warning alarms in his heart. Only his faith, friends, and Mary had seen him through those dark times. He had planned to give his grandmother's diamond ring to Debra that Christmas. Seven years later, it still sat forlorn in his safe, serving as a reminder to him each time he opened it.

Finally, another woman had stirred something deep in his heart. Few had affected Dirk as Rachel had, and it scared him to death. He gave up on his paperwork and walked outside, climbing the hill behind his house toward a small chapel. He met up with his current foreman, a deacon from his church.

"Ah, Dirk. I was just coming to talk with you."

"I'm headin' up to the chapel, Frank. Why don't you walk with me?" The path was steep, but both men, used to physical exertion, paid it little heed. They talked about the afternoon's job of fencing a sinkhole in the southwest pasture and discussed who should be involved. Frank got the answers he needed and then paused outside the one-room stone chapel.

"Incredible view from here," Frank said.

"This place always brings me peace. Use it anytime you want."

Frank sighed, still looking outward to the valley. "Sometimes the beauty of this place catches me off guard. It makes me remember why I live here."

"I know what you mean. I'm going to catch some one-on-one with God, Frank. Thanks for the company up the hill."

"Sure. See you at supper." Dirk watched his foreman walk away. The man was excellent at his job but making noises about retiring.

Dirk would be sad when he left Timberline. He would miss his quiet, understanding ways and friendship as much as he would his expertise on the ranch.

Dirk entered the small chapel, which was furnished with two large, plush chairs, a small table, and a wood stove. At the front a huge window overlooked the valley. But it was an intricately hand-carved cross from Italy that commanded one's view. Dirk came to the chapel often to find direction and recover his appreciation for what God had given him. Sometimes he came just to rest and meditate in prayer, finding peace and security within the building's four walls.

After his parents' death, Dirk had built the tiny sanctuary himself, lugging the native slate up the hill to constructively work out his anguish. The manual labor transformed his fury and pain into something of peace. And when Debra left him, he rediscovered the need to retreat to the chapel frequently for meditation, direction, and spiritual healing.

After spending an hour with God, Dirk felt calm and ready to find out more about Rachel, despite his fears. His rumbling stomach directed him to Mary's kitchen. Then, after eating, he headed out to the fields. Reaching the Jeep, he radioed his foreman. The men had already eaten and headed out to work at the sinkhole. "Frank, I'm comin' out to join you boys for the party. Need me to bring anything?"

Frank responded, his voice serious and low. "You better hurry, boss. We got a mother and her baby going fast."

Four miles out on a road that was severely bumpy, even for the Jeep, Dirk found his men. Frank and a team of eight others were working to extract a cow and her young calf from a black mud sinkhole. Every year they filled, covered, and bordered the hole, but each spring it reemerged, claiming border fences as well. In Dirk's memory, the sink-hole had claimed the life of one of the ranch's cows every other year or so. But a cow and her calf were an intolerable loss; the ten men were set to battle the muck until the end. Four men were up to their knees in the sludge, each with a rope tied around his waist and a man on the edge holding the other end. Years before, Dirk's father had watched two of his best hands go down with a bull, tragically suffocating in the muck when the bull rolled over one in the struggle and the other tried to save him. Neither the men nor the bull survived. From that point on, safety had become paramount in every rescue on the ranch.

One burly man named Joe had almost reached the calf before it went under. Its eyes rolled in terror, an awful bleat escaped its lips, and they all watched in horror as the calf's soft ear tips and nose sank from view. Letting out a cry of anger, Joe dove forward to grab the calf and lost his footing.

His sudden movement pulled his safety rope taut, and his mate, Ben, gave it a mighty yank to counteract the fall. As if in slow motion, Dirk saw that the rope was unraveling in the center two seconds before it gave way, leaving Ben staring blankly at a frayed end and Joe sinking deeper into the hole. The mud was heavy, and Joe could not regain his footing before his face slipped under as well. The men shouted and swung into action. The men closest to Joe abandoned the cow and moved with agonizingly slow, exaggerated motion through the heavy muck.

Their calls of Joe's name echoed in Dirk's mind as he sought frantically for a way to help. He remembered his father's policy that in any emergency the boss should lead the way. "The captain stays on his ship to the bitter end, son," his father had always said. "So it must also be for the rancher and his hands."

Snapping into action, Dirk slid down the embankment, grabbed the other half of Joe's safety rope, and pulled with Ben. Joe emerged briefly before he was sucked downward again.

Seconds seemed like hours.

Inside the hole, Joe's two closest companions finally reached him and helped hold the now-unconscious man upright after Dirk and Ben's next heave. All seemed to be chaos as the men shouted and screamed commands and pleas at once.

Dirk immediately saw that Joe was in trouble as the men laid him on the ground. Frank cleared the man's mouth of mud, and Dirk ripped open his shirt to expose the heartbeat he desperately hoped to hear.

None. He shook his head at Frank, unable to speak.

"He's not breathing!" Frank said grimly. Without another word, Frank positioned Joe's head, and they began cardiopulmonary resuscitation, Frank forcing air into Joe's lungs and then pausing every eight breaths to let Dirk compress Joe's chest.

They looked for a heartbeat or breath.

Nothing.

The others stood in silence around them, anxiously twisting their hat brims and biting their lips. At that moment Joe coughed deeply. The men cheered, but Dirk waved at them to hush.

"Joe," he said quietly, "are you okay, man?"

Joe nodded, somewhat dazed and slightly embarrassed. He looked at Frank and croaked out, "Do you think you could do that to the calf if we get her out?" The men burst out laughing, shouting Joe's name and patting Frank and Dirk on the back in congratulations.

Dirk got up off his knees, leaving Frank to care for Joe, and walked a few steps away to catch his breath and his composure. After steadying himself, he returned to the men beside the sinkhole, where the mother cow had also sunk beneath the surface.

"Six of you get back to the stables," he ordered. "Load up another posthole digger, more fence posts, and barbed wire. Then get back here and section off this hole for good. Go out a quarter of a mile around it if you have to! We'll never beat it by filling it, and I swear I'll never lose another head of cattle—or a man—to it again."

He picked up the frayed end of Joe's safety rope. "You others go through every rope in the stables—I don't care how many there are— and examine every inch of 'em. If this ever happens again because of blatant *negligence*, you don't want to know what will happen. Frank, I'll trust you to make sure that all gets done." His voice softened. "C'mon, Joe. I'll give you a ride back to the bunkhouse. You're in serious need of a shower and a visit from Doc Harmon."

Supper that night at Timberline was somber. The loss of the cattle and the scare of almost losing Joe cut conversation to a bare minimum. The food was hearty, however, and Mary rolled out her special apple cobbler after the meal, raising everyone's spirits. As the men ate their dessert, Dirk shared coffee with Mary in the living room, finally letting her in on the drama in the south fields that afternoon. Mary had known he would eventually tell her. She just needed to wait patiently; the proper moment would come.

When it did, Dirk's emotion was evident. "I can't believe it, Mary. We could have lost more than Joe out there! We could have lost three others in trying to save him. It was so stupid! If they had just thought for a moment..."

"It wasn't a time for thinking clearly, Dirk. Saving the cattle meant rushing in, acting fast."

He still was sickened by the memories of the afternoon, even as he listened to her.

"Dirk," she began gently. "They're fine. It's all over."

"I know. I just don't want to lose anyone else."

Mary put her hand over his own reassuringly. "I know, Dirk." She looked outside at the fading sunlight. "Didn't you say something about going to see our neighbors tonight? Go on, get out of here. I think a visit to the Double M is just what you need." She smiled until he returned her grin.

Feeling better, Dirk took a quick shower, changed his clothes, and climbed into his Jeep to go visit the Morgans—and their pretty houseguest.

*

"That'd be Dirk," Beth said as they spotted the Jeep kicking up dust on the road as it approached in the soft twilight. She squeezed her friend's arm and then turned to her husband. "Honey, you and I oughta go inside and think of something to do."

Matthew laughed and leaned toward Rachel. "My wife is subtle, isn't she?" He looked back at Beth. "Just what do you have in mind that we should do inside on this beautiful evening?"

Beth got up and pulled at his arm. "I don't know. We could write your mother in Florida or play a game." Matt made no move to rise.

Beth tried playing the bossy wife. "Matthew Morgan! You come inside right now!" Still, he made no move, simply smiling at her as Dirk pulled up. She decided to outmaneuver him.

"Matt," Beth whispered seductively, "it's rather cold out here, and we have that big inviting bed upstairs that could warm us right up."

Matthew rose quickly, grinning. "'Night, Rachel!" he said. "Hi there, neighbor," he called as Dirk walked up the steps. "See you later."

"Uh…good night," Dirk said, watching his friend disappear into the house. He smiled at Rachel sitting on the porch swing, curiosity evident in his eyes.

"Ah, you probably know how discreet Beth is when she gets an idea in her head," Rachel explained. "They *retired* a bit early."

He glanced at his watch and cocked a brow at her. "They went to bed at seven-thirty?"

"Uh-huh."

Dirk nodded, comprehension evident. "Very subtle, Beth," he said loudly, hoping she would hear him from upstairs. He sat down beside Rachel on the swing, but not too close. The morning's memories of him had faded enough that Rachel found herself surprised to see such a handsome man so near at hand.

"Would you like some coffee or dessert?" she offered.

"Coffee would be great, but no dessert. I just finished some cobbler at Timberline with Mary."

Alarms rang in her head. "Mary?" she asked, trying to keep her voice casual.

"Mary, my housekeeper," he said gently. "I'm not married and have no girlfriend. You?" His smiling eyes held no look of disapproval, just amusement at her reaction.

"Me either," she said nonchalantly, slightly embarrassed at their frankness but relieved by the information. For a moment she was afraid Beth had failed to get her information right. She should have known her friend would not have made such a gaffe.

Rachel got them both some coffee. Then they talked politely for a while, maintaining their distance. Their conversation was just warming up when Alex bounded up the steps, interrupting Dirk in midsentence.

"Evenin', Dirk, Rachel. Heard you had some trouble at Timberline today." He stared at Dirk, obviously waiting for more information.

Dirk reluctantly turned his attention toward Alex. By his clipped manner, Rachel surmised he hoped to get rid of the man quickly. She swallowed her irritation with Alex, certain that his action was a blatant move to interfere. She hoped Dirk would soon end their conversation.

But just as Dirk finished one sentence, Alex fired another question at him, leaving Dirk no room to end the conversation politely. After an hour of talk that turned from the day's adventure to the weather, Dirk caught Rachel in a yawn. He soon excused himself and waited a moment for Alex to leave. When the man did not move, he simply said, "Well, Rachel, it was nice talking with you. Sleep well. G'night, Jordan."

"Evenin', Dirk," Alex responded with a fake smile and a wave as Dirk walked to his Jeep. "It's gettin' real dark. You drive careful." Alex's voice dripped with sarcasm. His tone made Dirk pause and look back at Alex as he moved to join Rachel on the swing. As he did so, Rachel rose and stretched as if stiff, walked to the steps, and leaned against a post, determined that Alex not see her uneasiness.

"You all right, Rachel?" Dirk asked, obviously concerned about leaving her alone with the man.

"I'm fine, Dirk. Thanks for stopping by," she said, pretending not to have a concern in the world. Her hands were perspiring.

Dirk looked back at the house as if to reassure himself that others were still about, then reluctantly turned and climbed into his Jeep and slowly pulled away.

Rachel mumbled, "Guess I'll turn in too." She moved to the porch door.

Alex cleared his throat. "Please. Sit with me for a bit and talk.

That's all I want." His voice was almost pleading, and Rachel's heart softened a bit. *It won't kill me to stay and talk a few minutes. Maybe I've got him pegged wrong.*

She sat down on the porch railing directly across from him. "All right. I'll stay for a little bit."

"Good," he said, grinning. "How do you like Montana so far?"

"It's nice," Rachel said noncommittally. "How long have you lived here?"

"I was raised in Helena and moved to the Elk Horn when I was eighteen, looking for work."

"You've been on the Double M since you were eighteen?"

"Nah. Been lots of places. Seen a lot. Guess I like it here best. If I could find myself a good woman, I think life would be just about perfect." He eyed her more boldly.

"I'm sure you'll find the right person someday."

"Maybe I already have."

"I think you're getting the wrong idea, Alex. I'm here on vacation, not to settle down." She tried to keep her tone light, playful.

"H'm, too bad." He looked her up and down as he said it, sending a shiver down her spine.

"Brr. It's chilly again tonight," she said, covering her unease. "I think I'll turn in."

Alex looked at the ground as she stood.

"Good night," Rachel said.

"Stay, Rachel." His voice was low, his manner changed. He rose.

"No, thanks. I'm gonna call it a night." She walked toward the door, but Alex suddenly reached out and gripped her arm, then pulled her to him.

"City girl. Think you're too good for me?"

"Let go of me," she ground out slowly.

He laughed, seemingly unthreatened by her serious demeanor. He looked as if he was contemplating dropping his hand, and Rachel relaxed a little, trying not to overreact. This was one of Matt's men, and Matt had warned—

Alex used the opportunity to yank her around so that she was staring out at the valley instead of the house, his body tense and hard as a brick wall behind her. A strong arm wrapped around her from shoulder to shoulder, brushing her chin, and his warm breath filled her left ear. "No need to get all hot and bothered. Like I said, I just want to spend a little time talking." He moved to kiss her on the neck, but she elbowed him in the stomach. He immediately released her, doubled over in pain.

Rachel jumped away from him and said, "You ever do that again, I really will hurt you."

Alex walked around her from a distance and clomped down the porch steps, his hand rubbing his side. Then he turned and leered at her, saying only, "I like a woman with fire."

Rachel trembled as he faded into the pitch-black night, willing her heartbeat to slow down. She could have yelled for the Morgans, but she didn't want to be in the middle of another scene between Matt and Alex. *Besides, I can take care of myself. Didn't I just prove it?* With one last look to make sure he was really gone, Rachel entered the house quickly and locked the door behind her.

CHAPTER THREE

*R*achel...Rachel! Rachel, wake up!"

"All right, all right! What are you *doing?* The sun's barely up."

"Welcome to ranch hours, Your Highness. Vacation's over, and now the fun really begins for you. If you think this is early, wait till tomorrow. But first, how did last night go?"

"Oh," Rachel groaned. "Don't ask."

"What do you mean? I had such a good feeling about it."

"My time with Dirk was just fine," Rachel said, rubbing her eyes. "That goon Alex interrupted us, though, and never did leave us alone."

"Oh no! Why didn't you just tell him to get lost?"

"In front of Dirk? I didn't want him to think I was rude. Besides, he was the one who kept talking to Alex. If he wasn't going to tell the guy to leave, I sure wasn't about to."

"Well, you'll see Dirk again soon."

"What do you mean?"

"You'll catch him at church."

"We're going to church? My, haven't you gone backward in time since you came to the mountains?" Rachel taunted her friend. She and Beth had always slept in on Sundays in San Francisco. The last

33

time they had been to church together was in tenth grade, and then only because their parents had made them go.

"Don't prejudge it, Rachel. Just keep an open mind, okay?"

"All right, all right. Especially if Dirk is a loyal member too."

"He'll be there. You've got about an hour and a half before we go. There's hot coffee and biscuits downstairs to munch on. We'll do brunch after services."

"Got it. I'll be ready."

Rachel didn't tell her friend about Alex's shenanigans. She didn't want Beth, or worse, Matt, to baby-sit her the whole time she was at the ranch, especially since her friend seemed to have enough responsibilities.

She got out of bed, groaning inwardly as she gazed out the window and saw the sun just cresting the eastern horizon, casting pink hues upon high cirrus clouds. Her body cried out for more sleep, but it did feel good to observe the quiet beauty of the unspoiled morning. She was here to gain new experiences as well as to visit her friend, and a new day was before her. She even resolved to give "the church thing" a level of grace before judging it. *It might even feel good to go again*, Rachel thought.

She slipped on jeans and a T-shirt and went downstairs to grab some coffee and find out what to wear to church.

Entering the cold kitchen, Rachel saw Matt at the stove pouring Beth and himself cups of hot coffee. "G'mornin', Rachel," he greeted her. "Sleep well?"

"Good morning, Matt. I slept like a bear in hibernation. Boy, it's chilly this early! I think I'll grab some of the java to warm me up. This girl's used to California mornings in a small, toasty apartment."

Beth pulled a sweater off a wall peg for her as Matt waved

Rachel away from the stove and poured her a cup of coffee as well.

"A man of the new millennium," Rachel remarked appreciatively. "Maybe I can find one through *Rancher's Journal* too."

"Have you met anyone special lately?" Matt asked with care. "I mean, besides my wife's best 'Love Connection' efforts here. What about love in the city?"

"Sadly nonexistent. As they say, they're all gay or married. And who has time to look? I'm not into bars, dating services, or personal ads. The Internet scares me—too many loonies. My conversation with Dirk last night is the closest thing I've had to a date in a year."

"That's ridiculous! There oughta be plenty of guys wanting to go out with you. You've got your act together. You're attractive and funny." He gestured broadly as he spoke, his big hands threatening some of Beth's china on a nearby shelf.

"It's not that there aren't any interested in me, Matt. I'm just not interested in them."

"You should move out here," Beth said.

"And do what? There isn't a big need for an ad exec at the local paper, is there?"

"Now that you mention it, you *could* pull together ads at the paper, besides doing a lot of other things. What about telecommuting? More and more companies are letting some of their employees work out of their homes."

As they chatted comfortably, Rachel gradually felt warmer. The early sunlight gave the kitchen a crisp, clean feel, and Rachel was utterly content in her surroundings. It felt good to have her friends want her near, and it was fun to entertain the idea of moving—as ludicrous as it was. Perhaps there was a greater reason for her to be here. It had been a long time since she had felt close to peace.

Her life in San Francisco had grown continually more hectic, and although she defended her lifestyle to others, inside she craved more than her sixty-hour workweek. But the thought of giving up the security of her career confused and frightened her. Since Beth had left the city, Rachel's frustration had risen with each month that passed. She wanted the happiness that Beth had obviously found, yet she loved her job and was reluctant to leave it.

She finished her cup of coffee as Beth rose to change clothes.

Rachel asked, "What is the proper Sabbath attire?"

"We're pretty casual here. Some nice slacks or a casual dress will be fine."

"Gotcha. I'll go and shower too. What time does the horse and buggy leave?"

"Cute, Rachel. The truck leaves in an hour."

The hot water coursing down on her head and bare shoulders felt wonderful to Rachel. The faucet had an old-fashioned wide head with no water conservation spout attached, and it allowed a torrent of water to come through. Beth had told her she had redecorated the guest bathroom, putting a small, shoulder-high window in the shower, which permitted steam to escape and afforded an incredible view of the mountains. *This is what it would be like to bathe in Eden,* Rachel thought. She decided she'd take another shower that night and pushed herself to get out.

As Rachel dried herself off, she glanced at the clock. Alarmed by the time, she hurried through the rest of her preparations. She hurriedly dried her hair, then put on some makeup. Finally, she slipped on a soft, flowing dress and sandals. She was a little wrinkled, but she decided that she would pass.

Matt whistled as she descended the stairs. "You'll get a few offers for the dance on Friday, in that getup."

"Dance?" Rachel asked.

"Our annual Sweet Pea Festival town dance. It's the event of the summer, and you're here for it."

Beth grabbed her arm and steered her to the door. When Rachel winced, Beth asked, "What's wrong?"

"Oh, nothing," Rachel said. Pulling away, she lifted her sleeve to privately examine the bruises Alex's fingers had left on her upper arm. She quickly pulled the material back down again before Beth could see the marks. "See? I'm already sore from ranch work, and I haven't even started." She distracted her friend, saying, "Could I borrow that sweater you gave me earlier? I'll probably be fine, but just in case…"

"C'mon, ladies, we're gonna be late," Matt urged, standing at the front door.

Beth went to get the sweater for Rachel, and then they jumped into the truck and headed for church.

They drove up to a quaint country chapel, complete with a steeple and fresh white paint. Many vehicles were there already.

"You don't have a fire-and-brimstone preacher, do you?" Rachel whispered to Beth as they hurried up the steps.

"You just give it the fair shake you promised, woman," Beth answered with a stern glance.

The sanctuary was filled almost to capacity, and the people were either in prayer or sitting quietly. Matt, Beth, and Rachel took their seats in a pew next to Jake. Rachel was surprised to see him there. She knew the Rierdons attended church, but she hadn't thought Jake would continue to go in Montana. He smiled and greeted her as they settled into the pew.

A distinguished-looking pastor entered and paused at the cross in front. Turning, he welcomed everyone and made announcements. "I especially want to welcome Rachel Johanssen, visiting the Double M, and Rick Felt, a visitor to the Thompsons this week," he said. "All are welcome in the name of Jesus Christ. Let us come and worship." Rachel's face burned at the surprise of being named out of the blue in a crowd of strangers. However, she saw nothing but kindness in the faces around her, and she quickly forgot her embarrassment.

The congregation quietly sang a song they knew by heart, and after the second verse Rachel cautiously joined in. With each verse, the voices grew louder and more confident, drawn by a spirit of worship. The experience was moving and powerful to Rachel, who joined them in singing even though she still felt like an outsider. Under Pastor Lear's graceful leadership, she gradually became more comfortable.

Rachel was astonished when the pastor announced his topic. She found herself riveted by a sermon that sang to her, and every word seemed to physically enter her heart.

Pastor Lear began, "Peace to you, brothers and sisters, in the name of Jesus, our Lord and Savior. What did I just say? 'Peace to you.' Is there any greater wish for a dear friend? Is peace not what every person yearns for?

"I once knew a man who lived in forty-eight different cities before he moved to the county in which he died. I was a young intern pastor in that county, so I went to his home, where he planned to spend the last few weeks of his life. His body had been eaten away by ulcers and cancer, and he had little strength to continue living. A man who had once been strong and virile lay shriveled in his bed.

"I talked with him for a long while. There is nothing more powerful than sitting next to a person preparing to pass on to everlasting life. I asked him why he had moved so often in his lifetime. He had no family, no wife. His rootlessness kept him from establishing any lifelong friends. Was it because of his job? The military? I asked.

"'No,' he told me. 'I never had much of a job to speak of. I just grabbed the first thing that came my way when I got to a new place. I wasn't in the service. I moved so much because I was seeking the gold.'

"'The gold?' I asked him blankly. 'You were a gold miner?'

"'Ah, no, son. "The gold" is the peace I finally discovered in Christ. I looked all over the place, seeking, wanting…wishing for something I could not even name. It became the gold to me. The prize. The end of the rainbow. The medal at the end of the race.'

"I thought on that awhile and realized just how much sense the longing he described made to me. How many people are looking for that same peace? How many seek the gold? Anyone outside the grace of God. Anyone who has not fully allowed Christ into his life."

As Pastor Lear continued speaking, Rachel's mind whirled. *Could this be true? Could this be the answer I seek? In church?* The thought was too overwhelming to assimilate at once. She began to think about her life, her goals. Rachel tuned back in to the sermon just in time to hear the pastor's closing remarks.

"I never asked that man how he finally discovered what was available to him all the time. I don't even know how he came to Christ in the end. How many of us will seek for the gold until we're on our deathbed? How many of us will move, change jobs, divorce…anything to try to find it? How many of us cannot even name that which we seek? Peace. It is this most precious gift that I wish for you, my friends, found in our Savior, who walks right beside us. Amen."

The people moved and coughed, breaking their careful attention to the pastor's words and warming up for a song. Again they broke into a hymn, this time reading from an old red hymnal. Rachel followed along, numb from her revelation, but excited by the idea as well. *Maybe, just maybe, the answer is as close as the old stone church on Van Ness Avenue at home.*

As they finished the hymn, Rachel carefully looked around for Dirk. He glanced up and smiled at her while he sang. His eyes were caring and warm, and Rachel was even happier she had come to church with the Morgans. *What a morning!*

The offering plate was passed, and Rachel put in her share, deeming the service more worthwhile than her last five self-help tapes combined. She thanked the minister as she exited with the Morgans, noting their friendly, happy demeanor compared to the stiff way her parents had acted around her childhood pastor. Her friends were at ease around the man, and he seemed completely real and comfortable with them.

"That was the first pleasurable church service I believe I've ever experienced," Rachel said to Beth as they descended the stairs.

"Oh, good!" her friend responded. "I'm so glad you liked Arnie and the service."

"Arnie?"

"Pastor Lear. He comes over to visit with his wife, Anne, every couple of weeks or so. It was Matt, Arnie, and Anne who really showed me religion could be more of a gift than a burden."

Neighbors and friends who wanted to meet Rachel interrupted their conversation.

Everyone was friendly, and Rachel felt very much at home. She paused to look again for Dirk and, for the first time, really embraced the beauty of the valley as something more three-dimensional than what she had been seeing as a two-dimensional postcard picture. Slowly her eyes covered the cascading, slate blue mountains sweeping into gentle, heavily forested hills, silky in the morning light. Everything was a lush green, and the fresh breeze and early summer sunshine invigorated Rachel.

"Good morning, neighbor." Dirk's voice made her neck tingle as it tickled her ear. She turned to face the man, who looked even more stunning up close in his crisp shirt and perfectly chosen tie.

"Hello, Dirk. I was sorry we got interrupted last night. I was looking forward to talking more with you."

"Me too. Maybe we can get together again sometime." He kept his voice purposefully casual and seemed to hesitate. *Don't let her in. She's leaving in two weeks. You'll only get hurt.*

"That would be good." Rachel waited with anticipation.

"Well...have a great day. It should be a beautiful one." He turned on his heel with a confident smile, and Rachel watched as he strode away, a little startled by his abrupt departure. He was almost nervous around her!

Beth linked her arm in Rachel's and turned her toward the truck. "Well...?"

"Well, nothing. He told me to have a nice day. I was probably too forward—told him I wished we'd had more time alone last night. He probably thinks I'm a floozy, saying something like that after we just left church."

"Don't be ridiculous. I'm sure he thinks no such thing. But I don't understand. No date for the Sweet Pea?"

"No date for the Sweet Pea."

The trio reached the Double M, climbed out of the truck, and headed directly for the kitchen. Brunch would be a smaller affair than usual, with only the Morgans and Rachel there.

Matt left to collect the newspaper from the end of their lane, opting to walk and get a little exercise while the women cooked.

"The ranch hands have Sundays off," Beth briefed Rachel, "except for a couple who keep the cattle in line. The men living in the bunkhouse cook their meals in a small mess hall that's attached to it. I enjoy the break, and Matthew and I finally get a little privacy." Beth took eggs out of the refrigerator and began cracking them open into a large pottery bowl.

"It's a well-deserved break, as far as I can tell," Rachel said.

"The work is constant, but it's worth it," Beth responded. "I love going to bed tired at night and feeling like I did something worthwhile."

"*Is* it worthwhile?"

Beth paused. "Yes. I'd much rather feed fifteen hungry men than push papers around in an office. When the guys leave satisfied, they let me know. I'm appreciated. And when I'm not cooking or cleaning up, I can do whatever I want. Sometimes I go with Matt to work in the fields. Other times, I just curl up in the living room and read a good book."

"I hear you, Beth," Rachel said, leaning against the counter while bacon sizzled in the pan beside her. "But I can't quite believe my ears. What happened to the whirlwind ad exec on her way up in the world? The one who won five awards last year alone? You and I were going to be the star female ad team of our generation. How did you switch gears like that?"

"That's exactly it. Switching gears. Once I did, I found a peace I never had in San Francisco. And I'm telling you, there's no award I would take to give it up again. I don't know if I can explain it. It's more of an experience. When I cook for the guys, I know it's considered simple and backward in terms of being the modern woman. But it's real satisfaction. I'm helping Matt so we don't have to hire a cook. I'm helping him build the Double M into a ranch that will support us and our children for decades."

"He doesn't make you cook and clean?"

Beth laughed. "Heavens no. He offered to hire a cook and a maid when we got married, but I refused." She turned to stir a pitcher of orange juice.

"Why?"

"I was switching gears."

"But what about your career?"

"I was working sixty-hour weeks. My career was my life."

"But you were appreciated by lots of people—not just fifteen hungry men."

"The appreciation I get from the guys goes beyond a full stomach. They're my friends now. I'm part of a team with Matt, and the men all look at me that way. I'd rather touch a few people on a deeper level than a million consumers or ad execs on the surface."

Rachel flipped the bacon. "Don't you miss the world?"

"H'm, mostly no. I like this world. There's no smog. No traffic. People are *nice*."

"There's more to the world than San Francisco smog and traffic."

"Matt and I will travel once or twice a year," she responded, a bit of defensiveness evident in her voice. "He wants to go anywhere I want to see. He thinks it's a fair exchange, considering that I left my world to come to his. Now, are you done interrogating me?"

"I'm just asking," Rachel said, raising tongs and oven mitt in surrender. "Trying to get a grip on why you'd leave the best shopping partner you'll ever have to come to the country where"—she glanced at the oven mitt decorated in cornball pseudocountry appliqué— "JCPenney is your only fashion option."

"There's definitely more to life than shopping, my friend. Maybe you'll see more of what I mean while you're here." She joined Rachel at the stove and poured the eggs from the bowl into a cold cast-iron skillet, getting them ready to cook. Her cheeks were rosy, and Rachel noticed again how great she looked. "You'd better get those biscuits in the oven, or we'll be eating at two o'clock," she directed.

CHAPTER FOUR

That afternoon Rachel left her book and comfortable reading chair to go explore. The fresh air felt even better than she anticipated. Alex was not in sight. She breathed deeply and smiled to herself. It was really starting to feel like a vacation. Gazing around the abandoned complex, Rachel didn't see another soul. She spotted stables connected to a large, well-kept barn and headed off to snoop.

Rachel opened a wide red door and entered a dimly lit hall covered with straw. On either side were horse stalls, all empty except the last. She discovered Jake there, speaking softly to a mare. As he stroked the horse, a shaft of light from a window in the sidewall illuminated his arm and hand. Rachel felt like an intruder as she watched him administer his careful attentions.

He glanced around, slowing the steady rhythm of his stroke. After a moment he stopped, yet the mare stayed where she was. She seemed uneasy, skittish.

"Rachel," he spoke in a hushed voice. "Would you like to help?"

"I don't know much about sick horses, Jake."

He dismissed her excuse with a wave in the air, stood, and opened the door for her. "Come in."

She saw no choice but to do as her younger friend asked, so she entered the stall. He placed his hand gently on the horse's swollen abdomen and nodded for her to do the same. He rubbed the mare back and forth in an even fashion. As soon as Rachel's hand joined his, she discovered what truly was wrong.

"She's pregnant!" she whispered with a smile, feeling the outline of tiny legs within the mother's bulbous womb.

He answered with a grin, his brown eyes sparkling with delight. "She'll bring her foal into the world tomorrow at the latest."

"What were you whispering to her?"

"Anything soothing. 'It'll be okay.' 'Breathe easy.' Things like that."

"You're pretty good at this, Jake."

He met her gaze. "You sound surprised."

"Surprised? Nah. You've always been good with animals. And I knew you'd spent summers working on ranches. It's just, seeing you here, actually in your *element*... It's illuminating. I finally see Jake Rierdon as he was meant to be."

He grinned. "Wish my folks did."

She laughed under her breath. "Then you really would have everything, and that wouldn't be fair to the rest of us, now would it?"

"Guess not," he smiled back at her. "Come on. Let's go see the piglets that were born this morning."

She followed him to another stall, and he gently opened the top portion of the door so as not to startle them.

Rachel and Jake laughed at the tiny, wriggling round bodies suckling hungrily at their weary mother's abdomen. They watched for a minute or two.

"All these babies!" Rachel said, shaking her head. "What about you, Jake? Do you want children someday?"

"Are you proposing?" he teased.

"Uh, not yet," Rachel said, playfully cocking her head. He was a good friend, but more like a younger brother than a potential date. "Can I hold one of those?" she asked, pointing at the piglets.

"Sorry. Sows can get aggressive and mean when protecting their young."

"My, you have become Joe Expert on the ranch!"

He shrugged off her indirect compliment, smiling. "Now you *are* surprised. I've been picking it up as I go. Matt and Dirk are good teachers."

"I'll bet."

Jake led her out of the stables and to a barn located across a narrow path. It contained various supplies, several tractors, and some huge machinery that Rachel could not identify.

"So, you want to be a cowgirl, huh?" he challenged.

"This week and next anyway."

"Well, I better teach you how to ride then. If that idiot Tanner is going to be so slow, I'm sure not going to hesitate."

She enjoyed his idle flirting—a part of their relationship for years—and watched, fascinated, as he moved to a nearby corral, separated a solid-looking mare from the other horses, and quickly slipped a halter over her head. He walked her over to Rachel, briefly introduced the horse as "Kala," and left to catch another mare for himself. He then led the two horses to the stables and saddled them up in what appeared to Rachel to be a very long and complicated process.

The ease of riding the mare around the corral amazed her. She grew accustomed to the horse's rolling gait and found it relaxing and invigorating at the same time. When Jake proudly opened the gate to allow her through, her heart leaped with excitement and anticipation of the new experience. The horse seemed bored and readily took advantage of her rider by grabbing a snack of weeds every few minutes.

"No, Rachel. You cannot give the horse free rein. If you give her an inch, she'll take a mile. Kala is to do only what you want her to do. Now look at my position. See how I hold the reins firmly?" Rachel saw that Jake's horse was unable to bend down and munch on green edibles. He dismounted and opened the horse's mouth, showing Rachel the bit inside. "You have the control," he said, looking up at her.

After a few pointers, Rachel felt more at ease with Kala. They remained in the haven of the front yard, waving to the cheering hands as they walked or drove by. She was beginning to feel at home.

An hour later Jake helped her dismount, promising her another lesson the next day and reluctantly agreeing to teach her how to trot and then canter. As she left the stables and walked up to the house, she felt the muscles involved in horseback riding. After more than an hour on Kala, her legs ached. She laughed as she imagined herself walking with a permanent inverted U to her stride and painfully climbed the stairs.

Rachel heard Mary's matronly, rolling laugh before she could actually see her, and she felt drawn to the woman immediately. "This must be your guest!" Mary exclaimed to Beth, catching sight of Rachel. By her tone, it was clear why Mary was visiting. As soon as the weary Rachel sat down, the questions came, one after another. She answered them calmly, quickly ascertaining that Mary was checking up on her. The woman was well-meaning and amusing, so Rachel went with the process.

"I didn't mean to be so nosy," Mary said after taking a breath. "I don't get much of a chance to talk to city folk."

"I bet you get more of an opportunity than you claim, Mary,"

Beth said. "Just tell Rachel that you're like Dirk's own mother. It's your duty to check out all the eligible women, isn't it?" Beth smiled and laughed at Mary's blush as she attempted to deny the "preposterous idea." After seeing she would not convince either woman of her innocence, Mary gave up and started talking about Dirk. In an hour, Rachel knew of Dirk's lost parents and lost love. *No wonder he is so hesitant to make a move,* she thought.

After Mary left to go home and plan supper, Beth and Rachel laughed and chatted about her visit, speculating about Dirk's involvement.

"If I know anything about Dirk Tanner," Beth said, "it's that he would never send his housekeeper on such an errand. He's very independent, and when he does decide to pursue a woman, it will be slow and sure. It will take a patient woman to woo Dirk into taking the first step," she finished, nudging her friend in the side.

Rachel snorted indignantly. "I don't woo."

They spent an hour making a special dessert and marinating a roast for Matt to barbecue outside that night. The evening air was a perfect temperature, and as she watched the late northern sunset after supper, Rachel tried envisioning herself in Montana permanently. The image surprised and scared her a bit.

Her mind raced with new visions, and that night she dreamed she ran the town's tiny newspaper, reported on birthing rates of horses and cows in the county during the day, and returned home at night to Dirk's arms.

TUESDAY, JULY 20
Determined to go faster than during her last two lessons and contemplating a casual ride over to Dirk's, Rachel bypassed Jake's

watchful eye and asked another hand to help her saddle Kala. The man warily watched her mount and then shrugged, as if refusing further responsibility. She politely thanked him, and then, nudging her horse out of the stable, she rode out into an incredible mountain summer day.

Rachel smiled broadly and waved at Beth on the porch, who had refused to accompany her on the ride. "You're missing some fun!" she yelled.

"There will be more!" Beth hollered back. She motioned for Rachel to move closer. "You're not going over to our neighbor's by any chance, are you?"

Rachel grinned. "Now why would I consider doing that?" she asked with mock indignation.

"No reason," Beth said slyly. "Don't be gone too long, you green maverick."

"We'll see. Kala asked me for a long ride today." As if on cue, the mare snorted, and both women laughed.

"Talking to the horses," Beth called after her departing friend. "Not a good sign. Not good at all."

"I told you we should have gone to a tropical island," Rachel retorted over her shoulder.

Most of the hands were working in the boundary forests of the Double M, clearing dead stands of trees that had recently succumbed to a red beetle and cutting timber to repair fences on various parts of the ranch. Alex and another man, Ted, stationed on the western border, were directly along Rachel's path as she passed. Catching sight of her, Alex wiped the sweat from his brow, grinned widely, and let out a long, low, appreciative whistle.

Embarrassed by his companion, Ted ducked his head and said angrily, "Jordan, shut up! Matt will bust your chops and mine, too!"

Rachel nodded curtly to Alex's companion, "Good morning, Ted. Hope you don't have to work too hard." She ignored Alex completely.

"Oh no, miss. All part of a day's work," he said as she rode on by.

"What a woman," Alex said offhandedly, leaning on his ax handle. "Like to find a way to spend more time with her."

"She's not interested, Jordan. Leave her alone. Matt's made it clear that you're to stay away. Now you're probably gonna go off and do something stupid as usual and bring me down with ya," Ted hissed, his face flushed with anger.

"Ah, calm down, buddy. If Matt ever tried to cross either of us off his list, I'd fix him," Alex said meaningfully as he swung his ax into a dead sapling.

"I'm not your buddy, Alex," Ted said, swinging his ax as well. "You leave me out of your plans."

Except for Alex's rude interruption, Rachel thoroughly enjoyed her new experience out on the range. Alex Jordan seemed bent on getting under her skin, but Rachel would not allow it. Kala behaved quite well, and Rachel rode directly north, following Beth's directions to Dirk's house. The sun's warmth was pleasant to her. But the ride took over an hour, and by the time she reached the Tanner ranch, she was ready for a drink of water. As she detoured east to enter the front gate, her heart started to pound and her mind raced to find an explanation for her visit.

Make it a good one, Rachel, she told herself.

Like the Morgans' ranch house, Dirk's huge log home sat against the valley's western hills, predominantly facing the Rocky Mountain range. As she looked over her shoulder at the view, she sighed, admiring the scenery Dirk awoke to every day. A lovely porch bordered three sides of the house, and the wall on the eastern side was made mostly of windows. Dirk obviously appreciated the beauty that surrounded him.

Mary spotted Rachel first and greeted her profusely as she came out on the porch. "Come in, dear, come in. You must be parched, and probably hungry, too."

Rachel gratefully dismounted and entered Dirk's home. It was decorated similarly to the Morgans' but with darker, more masculine tones. It was attractive, but not inviting. *Needs a woman's touch*, she thought. She was surprised that Mary didn't have more control over the decor.

The woman settled her guest into the living room and bustled off to get some lemonade and gingersnaps. When she returned, Rachel took a large bite from a freshly baked cookie just as Dirk entered. Embarrassed, she chewed and tried to swallow too quickly. In doing so, she started choking on the crumbs.

"Whoa, neighbor! Easy there," Dirk said with a laugh. "Can't have you choking to death here on Tanner land. Beth would kill me."

Rachel's eyes streamed tears. Thoroughly mortified, she couldn't think of a thing to say. All her smart excuses for the visit escaped her.

"I like a woman who blushes," Dirk said with a smile. His eyes were the color of oil, and they sparkled happily. "I once spoke with a man from India who told me, 'The trouble with you Americans is that you've lost the ability to blush.' There's a lot of wisdom in that statement." He studied her thoughtfully for a moment, then quickly changed the subject to alleviate her discomfort. "How is the riding coming along?"

Regaining her composure slowly, Rachel asked, "How do you know I'm not an expert?"

"Well, for one, I got the scoop from Matt this morning on his guest's progress. I also watched you coming from the barn. You looked saddlesore after only four miles."

"*Only* four miles?"

They laughed and talked easily about a number of subjects, mostly ranch life and Rachel's job in the city.

"Oh no!" Rachel exclaimed, looking at her watch. "I have to be going. Beth will think I got lost." She'd been chatting with Dirk for over two hours, unaware of the time passing.

"How about a ride home?" Dirk offered. "I could bring your horse back to the Double M tomorrow."

"No thanks," Rachel coyly refused. She bid Dirk good-bye and, once outside, congratulated herself on her smooth exit. *Almost counterbalances that lame introduction today, Rachel.*

Mary leaned out the kitchen window. "You're not staying for supper?"

"Not tonight, Mary. Thank you though." *Guess I passed her inspection,* Rachel thought.

"Maybe later in the week…," Dirk called after her.

"Maybe. If you're lucky," Rachel said with a smile.

WEDNESDAY, JULY 21

"Take a breather, Beth. Come with me. Please!"

"Oh no. You see how messy this house is? And I thought I'd make a special dessert for tonight."

"The boys can deal with ice cream this time. You're forever making them a special dessert. Come for a little ride with me. We can picnic by the river and soak up some sun. When was the last time you were out of this house just for fun?"

"Too long ago," Matt said as he entered the kitchen. "Go have some fun with Rachel."

"Well, all right. It would be good to get outside for a while. But no horses. I want to walk."

"Some rancher you turned out to be! No horses... What should we do for lunch?"

"We'll leave out plates of sandwich makings for the men, and they can fend for themselves. We'll make our own. I'm getting more into this idea all the time."

They made large sandwiches of peanut butter and fresh strawberry jam and cut up fruit to take along as well. Rachel couldn't stand to wait, it all looked so good. She took a large bite out of her sandwich, and when Beth turned around, Rachel took a bite of her sandwich, too. Discovering the perfect bite in the corner, Beth put her hands on her hips, feigning indignation.

Rachel stuck her hand into the peanut butter jar and brought out a huge glob of the light brown paste on the tip of her finger to eat. Laughing at the look Beth gave her, she said, "I think you are getting way too prudish as a married lady." With that, she swiped Beth's nose with the peanut butter.

Beth choked, laughing and yelling at the same moment. She turned around, grabbed a cold glass of water and launched it at Rachel. "Still think I'm too prudish for a little mischief?" she asked, a self-satisfied grin lighting up her face.

Rachel screamed as she looked down at her soaked T-shirt and shorts and the little streams of water running down her legs. She grabbed her glass of water and returned fire. Beth retaliated with a handful of flour. Reaching into the cupboard, Rachel grabbed the oatmeal and let the whole cardboard container fly. Beth returned to her flour arsenal and covered them both in a thick cloud of white dust. Laughing hysterically, Rachel grabbed the peanut butter and threw fat bombs at her friend, who shrieked each time they came at her.

They finally sank to their knees, laughing so hard they cried. The two women lay on the floor amid flour, oatmeal, and globs of peanut butter, struggling to get their breath. Each time they got a little air, the laughter started again.

Matt came back in, alarmed by the barks of Chad and Wellington. "What in the world...?"

Sitting amid the chaos, Beth was struck by a fit of giggles when she saw her husband's face. "I guess I'll take you up on the maid idea, honey," she said, and with that both women sank into laughter all over again.

They were still giggling two hours later when they finally reached the river. They had cleaned up the mess, as well as themselves, and set the noon dinner out for the men before they left. *The walk was worth it*, Rachel decided as soon as she saw what awaited them. The Kootenai River was glorious, the color of jade amid brightly dancing whitecaps. Beth led her to a lush, grassy bank, perfect for catching a little midday sun. The bank jutted out a bit into the river, catching the flow and making an indigo blue pool.

They unloaded their dinner and started munching right away, hungry after their food fight and mile-long walk. "I've probably eaten over a thousand PB&J sandwiches in my life, but I swear this is the best one I've ever had," Rachel said.

"It's nothing compared to this view though, huh?"

Rachel returned her attention to their surroundings. The river ran directly south, forming the western edge of the Double M and Timberline. From where they sat on the bank, they looked up at the hills behind the ranches and the gentle mountains beyond. Over their shoulders were the western edges of the Rocky Mountains, forming the Continental Divide. They sat in the middle of a verdant forest with junglelike underbrush. Above was a brilliant blue sky.

"Do you live in heaven?" Rachel asked between bites.

"As close to it as it comes, I've decided."

They stared back at the mountains and finished their sandwiches in silence. Rachel rolled over onto her stomach and peered back at the Great Divide. Few of the crags and ravines showed, and it looked flat and austere in the harsh noon light. Flanked by mountains on either side, Rachel felt a sense of cozy security. The peaks seemed to form a fortress, and she felt invincible inside its walls. She thought of home but dismissed the image quickly. Thoughts of San Francisco seemed foreign, and she had no desire to dwell on them.

"Wanna take a dip?"

"Rachel! The water comes right off these mountains! It would be like swimming in ice water. *Glacial* water."

"Sounds divine. Come on, let's get the rest of that flour out of our hair." Rachel bounced up and stripped down to her underwear. Looking over the edge of the bank, she studied the pool for any underwater obstructions. Not seeing any, she took a huge breath and dove into the clear pool. She plunged downward until the water slowed her progress to a stop. Then she turned a half-somersault and swam toward the surface, eager for air. "Whew!" she said with a shiver, breaking the surface. "This pool is *deep*. And you're right.

The water is very…*refreshing*." Treading water, she begged Beth to join her.

"No way. I'll soak my feet, but that's it."

"You're missing it, bud. This feels like swimming in a pool of the gods."

"One God. And he *has* created beauty here," Beth said reverently.

Saying nothing, Rachel paddled out to the current. She swam against it for fifteen minutes, enjoying her workout. When she tired, she returned to the pool and struggled to get out onto the slippery wet bank.

Beth laughed at her and finally lent a hand. "You're a lot more graceful *in* the water than out," she said.

"Careful, or we'll see how well *you'd* do getting out of the water," Rachel warned.

Beth put her hands in the air. "Oh no. Truce. No more battles today."

They lay back on the bank, soaking in the sun as Rachel dried. She put on her clothes after an hour, her underwear already dry in the hot, thin mountain air. Minutes later, Dirk rounded the bend on his horse, and both women giggled at his timing. He was at a loss to know the reason for their laughter but shrugged it off when they would not explain.

He looked devastatingly handsome astride his horse, Caleb. Fine stubble covered his face, and his chambray shirt was unbuttoned at the neck, exposing tanned skin. Over his jeans were worn leather chaps, and his cowboy boots fit neatly into the stirrups. Dirk sat astride his horse in a casual, practiced manner, looking as though he could remain there all day if needed.

"I was just on my way over to the Double M when I heard you

two laughing," he said. "Since you've been so happy about riding Kala, I thought you might want to go for another ride today, Rachel."

"Is this a rancher's version of a date?"

Dirk shifted uneasily in his saddle. "Let's call it a *neighborly invitation.*"

"Ah." She let their conversation pause for a moment, enjoying his discomfort.

He couldn't stand it for long. "Well, Ms. Johanssen, would you like to go riding with me this evening or not? I'll take you to a spectacular point of the valley and even provide supper."

"Well, Mr. Tanner, that sounds like an offer I can't refuse."

CHAPTER FIVE

irk drove up to the Morgans' ranch house in a large blue truck, pulling a horse trailer. Matt helped him put Kala in beside Caleb. Rachel tried to keep her pace casual as she walked out onto the porch to say hello to Dirk. She wore a lavender V-neck top with her blue jeans and boots. Dirk noticed that the color brought out her bright green eyes, and he fought the desire to stop his work and stare at her in front of everyone.

He had changed shirts but otherwise wore the same outfit she had seen him in that afternoon by the river. As they climbed into the truck, waving to the Morgans, Rachel remarked about the picnic basket. "Slaved over supper all afternoon?"

"All afternoon," he said with a smile.

"Mary?" she asked.

"Mary," he answered.

They drove out the ranch road and onto the highway, heading south past the town of Elk Horn. About five miles later, Dirk turned east onto a dirt road, and they quickly started climbing. Back and forth they drove up the switchbacks. Several times Rachel used the excuse of looking back at the scenery to peek at Dirk, his proximity making her heart pound. He had a movie star's jaw line, she decided.

They continued to casually converse about their lives, gradually getting to know each other better.

"Beth tells me you two go way back."

"Second grade. We both were raised in San Francisco, and our parents were friends. We were as close as sisters as soon as we sat together in Miss Hunter's class."

He smiled over at her. "Matt and I were like that too."

About thirty minutes later they reached the top of the forest-service road and parked in a small clearing. Dirk backed the horses out of the trailer and began the tricky business of turning the trailer around on the narrow road, explaining that he wanted to do it before dark.

Guess he's planning on a successful supper if we're to be out here until dark, Rachel thought.

After a moment Dirk got the trailer expertly positioned behind the truck, which was pointed downhill. "There we go," he said. "Now we can just load Caleb and Kala when we return and head home."

"Sounds good," she agreed. Dirk lifted her saddle and threw it across Kala's back. When he returned to the truck for his own, Rachel began the process of positioning and tightening her girth.

"Pretty good for a city girl," he quipped, watching her concentrated efforts.

"Jake's a good teacher," she said.

"And a good man, from what I know of him," he said agreeably. "I'd like to recruit him to Timberline, if Matt will let me." They mounted the horses and continued their conversation as they ascended a small trail. Dirk led, and Rachel followed close behind.

"He seems to have adapted to ranch life like a duck to water," Rachel marveled.

"That's true. He's a natural. It's hard for me to imagine him back in some city office. I don't quite understand a man who can do that."

"Shuffling papers and schmoozing with clients?"

"Yep."

"What about a woman who does the same?"

He turned to study her quizzically for a long moment. "No. I guess I can't quite understand *anyone* who wants to do that all day." He threw her a mischievous smile. "At least, not yet anyway."

"Jake's a good man, and sharp," Rachel said, pulling her eyes away from his dark, mesmerizing gaze. "He was a promising architect, and he gave up a lot to come here."

"I know. Hey, I'm not criticizing. It's just that he's got such great instincts for ranching. I can't imagine him anywhere but here." Dirk looked thoughtful. "But it's more than that. He loves it on the ranch. He knows who he is and where he wants to be. You have to respect a man like that. So few people have the courage to pursue their dreams. I'm glad Jake followed his heart. He deserves to be happy."

Rachel softened at the warmth in his voice. *This man really cares about others*, she observed. She returned to something else he had said. "How do you know *you're* in the place you ought to be, Dirk?"

"Because I feel totally at peace," he said easily. He turned in his saddle to look at her as Caleb carried him ahead. "Except when you're around." He faced forward again, leaving Rachel with a deliciously sweet smile of surprise.

They rode on in comfortable silence as they sorted through their feelings. Dirk's leading statement sent Rachel's mind whirling. "I have to leave in ten days, Dirk." Her voice held a sad warning.

"I know," he said, reading her concern. "It scares me, too. I don't have the time or the energy to be hurt again, Rachel. But let's just see where those ten days lead us, okay?"

She paused and then answered quietly. "Okay."

They stopped at another clearing on the south end of the valley, where the mountains on either side merged briefly before heading their separate ways. Dirk unpacked a blanket and poured Rachel a glass of wine. Standing close together, they stared at the beauty around them and watched as the sun slipped over the western mountains. Dirk pointed out the Double M and Timberline ranches, as well as other landmarks Rachel knew. The Kootenai River wound along the valley floor on the western edge, rather than running straight south as she had envisioned. It straightened out briefly along Dirk's and Matt's ranches, forming a handy boundary line, and then resumed its winding coil.

As the sky turned color, so did the water. The green of the forest deepened as dusk enveloped the sky, and the fields of the valley were painted with rich shadows. The mountains she had seen all week appeared completely different from that height and angle. "Look," she said, pointing at the stone monsters. "They're like huge triangular men standing in a line. Each shoulder juts out and then disappears into the next. It's as if they were born in that position."

Dirk smiled at her observation. "They were born together," he said in awe, staring out at them as if he could see back in time. "In a huge, fantastic eruption they came, screaming out to the sky upon their arrival. Can you imagine? What a wonder it must be to be God. To create and then stand back and marvel at your work."

She smiled in return at his poetic vision of the mountain birth.

"Let's see what Mary made us," he said, breaking their reverie and turning away. They went to the blanket and dug in to a basket full of delicious treats. They dined on lasagna, carefully packed in foil and newspaper to retain its heat, a fresh tossed green salad with parmesan cheese, and Mary's own French bread. "Mary's cooking is divine," Rachel cooed. "I think I'd weigh two hundred pounds if I ate her food all the time."

Dirk said nothing, grinning at Rachel while he chewed his fourth piece of bread. She looked glorious. Her hair shone in long, sumptuous waves of chestnut, her green eyes glinted in the fading light, and the hollows and curves of her face took on deeper shadows.

"What?" she asked in exasperation as he studied her. "Do I have tomato sauce on my nose or something?"

"No," he said. "I was just thinking how stunning you are, and how you would still be beautiful, even if you did weigh two hundred pounds."

She smiled. "You do know what to say to a woman, don't you?"

"I know enough not to say anything I don't mean." He rose and returned to his saddle. From a large saddlebag he pulled out a radio and turned it on with a grin. The music was quiet and melodious, fitting perfectly with their surroundings. He bowed before her and held out his hand. "Mademoiselle?" he asked formally.

"Oui?" she answered coyly.

"May I have this dance?"

"You most certainly may." Taking his hand, Rachel rose and stood next to him. He drew her near as she put her hand on his shoulder and swayed with him to the music. The horses continued chewing wild grasses and looked over at them with bored expressions.

But Dirk was not bored. His entire being seemed to be drawn to this woman. She felt right in his arms… She spoke to him in such a forthright, honest manner… She even looked at him right, all alluring eyes and mystery and playfulness. They stared at each other as they turned in their own intimate little world, communicating without words. Instinctively both fought fear as they recognized something neither had felt in some time. Rachel broke away first and sat down on the blanket again. Dirk joined her in silence. They watched the moon rise soon after the sunset, following the same path as its predecessor.

"This is the most beautiful place I've ever visited, Dirk," Rachel whispered. "And I'm scared to death."

"Is it the valley," Dirk asked, gently turning her face toward his, "or me?" He kissed her softly before she could answer, drawing her close, then allowing her to slip back out of their embrace. They sat for a moment, dazed by the whirlwind of emotions, by the romantic setting, but most of all by the kiss.

"It's you," she finally answered.

Thursday, July 22

Beth pounced on her guest's bed, bouncing the mattress wildly. "Up, up, up! You have stories to tell, judging from how late you got in last night."

Rachel rubbed her eyes sleepily and gazed at her friend and then the clock. She groaned and put her pillow over her head. "I'll tell you about it in three hours," she said, her voice muffled.

"Three hours? No way. Remember ranchers' hours?"

"Beth, you haven't made me do anything on the ranch all week," she said, poking her mouth out to speak. "You just want company."

"True. But I want you to get up anyway. I particularly want company that can tell me juicy romantic stories. I'll get you a cup of fresh coffee," she said enticingly.

"I'm going to kill you, Beth Morgan. I need to go home so I can get some sleep after this crazy vacation. Give me two minutes and I'll be down."

Beth jumped up and walked to the door. She watched silently as Rachel closed her eyes and buried herself back under the covers. "Rachel!" she said loudly.

Rachel sat up, startled. "I'm coming, I'm coming!"

Over coffee Rachel shared the whole romantic evening with Beth, leaving nothing out. They laughed together at the funny little moments when things were awkward, and Beth squealed with delight when Rachel told her how they had danced and kissed and talked for hours under a bright, moonlit sky.

"I think I'll direct Matt over to Timberline for some weekly Romance 101 classes from Professor Tanner."

"No kidding. I've never encountered a smoother guy. He is a dream man, from what I can tell about him. How come some woman hasn't grabbed him?"

"He hasn't let anyone close for a very long time," Beth said. "You're the first woman he's made a move toward since Debra. Women have come after him, but he never looked their way, never encouraged them. This is the first crack in the armor that I've seen."

Rachel looked out at the mountains through the living room picture window and then turned back to Beth, her face anguished. "But what am I gonna do, Beth? I'm only going to be here for nine more days. I live so far away...and I don't see Dirk tolerating a long-distance romance."

"Whatever's to be, will be," Beth said. "It's a little late to worry about a ball that's already rolling. You just have to play the rest of your time out and see what happens. Make the hard decisions after your whole hand has been dealt."

"I suppose you're right. What if I got a totally wrong message? What if he sees the evening as just a fun date?"

"Rachel, Dirk isn't like that. He doesn't casually date. I don't think you have to worry about that angle."

Rachel's stomach was rumbling for breakfast, so the two friends headed toward the kitchen. "Did Dirk tell you when he'd pick you up tomorrow?" Beth asked.

"Tomorrow?"

"The Sweet Pea Festival kicks off with that dance tomorrow night." She paused, then frowned. "He didn't ask you?"

"No. You see? He's probably not as sure about me as you seem to think he is."

"Yes he is."

"Then why didn't he ask me to the dance?"

"I don't know. Maybe he thought it was too soon. Maybe he had other things on his mind," Beth said meaningfully. "Either way, I do know Dirk Tanner likes what he has seen in you so far. I can see it in the way he looks at you. And Matt says he just starts blabbing when your name comes up."

"Still, he didn't make a date with me."

"He's scared. You're scared. That doesn't make it easy to ask for a date. Why don't you ride Kala over there today? Surprise him."

"That's a good idea," Rachel said as she bit into a freshly baked biscuit. She chewed and swallowed. "I'll go as soon as I eat twelve more of these baked marvels and take a shower."

Rachel dressed and headed toward the stables. Beth had again declined Rachel's offer to accompany her on a horseback ride. Rachel was disappointed but shrugged it off. Her time alone was enjoyable too.

As she entered the stables, Alex stepped out from the shadows and caught her arm. "Mornin', Rachel. Didn't see you at supper last night. Seems like days since I've gotten a good look at you."

She shook her arm free from his grasp and walked away without responding. Rachel had decided that she would just ignore him and not ruin her vacation by repeatedly tangling with him.

He caught up to her and walked along with her to Kala's stall. "Now that's not a nice way to act toward me, an earnest admirer 'n' all," he said sternly.

"Sorry," Rachel muttered without remorse. She turned, grabbed a halter off a peg, and opened the stall door. She approached Kala quietly and gently slipped it over her nose and ears, aware that Alex still stared at her. He blocked her path as she led the horse toward the door.

"I'm getting tired of your games, Alex," she warned.

"Do you have a date for tomorrow night?" he asked.

"Yes," she lied, moving to push past him. Still, he blocked her way.

"You're not telling me you're going with Tanner, are you?"

"It's none of your business, Alex. Excuse me."

"I'm not moving till you tell me who you're goin' with."

"And I said I'm not going to tell you." She raised her boot high and came down hard on his toe with her heel, causing him to wince. "Sorry, Alex, your foot must've been in my way." Rachel pushed past him, still leading Kala by the halter. She entered the tack room and took her saddle from the rack.

Alex followed her and watched as she tossed a saddle over Kala's back. His eyes were hard and angry. "Now look here, I'm just tryin' to be friendly. There's no cause for you to be nasty."

"On the contrary, Alex. Your boorish behavior demanded a like response. If you stoop to a nasty level, it brings me down too."

His angry eyes became lecherous. "Why don't we…start over." He took a slow, thoughtful step toward her, and Rachel backed up.

"I think you ought to go now, Alex. Matt's just outside."

He kept advancing, and Rachel kept backing away, her heart hammering in anger and alarm. "Matt is five miles south," he corrected her. Rachel abruptly bumped into a wall, and Alex moved close to her. "Now don't you think you should apologize for stomping on my foot?" His breath was hot on her face, and something wild and menacing in his eyes told Rachel to flee.

Rachel's hands felt the rough wood behind her and fanned out in search of a weapon. To her left she discovered a wooden handle, and taking a chance, she leaped to the side and brought it up between them, pleased to discover the metal tines of a pitchfork on the opposite end.

Alex paused to consider his next move, glowering at her. His chest began to heave, and his neck flushed in anger.

Just then, Rachel heard Jake enter the stables whistling. He apparently sized up the situation as soon as he saw them, his whistle fading away. Walking over to the stall where Rachel held Alex at bay, he leaned casually over the rail and tried to gently defuse the situation. "Trouble, Rachel?"

"I'd call it that."

"Back off, Rierdon," Alex said. "We just have a little misunderstandin' here. It's between *us*."

"It looks like more than a misunderstanding, Jordan. I thought Matt told you to steer clear of Rachel."

"He didn't use those words exactly. Besides, I can see whoever I want. It's not up to Matt."

"Okay, then. Rachel, do you want to see much more of Alex?" Jake asked sarcastically. He walked into the stall, taking the pitchfork from her trembling hands and easing her away from Alex.

"I think not."

"Why don't you come see the new foal?" Jake took her hand and pulled her toward the other end of the barn. Alex hesitated to follow.

The colt somewhat distracted Rachel, and she exclaimed in pleasure. Quietly Jake placed the pitchfork within easy reach and approached the tiny foal. He looked on like a proud papa and then turned to smile at Rachel as Alex watched them. After a moment Alex stomped off angrily.

"You better stay away from him," Jake whispered to Rachel as she stroked the colt's nose. Her hand still trembled.

"Believe me, Jake, I try. He seems to always be around. Does Matt realize what a creep he is?"

"He's not as bad around Matt. He's a hard worker. The only time he's been any real trouble was your first night, on the porch." Jake nodded at the look she gave him. "Yeah, Matt told me. Be careful, Rachel. Alex has his eye on you, and that's not a good thing."

"I know it. I'll try to watch out for him. And thanks for saving me, Jake." She looked back at the colt. "What's his name?"

"Nothing yet. Maybe you can think of one."

"I'll give it some thought on my ride." She left the stall and walked back to where Kala was tied and took off her halter. Wordlessly, Jake slipped on the bit while Rachel put on the saddle, tightened the girth, and climbed on. "Thanks again, Jake," she said meaningfully.

He waved it off, but she was impressed with his grace and poise in handling the tense situation.

Rachel relished every minute of her beautiful late-morning ride, gradually relaxing. She took deep, restorative breaths, feeling more alive than ever. The sky was a glorious blue, and white fluffy clouds dotted the horizon. Looking around her, Rachel truly understood why Montana was called Big Sky country.

She reached Dirk's ranch an hour later and rode up to the house. Mary came out, wiping her hands on an apron. "Oh dear, I don't think Dirk is around. He told me earlier that he was heading into town to run some errands."

Rachel was disappointed but tried to hide it, saying quickly, "Oh, that's okay."

Mary was not fooled by her denial. "Why don't you come in, dear, and join me in a cup of coffee?"

"Thanks, Mary, but I've reached my caffeine limit for today with Beth. How 'bout a cold glass of water?"

"Sure. Come on up."

Rachel dismounted and tied Kala loosely to a post near the porch. From a corral a gray Appaloosa whinnied at the newcomer, and Kala answered, looking over at him. Rachel watched in fascination as the horse galloped around the corral, tossing his head as if showing off and calling again to Kala.

Just then, Mary came out the screen door. "Cyrano is quite the ladies' man of horses."

"Cyrano?"

"He's been after every mare since Dirk brought him home a month ago, and he's not much to look at—thus the name."

"I think he's beautiful." Rachel climbed the stairs to join Mary, who had seated herself on a swing. "Look at how strong he is. Practically every muscle in his body is sharply defined."

"Yes, he is strong," Mary agreed as she handed Rachel a glass of ice water from a tray. "Dirk's been having quite a time getting him trained, even though Cyrano was partially broken when he bought him. Because of his poor demeanor, Dirk just had him gelded rather than continue using him for breeding." Her eyes twinkled. "He should come around now."

Rachel and her hostess chatted amiably for a while before the conversation drew more serious. "Dirk seems to be quite taken with you," Mary said, carefully looking out at the horizon.

"I seem to be quite taken with Dirk," Rachel said, amused.

Mary grinned. "I'm so pleased to hear that! It's been a long while since Dirk has taken a serious interest in anyone." Her smile faded. "You will be careful with him, won't you?"

"Mary, relationships are always a bit scary. There are no guarantees. But if you're asking if I'll do my best not to hurt him, yes, I'll certainly try."

"You probably think I'm a meddlesome old fool."

Rachel grabbed her hand and squeezed it gently. "I think you're a woman who's cared for Dirk for a very long time."

Her answer obviously appealed to Mary, but the frankness of their conversation made her uneasy. "Would you like more water?"

"No, thank you. That was the best water I think I've ever had. You should bottle it and sell it to Californians."

"It's from a well Dirk's father dug forty years ago. Tapped into a natural high country spring. And I don't think we'll be selling any to California."

"Just a suggestion," Rachel said with a laugh. "Say, Mary, since Dirk's not here, do you think I could snoop around the ranch? I'd love to get a feel for where Dirk comes from, if you know what I mean."

"Snoop! Go to it for as long as you like. And if you need anything, just come holler at me." She put the empty glasses on a tray and moved to the kitchen door, opening it expertly with her foot.

Rachel left the porch after thanking her hostess and set off for the corral. She wanted to get a look at Cyrano before exploring elsewhere. The uniquely colored horse ran around the corral as she approached and even bucked his hind legs once or twice when she reached the fence. "Well, hello, you big show-off," Rachel said in greeting.

She climbed the first rail and watched him silently for several minutes until he finally slowed to stare back at her. Quietly, she stepped down, reached for a handful of long green grass beside her, and resumed her previous position. She extended her hand slowly, offering the horse a snack and cooing to him in even tones. "Come on, Cyrano," she said in a low, unthreatening voice. "Come on, baby. Don't you want some nice green grass? Doesn't that look good? Just take the grass, not my fingers. Come on."

Cyrano cocked his head slightly to the side, listening to her. His giant pink nostrils flared and snorted toward her offering. He took a few hesitant steps toward Rachel, prancing back and forth in place as if he was unsure what to do with her. His eyes watched her intently, never wavering. She called to him softly, and after a moment he covered the remaining steps between them, tossing his head. Then he reached out ever so gently, grabbed the grass from her hand, and chewed it, on alert the whole time.

Rachel pulled up some more grass and climbed to the top of the fence, temporarily making the gelding shy away from her. Again, she coaxed Cyrano toward her and offered him the grass, this time advancing into the corral with the gelding. She heard a screen door at the house slam, and knew Mary was probably on the porch, watching her, but ignored her. Her attention was on Cyrano, who approached Rachel and stretched out his neck to gently take the grass from her hand.

With care, Rachel reached out her hand so the horse could smell it without the grass. He turned his head as if uninterested but did not move away. When he turned back to her, Rachel quietly reached out to his nose, softly brushing it. Again, he turned away and then came back to her. She rubbed his nose a bit harder.

Rachel was entranced by the horse's response. She knew he was "green," as the men at the Double M called untrained horses, but she decided he was enjoying her attention. He lowered his head to allow her to rub even harder and moved closer to her. After a while she stopped and turned to climb back over the fence. She was startled by his nose rubbing hard along her back, almost lifting her up with each stroke. She laughed in surprise, and the horse immediately backed up at the noise.

"Sorry, Cyrano. We were doing so well. I guess I'll see you later." She turned to climb the fence and jump down on the other side, watching Mary's shoulders droop a little as if in relief. A grizzled, lean-looking man approached from the barn, muttering something about a "woman's touch."

Rachel greeted him as she brushed off fine gray horse hairs from her top and jeans. "Hi, I'm Rachel Johanssen."

"I'm Frank, the second man in command around here. I think it would be a good idea to stay away from Cyrano until he's totally broke, ma'am. I'm considering your safety first. I'd hate to see a guest trampled during my last year."

"Sorry, Frank. I'll stay away from any more untrained horses around here, okay? Mary gave me the go-ahead to snoop around, and I couldn't resist Cyrano. But I'll stick to looking at nonmoving objects if it'll make you feel better."

"Yes, it would, ma'am."

"You have to admit that I did all right with the horse."

He worked his jaw as if fighting a stubborn urge to refute the fact. Dirk had told her on their date about working for weeks on the gelding—who she knew now must be Cyrano—and not getting as far as Rachel had. "Hate to admit it, but you did mighty well," he said at last.

"Thank you, sir," she said, trying to keep pride out of her voice. "Now where's a nice, safe place for me to explore on Timberline?"

"See that path around the north end of the house?"

Rachel nodded in response.

"Follow it up the hillside. You'll be away from danger there. And if you want to meet any more of the horses, look me up in the barn, all right? No more self-introductions."

"Deal." Rachel headed off in the direction Frank had pointed. The hill rose steeply, and Rachel was soon out of breath. She wondered where the path led. The trees deepened in density, filtering out much of the sun but allowing a few beautiful rays to seep through. She paused in the hush that only an isolated forest could create and stared at the scene, transfixed. A doe and her fawn shyly walked amid the sunbeams, sniffing the air as if they knew someone was near but were unable to spot the intruder.

The fawn jumped a narrow log and stumbled clumsily. Rachel cried out softly, worried for the baby. But he quickly regained his footing and dashed after his fleeing mother.

Rachel smiled in wonder at her encounter, feeling as if she had entered another world. She resumed her walk and soon noticed a clearing in the trees. On a ledge ten feet away she saw what looked like a tiny hut made of rock. It almost appeared to be a playhouse, complete with roof and chimney. She drew nearer and walked in the back door, surprised by what she found inside.

The room was about fifteen square feet, with a potbelly wood stove to the side and a small altar with a tiny cross in the front. Beyond the altar a huge window framed a large portion of the Rocky Mountain range, and in front of the altar was a small kneeling pad. Closest to her and to the right were two big, overstuffed chairs and a reading lamp. Despite her inexperience in religious matters, Rachel realized the room was a chapel. She seated herself in one of the chairs, silenced by the utter peace the room held. For a long while she sat and stared, first at the view and then at the handcrafted altar and cross.

Looking over the side of the chair, she spotted a Bible. *Dirk James Tanner* was printed in the leather that covered the well-worn volume. She opened it to where a bookmark stuck out. It was in Psalms, the book Rachel remembered as her childhood favorite. She began with Psalm 28 and moved on to 29, meditating on the passages that spoke of strength and trust and peace. She continued with Psalm 30 and stopped after reading the concluding verses: "You turned my wailing into dancing; you removed my sackcloth and clothed me with joy, that my heart may sing to you and not be silent. O LORD my God, I will give you thanks forever."

Deep within her, something stirred. Her heart cried out at the familiar but long-forgotten words. With tears streaming down her cheeks, she again read the songs that David had written and felt a desire to know his Lord. "Why now?" she begged God to hear her. "I was happy. I didn't need you. Now I feel like I've been missing you for a very long time."

Rachel moved to the altar and knelt there. For the longest time she said nothing. The silence sounded deep and rich to her, as if a whole world lay just beyond her comprehension, and she sensed God's presence. "Hello, Father," Rachel said, smiling through sudden tears at the quickening in her heart.

She knelt for a long time, talking, listening, praying—even humming old hymns she remembered from her childhood. The feelings she experienced were incredible, even beyond those she felt for Dirk, which surprised her. When she finally left the chapel, Rachel knew something had changed. She looked back at the building in wonder and marveled that Dirk obviously spent time there. *You're an even greater man than I had thought, Dirk Tanner. I want to know you better. And I want to know your God better too.*

CHAPTER SIX

*Y*ou're going, Rachel," Beth said firmly.

"Oh, Beth, I thought I'd just relax here on the ranch. That's what I came on vacation for—a little R and R," Rachel said.

"Dirk will be so disappointed if you don't show up! The Sweet Pea Festival is the biggest event of the year around here. You also came on vacation for some fun. *Please* come."

"If Dirk Tanner cared whether or not I showed up, he would've asked me to go. I don't want to push myself on him."

Exasperated, Beth said, "He's probably assuming you're coming with Matt and me. No more arguments. Get your gorgeous body into a dress by suppertime. We'll leave directly after." With that, Beth confidently turned around and exited her friend's room.

Rachel groaned loud enough for her hostess to hear and flopped down on her bed. With her head resting on her hands, she gazed out the window toward the hills behind the house, thinking about Dirk.

It was then that she saw Alex standing outside among the trees, twenty feet from her window. His arms were crossed over his chest, and he wore a big grin on his face as he met her wide eyes. She jumped off the bed and quickly drew the shade. "Creep," she muttered under her breath.

Rachel stood beside the window, urging her heart to ease its pace, and glanced over to the bathroom. *Oh no*, she thought. *The shower.* She walked cautiously into the small room and looked out the shoulder-high shower window. As she peeked around the corner, Alex caught her searching face and hooted in laughter. Rachel quickly ducked back, acknowledging the fact that he had probably been watching her shower all week. The window only exposed her head and shoulders, but she still felt invaded. *This has gone too far. After the dance, I'll have a chat with Matt.*

She moved back to the bedroom, picked up a book, and sat on the bed, resolving to forget about Alex. However, her mind drifted from the story line, and she found herself thinking more about Dirk and Alex than about the characters.

At five o'clock, she rose and slipped on a soft red summer dress that fit her well and flared prettily in the skirt. She stealthily moved into the bathroom and pulled the shade down from the side. She couldn't see Alex anymore, but she was taking no chances. "The peep shows are over," she whispered. Once protected from her outside observer, she relaxed and freshened her makeup. Afterward she pinned her hair up in a casual knot. *Not bad,* she mused, looking into the mirror. *We'll show these cowboys how to dance!*

As she entered the living room, Rachel received appreciative glances from several of the men coming in from the bunkhouse. Matt had let them off early to give them time to shower, shave, and don their Sunday best. Alex, fortunately, was not among them. With any luck, he wouldn't show up that night at all.

"Come on! Hurry up and eat so we can get going." Beth directed them to the table, looking gorgeous in a lavender sundress. Matt walked in and picked her up in his arms with a hoot. "Darlin', you look beautiful."

Beth scolded him and blushed brightly as the men looked on with broad smiles, and then she joined in their laughter. All were bursting with anticipation for the evening ahead.

"It feels like Christmas around here," Rachel said.

The men talked more animatedly than they had all week, and a few even dared to ask Rachel careful and polite questions. She enjoyed the meal and promised several a dance. Afterward, they hurriedly cleared the table—leaving a monstrous pile of dishes in the sink—and moved to the front door.

Rachel ran upstairs to grab a sweater as everyone left the house and was the last one out. From her left, Alex emerged from the porch's shade.

She gasped in surprise and froze, glancing from him to the nearest truck. The men were bantering back and forth, and Matt was helping Beth into the truck. No one saw them. Alex waited until she looked at him again. He whispered closely in her ear, "Save *me* a dance, gorgeous." With a deep chuckle and a tip of his hat, he departed.

Rachel joined the Morgans in their vehicle. In caravan fashion, they all left the ranch, drove to town, and soon entered the grange hall drive. Rachel used the time—and the cover of Beth and Matt's idle wonderings over friends and neighbors—to convince herself that Alex only had power over her if she gave it to him. And she wouldn't do that. It was time to end the game.

Rachel looked between Beth and Matt to the grange parking lot. "Looks like a used-car lot for Ford trucks," she commented. The majority of the vehicles in the parking lot were indeed trucks, although there were also a few Buick sedans. "I didn't know Elk Horn had this many people."

"I told you, everybody comes out of the woodwork this weekend," Matt said.

"It's not exactly the philharmonic, Rachel, but my friends do say it's the most fun this town sees all year," Beth chimed in.

Matt parked the truck and came around to open the doors for the ladies. "I love it. I'm bringing the two prettiest women to the Sweet Pea, one on either arm. Life is good."

"Proud as a peacock, aren't you?" Beth chided him. "You just concentrate on teaching me the steps around these country dances. This is my first Sweet Pea too."

"I know it. But how will you take it when I leave you to whirl Rachel around the dance floor half the night?"

Smiling at her friend, Beth said, "You leave Rachel's whirling to Dirk Tanner, Matthew. Tonight, you're mine and mine alone."

Rachel enjoyed their banter. It was good to see her friend so happy and satisfied. But as they neared the grange hall, her heart pounded—anticipating seeing Dirk and dreading a confrontation with Alex. The old building glowed from within in the cool light of the mountain evening.

Matt frowned and stopped to stare at Rachel, obviously picking up her hesitation. "You okay?"

"Fine, fine," she said, pasting on a smile.

Vaguely mollified, Matt moved forward and opened the door for Beth and Rachel. It was fifteen degrees hotter inside the worn pine walls than out. A loud country band was already playing, and people merrily streamed in and out of the front door.

"I bet you'll be picking up the fiddle soon, Beth," Rachel joked.

"I'll stick to dancing, thank you," her friend retorted as she and Matt joined hands and moved deeper into the room. Rachel followed behind, delightfully pleased by all the sights and sounds of a good old-fashioned country dance.

Papier-mâché lanterns painted with bright colors swung in the breezes of open windows and passing dancers. Hay bales lined the room and served as benches for chatting neighbors and the weary. The band included two fiddles, a washboard, a bass and trap set, and a tiny upright piano with a high C that stuck. The members played wildly as an overweight woman in straining red gingham sang into an ancient microphone that squealed when she got too close.

Rachel watched the scene, observing couples weave and bob in delighted revelry. The song ended, and sweating duos clapped animatedly while heading toward the punch. A few waited for the next song, which was slow and melodic after the crazy beat of the previous number.

In the soft, dusty light, Rachel caught sight of Dirk across the room. He looked dashing in a crisp white shirt, rolled at the sleeves and unbuttoned at the neck, and well-fitted blue jeans that met brown suede boots at the bottom.

Two women stood on either side of Dirk, talking to him, but he only had eyes for Rachel.

He noticed how elegant she looked, appearing at once poised and out of place. The women with Dirk frowned, pouting at his sudden distraction and wondering how to compete with the pretty stranger. There was no need, he wanted to tell them. No way to compete with a woman like Rachel. He left them without a word and walked toward her, wanting to put her at ease, make her feel at home, take her in his arms, unpin that fantastic, sexy hair… He swallowed, hard, as he approached her. "Hello, Rachel. You look beautiful."

"Hello, Dirk. Don't look so bad yourself." She gazed up at him with a smile.

"Would you like to dance?"

"Your girlfriends don't mind?"

He ignored her playful barb and extended his arms. She joined him with a grin, and they twirled around the floor, each happy to recognize in the other a gifted dancing partner.

"Heard you romanced Cyrano yesterday."

"Well, you weren't around."

"You mean if I had been, you would have romanced me?"

Rachel smiled but didn't answer. They finished the dance, swept along to two faster tunes, and then slowed for another soft ballad. While they danced, they chatted about horses, the Morgans, the weather…measurably more comfortable after their shared afternoon and sunset picnic.

Dirk looked down into Rachel's bright green eyes and admired the sable tendrils of hair that had slipped from her careful knot and now clung to her damp neck. Her neck was strong and lean and met a pronounced collarbone. And her skin, softly tanned, seemed to call out to him for a kiss. He pulled her into his arms, rearranged their hands, and spun her out and away from him in an experienced dance move.

"Thank you, friend," Alex said smartly as he grabbed Rachel's hand from Dirk's. "Don't mind if I cut in, do ya?" he half asked as he pulled Rachel close.

Stunned, Rachel reacted too late to ward off the man.

Trying to be polite and not create a scene, Dirk stepped away from the couple. Unable to watch them, he turned his back and went to get some punch, impatient for the song to end. He silently urged the band to finish and despised each new verse.

At the punch table, Dirk overheard two middle-aged women talking. He only needed to hear one saying, "Who is that poor girl that Alex Jordan has himself attached to now?" to turn and finally look back.

Rachel was obviously struggling, trying to get away from Alex, her face red with anger and her voice rising. Other dancers were slowing to watch the scene, and several men from the Double M approached the couple, seeking to come to Rachel's aid.

Dirk roughly set down his glass teacup, cracking the handle. He ignored the red punch that spilled over its edge as he strode back to the dance floor. Seeing Rachel's anger made him instantly furious. Matt's strong hand gripped Dirk's shoulder from behind, stopping his advance midway. Jake stood beside him.

"Hold on, Dirk. Let me handle this."

Dirk shook off Matt's hand and continued striding toward Alex, wanting desperately to punch Rachel's offender.

"Dirk!" Matthew said more loudly. He pulled Dirk to a stop. "Do you want to ruin the dance? He's *my* man. Let me take care of it. If he were yours, I'd step aside, but this is my business too. I'll get Rachel and be back with her in a minute." He left Dirk behind, fuming, and met up with his men, directing them with a nod to stand behind him.

As they approached, Alex still swayed with the struggling Rachel in his arms. She relaxed when she saw Matthew come toward them, and Alex took it as a sign of acquiescence.

"That's more like it," he whispered to her wickedly, looking down her torso.

"Step away, Jordan," Matt's voice rumbled with warning. "I think Rachel's tired and is about ready for some punch with Beth. No more dancing for our guest right now."

Alex continued to cling to her as he stared at his employer. "I have the right to dance with anyone I want to."

"Rachel, do you want to dance any more with this man?" Matt asked pointedly.

"No," she said with distaste, giving him another futile shove.

"Hands off, Alex," Matt directed. "You heard her." After a tense pause, Alex released Rachel and moved to stand chest to chest with Matt. His face was red with fury, veins bulging at the sides of his neck. If anyone but his boss had confronted him, he probably would have lashed out.

"You're invading my personal space," Matt warned with a tight-lipped smile. "If you want a job tomorrow, you'd better head home right now and never ever come near Ms. Johanssen again."

Alex swallowed hard. He glared at the men standing behind Matt, took a last, meaningful look at Rachel, and walked out of the hall, swearing under his breath. "I don't need this," he muttered. "There's a better party goin' on at the saloon anyhow."

Matt put his arm around Rachel and led her to where Dirk and Beth stood. Beth placed a cup of punch in Rachel's shaking hand. "You're sure popular," Beth quipped, trying to lighten the moment.

"You might think about a personality test for new employees, Matt," Rachel said. She silently willed herself to handle the situation with grace.

"Alex just failed my test. I'll give him notice tomorrow where he can't make a scene," Matt answered decisively. "A man's got to respect others to be a part of my team." He looked around the room, which had grown quiet after the disruption Alex had caused, and then turned to his wife. "Come on, Beth. Rachel's safe with Dirk. Let's hit the dance floor and get this party going again."

"I'm sorry, Rachel. I should have seen it coming," Dirk said, as the Morgans walked away. "I should've asked you to the dance myself, been a proper escort." He frowned as he noticed her shaking hand when she lifted the punch to her lips.

"Don't worry," she tried to assure him. "You were just trying to be gracious, letting him cut in. No harm done, really, and I'll never have to see him again after tomorrow. I'd feel bad about his getting fired, but I don't think he's stable." Editing details, she confessed how Alex had harassed her all week.

Dirk seethed with anger, and he resolved never to let a harmful man near Rachel again. The thought surprised him. *How can I protect her from any evil at all when she lives a thousand miles away?*

Rachel leaned under Dirk's arm, seemingly taking comfort in his proximity. "Let's shake it off," she said. "The night is young and we have a dance to finish, mister." She bounced onto the dance floor, and Dirk joined her, smiling and slowly coming out of his anger.

The rest of the evening sped by as they danced and talked and danced some more. Rachel barely noticed the time when Matthew and Beth said good night. She and Dirk walked them out, glad for the chance to cool down. "I assume you'll be willing to drive our guest home, Dirk." Matt grinned.

"Yes, I'll bring her home," Dirk said, smiling down at Rachel. He casually looped an arm around her waist and pulled her closer. "Don't wait up though; we just might break curfew."

"Two o'clock at the latest, Dirk Tanner," Beth said, shaking a threatening finger in his face.

"Okay, Beth, two o'clock."

Beth and Matt walked out to the truck arm in arm, looking up at the brilliant night sky filled with stars. Dirk and Rachel followed suit. The sky was pitch-black with no moon, perfect for showing off the twinkling heavenly lights. Above them, the broad pale band of the Milky Way stretched from one edge of the valley to the other. To the south, a shooting star made a sudden, dramatic descent.

"Good friends, aren't they?" Dirk commented to Rachel, looking back at the Morgans as they drove away, the truck's headlights swooping past, momentarily blinding them both.

"The best." Their agreement on the matter seemed to solidify their closeness, and Rachel rested her head on Dirk's shoulder as they walked together, wordlessly returning to the dance floor.

"Hit me again!" Alex yelled at the bartender as he gazed at his empty shot glass.

"Sorry, Alex. Gotta cut you off for the night."

Alex slurred obscenities and demanded more whiskey.

"You better head home, or I'll have you booted outta here," the bartender threatened.

The bouncer loomed over Alex's shoulder. "Don't give me any trouble."

Alex swore again and slid off his barstool. His mind swimming from the alcohol, he stood for a moment to regain his equilibrium and then sauntered out of the dark bar. The cool mountain air refreshed him, and he turned back toward the Silver Moon Saloon. "No prob'em boys!" he yelled. "Got a pretty young gal waitin' on me atta dance!"

He staggered over to his truck and turned the keys he had left in the ignition. After nearly driving into a roadside ditch, he turned onto the highway and headed back toward the grange hall with one thought on his mind.

Rachel Johanssen.

The truck careened dangerously back and forth across the lanes as he picked up speed.

Beth was so excited about Rachel and Dirk's obvious chemistry she hadn't stopped talking about them after she and Matt left the dance. She was in the middle of relating visions of their wedding when Matt spotted a truck heading toward them on their side of the road. The headlights swerved unsteadily from lane to lane, making it impossible for Matt to counteract the other driver's error. Beth stopped her chatter and screamed as the oncoming truck lurched back into their lane twenty feet ahead of them.

Alex Jordan's mind barely registered the fact that an oncoming vehicle had slipped over the embankment and out of sight. After a few miles, he turned into the grange hall lane. He stood outside for a while, watching Rachel and Dirk as they bobbed in front of the windows, and then moved out of sight. His anger grew as the fog in his mind lifted.

That man's got his hands on my girl. Alex would teach him a lesson. Teach him good. Tanner and Morgan had always thought they were better than him, looking down their noses. He ran through every foul name he could think of. He'd show Dirk Tanner who the real man was, who really deserved a hot woman like Rachel. He'd show her. She'd come around, see that she was wrong. Beg him to kiss her and more.

At half past one Dirk looked around at the quickly dwindling crowd and told Rachel they should head home. "I want to have a few spare minutes with you before curfew," he whispered, and Rachel smiled with anticipation of another kiss, a sweet word, a tender good-night embrace. He left to get the Jeep as Rachel chatted with Doug, the editor of the local newspaper.

"We could use your expertise in ad work. Any desire to move to Big Sky country?" he asked, looking after Dirk.

"Oh no," she said. "It's beautiful, but I have a job back in San Francisco that would really be hard to leave."

"'Scuse me, Doug," a slurred voice interrupted. "This lady owes me the res' of a dance." With that Alex grabbed Rachel and dragged her to the dance floor.

"Alex! Alex, no! Stop this!" She looked back at the diminutive editor and around the room. *Where's Dirk?* she wondered. *He's been gone a long time.* "Alex, let me go!" she demanded loudly. She tried to pry his fingers off her arms, but he just pulled her closer. "Alex, please," she said, trying to soften her tone. "Let me go."

When he refused, her anger boiled up again. With all her strength, she shoved him far enough away to slap him across the face.

Alex winced, one hand moving from her to his cheek. His eyes met hers in cold fury, the desire to slap her back plain in his expression.

"Alex," Rachel said, "Get away from me, and stay away! I hate the way you act, and I never want to see you again."

"Go home, Jordan," said a man, coming to stand beside the editor.

"Get lost, Jordan!" called another.

Alex let out a roar—a mix of hurt and seething anger—and lunged at Rachel. He pulled her to him roughly, his grip on her like iron.

Rachel pounded at his arms and chest but was unable to pull away. Alex ignored her blows and the people's shouts as he stalked toward the door, taking her with him.

Just as they reached the entrance, Dirk filled the doorway. Rachel's eyes flew from his heaving chest to an alarming six-inch gash in his forehead. *Alex hit him. That's where he's been.* "Get away from her, Jordan!" he growled. Fury that equaled Alex's glowed in his eyes like fanned white-hot coals.

A smile spread across Alex's face, and his alcohol-laced, pungent breath floated over to Dirk. Rachel watched in horror as Alex reached into his back pocket and pulled out an army knife. She grabbed at his hand and screamed, but the weapon was out of her reach. Eight inches long with a mean, serrated edge, it glinted in the light. With horror, Rachel glanced from Dirk to the knife to Dirk again. *He means to kill Dirk,* she thought, feeling as if she were watching a bad TV movie rather than living it. *He might intend to kill me.*

Anger pushed away her fear, and once again, she lunged for Alex's arm and the knife.

As Alex struggled with Rachel, Dirk charged, knocking all three of them to the ground. He pulled Alex back up and punched him with all his might, throwing him to the floor where Rachel lay sprawled. Alex dove for the knife, grabbed the stunned Rachel from behind, and pulled her up to stand in front of him, his knife at her throat.

"Back off," he ordered Dirk. "Back off!" Sweat dripped from his forehead, and his eyes were wild. He stumbled and Dirk gasped, scared that in a fall he might hurt Rachel.

Pastor Arnie appeared in the doorway. Alex whirled around, trying to keep an eye on Dirk, as well as on the man blocking the exit.

"Alex," the pastor said calmly. "This is not the way. It won't make you happy or satisfied. Let her go. Do you think she's going to start liking you after you've treated her like this?"

"She'll like me just fine. Outta my way, preacher, or I'll cut her throat."

"Now, Alex, I know you're hurting. I've heard and watched you act out the rage that's eatin' you up inside. But you must know that taking Rachel away by force will not make it better. She cannot—"

"I don't wanna hear it!"

"Alex, please, let's just go talk. Just you and me."

Alex drew up the knife until it pushed against Rachel's larynx. Her eyes grew wider, and the movement alarmed Arnie.

"Okay, okay, I'm moving, Alex. But why don't you leave Rachel with us and head on home?"

"Yeah, sure, preacher. Sure," Alex mocked, dragging Rachel through the door and to his truck. As he fumbled for his keys, he loosened his grip slightly. Rachel took advantage of the moment to whirl around and bring her knee up to meet his groin. Dirk pounced from two steps away, pushing Alex to the ground and taking his knife away.

Close behind them, the pastor stepped forward and placed a foot on Alex's chest, holding the man down, as well as keeping Dirk from doing something he would later regret. "That's quite enough, Alex. I think you should just wait there until the sheriff comes. I'll come visit you tomorrow at the jail, and we'll continue our talk."

Alex started to struggle but backed down when he saw the remaining men join Arnie and Dirk.

Dirk dismissed any further thought of Alex, having eyes only for Rachel. Rachel stared blankly at Alex and the preacher. Her skin was the color of his mother's bone china. Dirk approached her slowly and led her to his Jeep. "Way past curfew, Rachel," he said gently. "I think we're both ready for some sleep. Come on. I'll get you home to the Double M."

CHAPTER SEVEN

*M*s. Johanssen!" a loud voice called again from beyond Rachel's guest bedroom door. Rachel awoke more fully after the third insistent knock and rolled over to look at the clock. Four in the morning. "This has got to be a joke," she mumbled to herself. "Who is it?" she asked irritably.

"It's Daryl, Ms. Johanssen. We're afraid something's happened to the Morgans. I was wondering if you knew where they were." Rachel recognized the voice of one of Matt's most trusted men. Adrenaline surged through her body at the urgent tone of his voice.

"Just a second, Daryl. I'll be right out." Rachel yanked on her jeans and an emerald T-shirt. She quickly opened the door. "What do you mean, you're afraid something's happened to them?" She reached for her boots and sweater.

"Their truck isn't out back, and they're not in the house. By this time, Matt's usually starting a fire in the kitchen to warm the place up before breakfast."

"I thought they were in bed when I got home last night. Where do you think they might be?"

"Well, I'm not sure they even got home last night. We've got four men out already, checking for their truck along the highway in both directions. They didn't say anything to you 'bout goin' anywhere?"

"No, no. Excuse me. I think I'd better call Dirk Tanner and the local hospital."

Daryl followed her downstairs and into the cold, dark kitchen. Rachel flipped on the lights and blinked against the sudden brightness.

Dirk's number was listed over the kitchen telephone, along with the other neighbors'. As she was dialing, Daryl's hip radio crackled to life. "Daryl?" came Jake's anxious voice. "We found 'em. You better come on down the highway, about five miles south. Call an ambulance!"

Dirk had answered Rachel's call and was probably just deciding it was a crank caller when she finally tuned in to his voice. "Hello?" he repeated.

"Dirk? Oh, Dirk! Matt and Beth… We didn't even look for them." Overwhelmed by the thought of her friends in trouble, Rachel fought to maintain her equilibrium. Daryl was already on the radio with the hospital, and he beckoned her to follow him. Rachel fought her dizziness and tried to concentrate on Dirk's words.

"Rachel? What is it?"

"Beth and Matt. They've been in an accident. Five miles south of here on the highway. In a ravine. Meet us!" She hung up without waiting for his reply, sped out the door, and jumped into the truck with Daryl. As they drove crazily out the lane, Daryl radioed the sheriff while Rachel willed the ambulance to hurry, knowing it must come from thirty miles away.

"Matthew!" Beth screamed as Jake pulled her out of the truck, sobbing. "Matthew!"

Her cries sent shivers down Jake's spine as he looked to his companion, who was trying to pry open Matt's crumpled door. Both of the Morgans had looked dead to them when they arrived, but Beth had moved when she heard their shouts. Matthew remained still.

The truck pointed downhill at a severe angle, the front end crushed against a large Ponderosa pine. Matt's side of the truck was wrinkled from the force of the impact, and the door remained stubbornly shut. One of the ranch hands finally ran around to the passenger side and leaned across to check Matt's pulse. "He's alive!" he shouted. "He's alive!"

Beth passed out when she heard the news. Only then did her rescuer notice the bloodstain spreading over her skirt. "She's bleeding! She's bleeding!" Jake's voice held a note of panic as he cradled her in his arms. He rocked her back and forth, silently praying that she and Matt wouldn't die. "Please, God, please. They're good people. Please, God, please!" he repeated.

Rachel and Daryl arrived at nearly the same moment as Sheriff Bill Taylor. As soon as he examined the Morgans, he radioed the hospital. "Better make that Life Flight," he directed. Within minutes, they knew the county's medical helicopter would take off in the early light of dawn in the direction of Elk Horn.

Dirk arrived to see Rachel checking on Matt in the truck's cab and directing others not to move him. He ran to check on Beth, side-stepping down the ravine until he reached them.

"She's bleedin', Dirk." Jake looked up at him miserably.

Rachel walked up, knelt, and held her unconscious friend's cold hand. She looked up at Dirk through eyes shining with tears. "She's bleeding internally, and Matt barely has a pulse."

"They'll be okay, Rachel," he said, pulling her up and close for a brief moment. "Hold it together. They need us right now."

At that moment the sun's rays broke over the lower crevices of the mountaintops to the east. The beautiful scene drew Rachel's attention for a moment and inspired her to pray: *Dear God, you create sunrises like this. You are all-powerful. Please hold Matt and Beth in your arms and heal them. I entrust them to you.*

In the distance the sound of helicopter blades chopped the peaceful early morning air.

Rachel awoke, rubbing her stiff neck. She sat up, away from Dirk's shoulder. He moaned but did not wake. It was half past eight in the evening, and the hospital emergency room was still crazy, as it had been most of the day.

She watched Dirk as he slept, not wanting to wake him. He had spent all day pacing, holding Rachel as she cried, and calming her when she talked about how angry she was. He had been patient and loving despite his own fear and worry. *What a terrific man,* she thought as she stared at the stubble that grew darker each hour. *I could get used to having him around.*

Their only information had come from the hospital staff earlier that afternoon. At that time, Rachel and Dirk learned that Beth had been three months pregnant and had lost the baby in the early hours of Saturday morning. Matt had sustained a traumatic head injury and was still unconscious. Dirk tried to get further information throughout the day, but the doctors had been evasive. Tired of waiting, Rachel resolved to get a status report on her friends if she had to tackle someone and hold him down until he talked.

Wearily she walked down the hospital hallway and slipped through the ER doors as someone was leaving. Once she was in, she tried to flag someone down.

"Excuse me…," she called to a nurse who rushed by. "Pardon me…," she tried again with an attendant who ran by, pushing a gurney.

Frustrated, she stepped in front of the next doctor who came along so that he almost collided with her. He scowled in irritation. "Yes?"

"Look, we came in here with my two friends, Matt and Beth Morgan, who were in an accident early this morning. Can someone tell me how they're doing?"

He turned and pointed. "ER nurses' station." With that, he turned his nose back to his chart and walked away.

Rachel set off again down the hallway. A young woman was behind the nurses' desk, her ear to the phone and her hands full of charts. Rachel waited patiently for several minutes and then spoke as soon as the woman hung up. "Excuse me. Can you tell me how Matthew and Beth Morgan are doing?"

"Friends or family?"

"I'm the closest thing to a sister that Beth's got," Rachel said flatly, daring the woman in white to challenge her.

The nurse stared at her for a moment and then shrugged her shoulders. "Mrs. Morgan was moved to room 312D an hour ago. She can't see anyone now. Maybe tomorrow. Mr. Morgan has been moved from ICU to critical. If things go well, he may be in a standard room by tomorrow morning."

"So they're both doing better?" Rachel questioned.

"Yes ma'am."

Sunday, July 25

Dirk and Rachel attended church together the next morning, to praise God for saving the Morgans' lives and to mourn the loss of their unborn child.

They solemnly shook Arnie's hand and thanked him for his prayers and support.

"How are they?" Arnie asked as his wife joined them.

"They'll pull through," Dirk said. "Matt has a severe concussion from hitting the windshield, but you know how hard his head is. Doctor said he'd be out of the hospital by Tuesday. Beth will take a little longer to heal. She'll be out within a week, but her miscarriage complicated things."

"She hadn't told anyone she was pregnant," Anne said.

"I didn't even know," Rachel said.

"Tell them we'll drop by this afternoon," the pastor said.

Dirk grabbed Rachel's hand and led her to the truck. He headed out on the highway toward home but stopped at a roadside café. "Oh, Dirk, I'm not hungry," Rachel began wearily.

"Rachel, you haven't eaten since Friday and haven't slept more than a few hours. I'm not hungry either, but Matt and Beth need us, and we have to stay healthy for them."

She resignedly got out of the truck and they walked into the café. Dirk ordered eggs, ham, and hash browns for them both. After forcing herself to eat, Rachel admitted that she felt better. She glanced at her watch. "Visiting hours start before long. Let's go, okay?"

"You've got it," Dirk said, with love and compassion in his eyes. Rachel looked as anguished as he felt. As they drove to the hospital, they took turns sharing stories about Beth and Matt. Their shared love for the Morgans made them feel even closer.

As Rachel entered the room, Beth stirred in her bed. Rachel stood and stared at her best friend, thanking God again that she had lived through the accident. Beth opened bruised, swollen eyes to see Rachel observing her. "I must look terrible..."

"You look more beautiful than I've ever seen you," Rachel said, taking a seat beside her and grabbing her hand. She chose her words carefully. "You didn't tell me you were going to have a baby, Beth."

She turned her face away from Rachel and looked at the ceiling. "I was waiting until this week. I almost told you when we were by the river, but Dirk came up, and I didn't want anyone else to know for a while, you know? I was so excited about the baby, I was almost afraid to say anything—like if I did, it would cease to be real. Only Matthew knew."

"That's why you wouldn't ride the horses?"

"Yes. I wanted my baby to be protected and have every chance to make it. I wanted him so bad. I loved him already."

The two friends sat in silence as tears streamed down their cheeks.

"The doctor said Matt could come wheeling in here for a visit tomorrow," Rachel said quietly. The news obviously lifted Beth's spirits.

"I could use a visit from my husband," she said. "He called me four times yesterday until the nurse told him he had to let me sleep."

"How's he taking it?"

"He's heartbroken too. But he's trying to concentrate on the blessing that we're alive at all. He's focusing on our future and the family we will have someday. I look forward to other children too, but right now I'm missing the one that never got a chance."

Her sadness made Rachel angry. "Why would God allow your child to die? Why would he let something this terrible happen to you? You're the most kind and gentle person I've ever known. Why would he hurt you like this?"

Beth turned her tear-stained face back toward her friend. "Rachel, God didn't do this to me. God didn't take away our baby. A person did. Someone forced us off the road. Our God is one of love and creation. He cries with me that this child will never be born. When people move against God's will, the result is pure havoc. We're seeing the impact of sin, not the shadow of God's back."

Beth spoke with calm authority through battered lips, and her words silenced Rachel's anger. They made sense, and Rachel remembered the sunrise at the scene of the accident. "I think he saved you two," she said soberly. "I think he actually spoke to me when we found you."

"What did he tell you?" Beth asked.

"That you'd be okay." Rachel felt sheepish for acknowledging such a notion but knew Beth would understand.

Beth squeezed Rachel's hand. "Are you telling me you've found God?"

"I'm telling you that he seems closer here than in San Francisco."

"Well, there's another miracle. It's been quite a week," Beth said wearily as she laid her head on her pillow. Rachel sat and watched as she drifted off to sleep, unwilling to pull her hand away and risk disturbing her friend.

Matt was watching football when Dirk entered his room. "I'm going to tell Arnie that you were watching the game instead of attending church like a loyal member," he said from the doorway.

"Gotta take advantage of my infirmity while I still have the chance," Matt said with a little humor in his voice. "Have you seen Beth?"

"No. Rachel and I each took on a different patient."

"Ah. Florence and Lawrence Nightingale."

"How are you feeling?"

"My head hurts like all get-out, but otherwise I'm ready to get out of here and back to the ranch."

"I can identify with that headache. The Double M will be personally supervised by me, so you just rest up and concentrate on you and Beth healing." He paused and said quietly, "Matt...the baby?"

"We were waiting until this week to tell everybody. The baby would've been three months along." Matt, lost in his sadness, stared out the hospital window.

"I'm sorry, Matt; I really am. You and Beth will make great parents."

"If we ever get to. The miscarriage was pretty hard on Beth's body. The doctors aren't sure she can have another baby."

"You have to trust, Matt. God has great things in store, remember."

"Yeah, buddy, I know. I was just looking forward to this kid so much, it's hard to focus on the future. I try for Beth's sake, but it's not that easy."

Dirk gripped his hand in silent support.

"When can I see my wife?" Matt asked sleepily, the medication starting to rule his body once more.

"Rachel and I are coming back after dinner tomorrow. I'll be glad to wheel you on over to her room then." Dirk's last words barely registered in Matt's groggy mind before he drifted off to sleep again.

Dirk left him after a brief prayer and went to locate Rachel. He found her in the waiting room, crying. Gently he pulled her up to stand in his arms, and the tears streamed from both their eyes as they stood holding each other.

"They're very strong people, Rachel. They'll pull through this."

She looked up at him as he spoke, wiping the tears and mascara from her cheeks. "I know that. It's just so unfair. They, of all people, do not deserve this."

"I know. The best thing we can do for them is just be ready to listen and help out in any way possible."

"Well, I have a week left to help around the Double M." The mention of her impending departure made Dirk doubly sad, and his pain was visible. Rachel changed the subject. "How do you think the ranch hands will like my cooking?"

"I don't know," he said dully, still thinking about her returning to San Francisco. "I haven't had a chance to try it out."

"I should cook for you tonight. My best dishes come from Kentucky Fried Chicken and McDonald's."

"You eat out all the time?"

"Mostly. When you get off work at seven-thirty or eight, it's hard to get fired up about going to the grocery store and cooking a meal straight out of the pages of *Bon Appétit*." She smiled at him, and he worked hard at returning the expression.

"I'll come over in the morning to help you cook for the men. I've picked up a few pointers from Mary. Cleanup will have to be up to you, I'm afraid. With two ranches to watch over for a while, I'm going to have a workweek that compares with that of a big city advertising executive I know."

He turned Rachel gently toward the door, leaving one arm around her shoulders. "Let's go home. We can come back tomorrow with some clothes for Matt. Maybe Beth will be feeling better and I can see her, too, while she's awake."

CHAPTER EIGHT

*T*he sheriff pulled up the Morgans' lane just as Dirk and Rachel were serving breakfast to the ranch hands. Plates piled high with steaming scrambled eggs, bacon, and toast were set out for the men to devour, but the workers said little outside of praying for the Morgans during grace. They dug in to the food in silence as Dirk and Rachel went out to meet Sheriff Taylor.

The tall, rangy man got out of his car and walked over. Rachel felt that she and Dirk had bonded on a deeper level through the weekend ordeal and that they now faced this lawman and every other thing in life together. As if on cue, Dirk put an arm around her waist.

The sheriff sauntered to the porch, taking his hat off and greeting them. "I came to see if you two wanted to press charges against Alex."

"Come on up, Bill," Dirk said. "We can talk about this sitting down."

Rachel asked if he wanted anything to drink, but the man declined.

"Alex Jordan was written up for assault with a deadly weapon and attempted forcible abduction. With all the craziness you two have been through with the Morgans, I couldn't get ahold of you for official statements. As the principal victims and witnesses to Jordan's forays, you were key to holding him in jail. We had to release him last night on bail. We could only hold him forty-eight hours."

Rachel's mouth dropped open. "You let him out?"

"Had to, ma'am. I tried to get you on the phone several times yesterday, and I kept thinking you'd be in as I asked you to be."

"We were at the hospital and my house yesterday. I got a message from Mary, but our focus has been on the Morgans. We put Jordan on hold while we took care of our personal priorities," Dirk explained.

"I understand, but I have some more bad news that relates to the Morgans' accident. After we released Alex, an informant told us that he had been driving a friend's truck the night of the dance."

"So?" Rachel said.

"It was bright yellow and was most likely the one that ran the Morgans off the road. Matt remembered the yellow truck and model, and when we dusted the steering wheel, sure enough, Jordan's fingerprints were all over it, and an empty whiskey bottle was on the floorboard. To top it all off, the bartender at the Silver Moon remembers cutting Jordan off that night. The bouncer had to practically kick him out."

"So, Sheriff," Rachel said, her anger building, "you're telling us that you have released the man who not only hit Dirk over the head with a crowbar and tried to drag me off to God knows where, but who also almost killed the Morgans? The man who killed their child?"

He nodded bleakly.

"Why are you here? Why aren't you out arresting him again?"

"We didn't just let him out. He posted bail and was told to stick close to town until this was all cleared up—"

"Why do I feel a *but* coming?" Rachel asked warily.

"But he skipped town," Bill finished miserably.

"What?" Rachel and Dirk cried in unison.

"I had a deputy keeping an eye on him, but he's young, and Jordan just slipped through his fingers."

Rachel sat back in the swing and stared blankly at the sheriff, who was leaning forward in his wooden chair. "So he could be anywhere?"

"Anywhere."

That afternoon Dirk and Rachel drove to the hospital in silence. When they drew near, Dirk said, "If you're worrying about Jordan coming after you again, try not to. I'm sure he won't. He's probably on his way to Canada or Mexico."

"He's a sick man, Dirk. I wouldn't guarantee anything he might do."

"If he comes near you again, he'll be sorry."

"That's sweet, Dirk, you big, wonderful thug. But you can't be with me every minute of the day. I just hate that on top of everything else, I have to be double-checking shadows. And it kills me that the man responsible for Matt and Beth's accident is free."

"He'll get his due one way or another."

"What do you mean? A nice little cabin in Canada and a cabaña on the beaches of Mexico don't seem like options a man like Alex deserves."

"We have a just God, Rachel. One way or another, he'll get what's coming to him." They pulled through the hospital gates and parked.

Hand in hand they entered the white building and went to Beth's room. She looked much better than the day before and sat up and smiled as they came into the room. "How dare you come in here without my husband!" she said, feigning anger.

"Sorry, madam," Dirk said subserviently. "I will go and fetch him immediately after obtaining a hug from the invalid." Beth laughed.

While they hugged, Rachel admired new bouquets that had arrived. "Whoa, who's this one from?" she asked, smelling a huge arrangement of roses, stock, delphiniums, tulips, and gardenias.

"That's from the guys on the ranch," Beth said. "See? I told you they liked me for more than my culinary expertise. Now go! Go get my husband!"

"Okay, okay, we'll be right back," Dirk said.

They reached Matthew's room and laughed when they saw him already in a wheelchair.

"It's about time!" he said, wheeling himself back and forth in place, as if pacing while sitting.

"You're about as cordial as your wife," Rachel teased.

"Yeah, yeah. Sorry, but you guys are old hat. I want to see Beth."

They left the room with Dirk pushing Matt's chair and Matthew griping about hospital policy that wouldn't let him wheel himself through the halls. "Even when they release you, they have to push you to the front door! Ridiculous!" As they neared Beth's room, he stopped Dirk. "Let me go in alone, okay, buddy? We need a little privacy."

"You got it. We'll be in the waiting room. Call us on the house-phone when you want our company." Dirk and Rachel walked by Beth's door, waving quickly and walking on.

"We have to tell them about Alex," Dirk said. They sat down in the waiting room, on orange plastic cushions split from hours of use.

Rachel agreed. "But only after they can enjoy their reunion for a bit."

They rejoined the Morgans after an hour, when the doctor came to see them. The news was happily received: Matthew could leave the next evening, and Beth earlier than expected—the exact time depending on a few more test results. The two couples celebrated with a bottle of warm sparkling cider from the hospital gift shop and saltine crackers pilfered from the cafeteria.

A nurse came and broke up their revelry an hour later, directing both patients to get some sleep and their guests to leave. She curtly informed them that she would wheel "Mr. Morgan" back to his room and waited for them to say their good-byes.

"We'll be back in the morning to collect you, Matt," Rachel said, making a face at the nurse when she turned away. The woman looked back after seeing the Morgans stifling laughter, and a straight-faced Rachel said, "We'll get the house all ready for your return, too, Beth."

Rachel and Dirk left before they got the Morgans in trouble and laughed at the uptight nurse. It felt good to get a release from all the anxiety of the past few days. Rachel even talked Dirk into stopping at Kentucky Fried Chicken for the ranch hands' supper. They came out with five buckets of chicken, thirty biscuits, and four plastic containers filled with mashed potatoes and coleslaw. "Well that set me back a small fortune," Rachel said. "I *will* have to learn how to cook this week."

When the men filed in to supper that night, Rachel filled them in on the Morgans' progress. Conversation was much more upbeat after hearing the good news. When it was time to say grace, the men praised God so long for the Morgans' recovery that Rachel worried all the food would get cold. *Oh well,* she decided, *at least it's getting cold for a worthy cause.*

Women from the church began arriving in twos and threes, confidently making their way into the kitchen and taking over the responsibility of feeding the ranch hands. Others helped clean the house, and Dirk came with Matt's foreman to check on the status of the Double M. A weight seemed to be lifted from Rachel's shoulders when the forces arrived. She couldn't get over how nice everybody was and how they were all so willing to help out. *Chalk up another point for church.*

After Dirk discussed things with the foreman and stopped to chat with Jake, he came into the house to invite Rachel to lunch. They were together so often that Dirk doubted that she would say no. When he entered the house, she was upstairs making up the Morgans' bed after washing the sheets. He came behind her and wrapped his arms around her waist as she tucked in a corner. She turned and smiled into his eyes and kissed him deeply. His touch sent shivers down her spine. "If only Matt and Beth were healthy and safely home, I think I'd be the happiest I have ever been, Dirk."

"I don't remember being so happy myself. I know we haven't known each other long, Rachel, but in these last few days I feel like we've forged the kind of friendship that takes years."

"And what a friendship it is," she said suggestively, leaning in for another kiss. Just then the phone rang.

"Don't answer it," he begged.

"Dirk! I have to! What if it's Beth?" She jumped across the bed to grab the phone, rumpling her careful work. Her smile broadened as she talked to the caller.

"Oh, Matt, that's great!" She covered the phone and said to Dirk, "Beth's comin' home with him tonight." She returned to her conversation with Matt. "We'll pick you up at seven. Bye."

Rachel and Dirk cheered at the thought of bringing both of their dear friends home from the hospital, and they hugged again in celebration.

"Beth must be doing a lot better," Dirk said.

"A lot of people told me they were praying for her. The doctors thought it would be tomorrow at the earliest," Rachel said.

"Well, they can heal even better here than in the hospital."

"Yes, we'll wrap them up in blankets and place them on the porch in rockers with a cup of tea to sip. A little babying and fresh air could do wonders." She laughed at the image of Matt in the picture she had just painted. Knowing Matthew, he wouldn't sit still from the time he exited Dirk's Jeep.

"Let's go celebrate. We'll take the horses out and have a picnic," Dirk suggested.

"Excellent idea. I haven't been riding since last week, and I'm already missing it. I don't know what I'll do when I go back to San Francisco."

Dirk's face sobered and darkened at her statement, but he said nothing. "Let's go make some sandwiches. I'll borrow Matt's horse for the afternoon. He probably needs the exercise anyway."

They made their dinner quickly, pausing only for a brief food fight after Rachel calmly spread peanut butter on Dirk's hand, which was innocently resting by the bread. He wrestled her to the table and held her down until she ate an entire spoonful of jelly, trying not to choke as she laughed and swallowed at the same time. He eased his hold on her and demanded an apology.

"An apology?" she said indignantly. "You were the one who just made me eat half a jar of jelly."

"You were the one who started the whole thing," he retorted, smiling.

"Oh, all right. I want to get going. I'm so *very* sorry that I missed the bread and got your hand instead with peanut butter, sir. I guess I just miss having Beth around for a food fight every now and then."

Dirk pulled Rachel up to stand before him. He cupped her face in his hands tenderly and then looked away, trying to find the words to express what he wanted to say. Finally, looking back into her bright green eyes, he said, "I'm falling deeper and deeper in love with you, Rachel Johanssen. I love your sense of mischief and play. I love your passion for life and discovery. I love your respect for others. I love *you*, Rachel."

Her eyes filled with tears at his intensity. Wet eyelashes fluttered, then opened as she looked directly at him without wavering. "I love you too, Dirk. You are the finest man I have ever known. But I'm so confused. What are we supposed to do when we live eight hundred miles apart? How can I leave my job? And if I don't, how can we spend the time necessary to know if we are supposed to go the distance together? The whole thing scares me. I just don't want to end up hurting, Dirk."

He pulled her close and held her silently for several minutes. Then he said, "Come on, love. Let's go have our picnic. Everything else will work itself out."

They spent the entire afternoon riding in the hills behind the Double M and parts of Timberline. Dirk showed her his favorite spots, and together they explored new hideaways. High in the mountains, they stopped at one small waterfall that rushed downward toward the river and valley that lay below. The falls paused to pool in a deep basin carved by centuries of erosion, then spilled over into another basin. The water was icy cold, and it felt good to splash it on their hot faces. They ate dinner and lay in the hot mountain sun with their bare feet resting in the warmer top inches of the pool's water. The heat felt especially good to Rachel as it penetrated her skin and warmed her, easing away tension in her muscles.

At last Dirk stood and picked her up in his arms. Before she could protest, he walked to the side of the pool and dropped her in without warning. She came up sputtering and yelped at the shock of exposure to the glacial waters. He laughed uproariously, obviously pleased with himself. "That is for the peanut butter incident."

"But you already got me back with the jelly!" she protested, treading water.

"Yes, but then I decided it wasn't sufficiently satisfactory."

"Ah. And now?"

"I think we're about even."

"Well then, help me out of this bowl of ice water." Dirk leaned over and gave her a hand up, easily pulling her out. As soon as Rachel had a good foothold, she turned and shoved Dirk toward the pool. He almost regained his balance after the shove, half-expecting such a move from her. But he overcorrected and went tumbling in, sending a large wave of water over the far side. He came up under the stream of falling water as Rachel laughed.

Laughing with her, Dirk swam out from under the gentle waterfall. She jumped into the water and joined him, pleased with her work and wanting to go back in before he came out after her. The pool was about six feet at its maximum depth and edged out slowly to form a perfect bowl. They stood on the bottom, ignoring the cold, and Dirk picked her up in his arms. She stretched out and floated on top of the pool, feeling delightfully free and wanting to remember the day always.

As he looked down at her, Dirk thought Rachel was even more captivating than when he had first seen her. Her hair spread out on the water in shining, red-brown waves, and her long limbs kept her balanced perfectly. She looked peaceful as she closed her eyes to listen to the pounding of the water rushing into the pool. The sound echoed in glorious thunder, and she turned to Dirk, unable to remember when she had ever been so happy.

He pulled her back into his arms. "You look like what I expect angels to look like, Rachel." He gently eased her to the edge of the pool. She lay back, resting against the slope of smooth rock beneath her, with Dirk very close. They kissed for a long time with increasing passion as each thought of their impending separation. Dirk stopped abruptly. "We'd better get out. We're both so cold we're nearing hypothermia, and things are *still* getting a little too hot to handle."

Dirk and Rachel lay beside the pool to dry off. They held hands and smiled quietly as they studied each other. "I'll bet it's around five o'clock," she said, noticing the sun's angle. "We'd better pack up and get going."

"Yeah. It's going to be a fun ride in soggy jeans."

"I'll pull our junk together, and you get the horses ready." Rachel rose and was walking toward the horses when her attention was drawn to the brush beyond Kala. She stopped and studied the place where she had seen movement—a flash of white and brown. A man? A bear?

Dirk noticed her hesitation and came near. "What is it, Rachel?"

"I saw something." Her pulse pounded, double-time.

"What?"

"I don't know. Dirk, don't go."

He rose and walked past her toward the horses. "I'll just check it out. Don't worry." He left her side and walked around the horses. From behind Kala he called loudly, "Back here?"

"That's it. That's the spot."

"I'll be right back. Just takin' a look around." Dirk pushed his way through the brush and then was gone.

She looked around warily, looking—expecting—Alex.

Nothing.

The gentle mountain breeze rustled the leaves, and Rachel started to think she was going crazy. *Come on, Rachel, get ahold of yourself.*

"Dirk?" she called. "Dirk!" she hollered again, louder.

He came crashing back through the bush, his face anxious as he looked for her.

She stood trembling as he took her in his arms. "You okay?" he asked.

"Yeah. Maybe I just got so cold I started seeing things."

"Alex?"

"It could've been. But then, it also could've been a deer."

Dirk moved cautiously around the clearing, glancing from Rachel to the thick stand of trees and back to Rachel. He obviously wanted to search further but was reluctant to leave her exposed again. "It'd be crazy for him to hang around, Rachel. He has to be long gone. Plus, how would he follow us way up here?"

"I know it sounds ridiculous to think he's still in Elk Horn. But he's scary, Dirk. Not right in the head. It may be stupid, but I can't help feeling like he's just over my shoulder."

"Come on, Rachel," Dirk said grimly, putting his arm around her shoulder. "Let's go home."

They left the mountain cautiously, wary of every sound in the forest and concentrating solely on getting home. Once at the Double M, they handed the horses over to Jake and went their separate ways to shower and change.

On the way to pick up the Morgans, they stopped briefly to talk to Bill Taylor, hoping the sheriff had captured Alex. He had not.

"Just do your best to get a hand on this man, Sheriff," Dirk urged.

"I will, Dirk. We'll send out a couple of men to check those woods. If they see any trace of him, we can try to track him. I can almost guarantee that he hightailed it outta of here though. As Rachel said, you're not even sure that's what you saw. But we'll show our presence and do a search with the county helicopter tomorrow. Even if we don't find him, he'll know we're lookin'—and hopefully that will keep him away from Rachel."

"Good enough. Let us know if you find anything," Dirk said.

"Will do."

Dirk walked Rachel to the truck, his arm around her shoulders protectively.

"I'd feel better if you spent the night at the Double M, Dirk," she said quietly.

He lifted her chin until she looked into his eyes. "I already have my name on their living room couch."

CHAPTER NINE

*R*achel woke at nine the next morning, showered, and came downstairs to find Dirk waiting with hot coffee and breakfast. She grinned and entered his waiting arms, happy to comply when he tipped her chin up for a good-morning kiss. They held each other for several minutes until Rachel heard and felt his stomach growl, protesting a lack of food.

"How long have you been up? Hope you got some sleep and didn't stay on guard all night."

"I'm a pretty light sleeper, so I figured I'd wake up if I heard anything. But I was up at five and helped Jake fix breakfast for the boys. Then I ran out and checked on some of the livestock with him."

"What'd you make this morning?"

"Oatmeal and fried ham. I made some fresh a little while ago to share with you and our patients."

"They're still asleep. Let's eat. If they're still not up by the time we're done, we'll go serve them breakfast in bed."

"Great idea."

The food tasted delicious. She didn't know what it was, but she seemed hungry all the time in this thin-air, high-mountain country. Rachel devoured two thick slices of ham and a huge bowl of oatmeal sprinkled with raisins, walnuts, and brown sugar. It occurred to her that in the chaos of the previous night, neither of them had eaten supper.

Dirk served himself a second bowl of cereal and commented on the same thing. "At three this morning, I had to get up and grab a snack out of the refrigerator."

They chatted over coffee after they finished eating and finally decided at eleven-thirty to check on the Morgans. Rachel knocked and entered after hearing Beth softly call, "Come in." The couple was still in bed, holding each other and talking quietly.

"Don't want to disturb our patients," Rachel apologized, "but we think you ought to eat something." She entered with the coffeepot, and Dirk followed her with a tray laden with food. With great flourish, he served the couple, making them both laugh at the sight of their burly friend with a crisp white towel over his arm. After serving them, Rachel and Dirk excused themselves, not wanting to interfere with Beth and Matt's reunion and homecoming.

"When you're ready, come on down. We'll be in the living room or right outside," Rachel said.

"Enough already," Matt said. "You guys have done plenty around here. Go and do something fun. We'll be fine."

Dirk and Rachel looked at each other, unsure whether they should agree. Dirk made a decision. "Rachel hasn't seen Dancara Lake. I'd love to take her out in the canoe and get stranded for a while."

"Do it," Beth said to Rachel with a grin. "Believe it or not, my friend, you still are on a vacation. Go have some fun. You can baby us tonight."

The idea of getting out of the house with Dirk was enticing, but Rachel was reluctant to leave the Morgans, and she feared running into Alex again. But she looked to Dirk, and his face convinced her. "Maybe just for a few hours. But we'll be back this afternoon. Don't overdo it, either of you."

"Aye, aye, Captain," Matthew said smartly. He turned to Beth. "We better heal quick before she takes over the whole ranch."

"That's for sure," Rachel said. "Mutiny on the Dub M." Dirk impatiently picked her up and carried her down the stairs with Rachel laughing and shrieking, "Okay, Dirk, we're going, we're going!"

From their bed, the Morgans laughed along with them.

Rachel fixed their lunch while Dirk went home for the canoe. He came back with the hardtop off and the boat strapped to the roll bar and back of the Jeep. Rachel had packed roast-beef sandwiches on whole wheat bread, fresh fruit, chips, and chocolate chip cookies sent over from Mary. Her stomach growled, and she nibbled on a cookie as she watched Dirk jump out of the Jeep and walk toward the house. Handsome and as sure of himself as Robert Redford, he made her heart pound. He caught her staring from the window and grinned broadly. When he reached her, he grabbed her by the waist and pulled her to him for a long kiss.

"You've been sneaking dessert before we even had dinner," he accused with a grin.

"I prefer to think of it as an hors d'oeuvre."

"Ah," he said, pretending to ponder the thought. "I prefer to think of your kiss as an hors d'oeuvre."

"Dirk! I'm shocked and appalled!" she said, her smile broadening. "I think we'd better put your excess energy to use."

"Agreed. Let's go."

They walked out hand in hand, and Dirk opened the door for Rachel and placed the picnic basket behind her. They drove off in the direction of their first horseback ride together, but took an earlier cutoff. The Jeep climbed the steep forest-service road, effortlessly spanning ditches dug by the runoff of spring rain.

"Looks like they could use a little road repair," Rachel shouted above the din of the engine as they swayed with the jarring motion of the road.

"Guess you don't hit many roads like this in San Francisco," he yelled back.

"You get 'em this steep, but not this bad!"

It was another hot, beautiful day in the valley, with not a cloud in the sky, and they drove without speaking, each thinking of Rachel's impending departure to California. Rachel breathed deeply, wanting to imprint in her memory the smell of pine and hot dust and mountain air. Soon they arrived at their destination as the road abruptly ended beside a small valley with an incredible lake.

Dirk pulled to a stop, hopped out of the Jeep, and came around to open her door. "Welcome to Dancara Lake, mademoiselle," he said, offering his hand. She took it and stepped out, barely acknowledging his comment as she stared in front of them.

"Dirk, this place is amazing! Just when I think I've seen all that Elk Horn Valley has to offer, you show me a new place that takes my breath away." She drank in her surroundings as Dirk encircled her with his arms. Dancara was a brilliant turquoise blue, due to the glacial silt that slid off the surrounding mountains and covered the shallow bottom. Never had she witnessed anything more pristine.

Dirk kissed her temple tenderly and whispered in her ear. "Let's go, Rachel."

They untied the canoe and carried it to the water's edge. Dirk went back for the picnic basket and his portable radio, tuning it to catch Vivaldi's *Four Seasons*.

"Perfect!" Rachel said, approving of the music. "Nothing else could measure up to this place." She gingerly stepped into the front of the canoe and Dirk pushed off from shore, easily climbing in at the last moment. They paddled out to the middle of the lake and took in the view of the mountains that towered on three sides of them. Dirk explained that Dancara was formed by an old glacier and that the remnants of the glacier could be seen on the eastern mountain. Over thousands of years, that glacier had carved out that tiny valley and many larger ones in the Elk Horn. "Much of Montana's geography is linked to those old monsters," he said, looking up toward the eastern slopes.

Soon Rachel's stomach rumbled, and she reached for the basket. "Hungry?"

"Starved," he said, delightedly watching her as she pulled out the sandwiches.

They ate and talked quietly, slowly drifting in the slight breeze. Looking at Dirk, Rachel knew she had never felt happier. His dark hair shone in the sun, and his eyes danced with warmth. He finished his sandwich and took a bite of apple, never taking his eyes off her. He swallowed and said, "You are the most incredible woman I've ever seen, Rachel Johanssen. You're more beautiful than these mountains or Dancara or Vivaldi's creation. You know that, don't you?"

She blushed at his praise. "You make me feel beautiful, Dirk. But I was just about to tell you how gorgeous I think you are," she said.

"Well then, we're quite stunning together, aren't we?"

"I like us together for reasons beyond looks," she said quietly.

"Me too." They listened to the music and stared tenderly into each other's eyes. After they had finished eating, they paddled around the entire perimeter of the lake, a distance of about eight miles. Rachel's muscles ached from the unaccustomed use, but it was a good feeling. Never had she felt more invigorated, cleansed, and whole. *It's got to be this place.* After a few hours, they canoed back to the Jeep and landed for the day.

"That was absolutely marvelous, Dirk," she said.

"Yes, it was," he agreed, smiling at her. He gave her a tender kiss as he took her into his arms. "I love you, Rachel. With each passing day, it becomes more and more clear." He released her and yelled at the top of his lungs toward the lake, *"I love Rachel Johanssen!"*

Rachel laughed as she looked up at him. "I love you too, Dirk." His shout continued to echo off the mountain walls, then finally quieted.

After they had emptied and tied the canoe back on the Jeep, she turned for one last look at the lake. Dirk's arms encircled her shoulders comfortingly.

"God has done wonderful things, hasn't he?" Dirk said softly.

"Yes, he has," Rachel said. "He really has." The truth of it all settled into her heart easily. This was the Creator whom she sought. This love developing between Rachel and Dirk was a gift from him. And Rachel smiled yet again as she accepted it.

THURSDAY, JULY 29

By Thursday the Morgans were doing even better, so Dirk reluctantly moved off the living room couch and back to Timberline. Despite a heated argument with Dirk, Rachel, and his foreman, Matt was out supervising the haying process on the north end of the ranch. Beth remained quiet, reading in the living room. The temperature was high, and everyone moved slowly, trying not to get aggravated by the heat.

"I thought that only California gets this hot," Rachel commented as she brought Beth some iced tea.

"It's a surprise for me, too," Beth said. "Last summer our high was eighty-five degrees, and today it's supposed to be over a hundred." The two friends chatted over their tea. Beth was still a little sore but was on the mend physically and spiritually. "So, Dirk finally broke himself away from you?" Beth teased.

"Yes, we had surgery to separate our hips, and I have to admit that all I can think about—aside from your health, of course—is when I get to see him again. Apparently he was worried about his ranch and thought he had better check on things."

"I see. Are you getting together tonight?"

"Yes. He said he wants to take me dancing. He'll be here after supper to pick me up, so I have all day to spend with you."

"Dancing? There isn't a dancing place around here within miles. The Sweet Pea is the closest thing we get to it all year."

"H'm. Well, he was really clear about it. Never said anything about having to drive anywhere far."

"I'll be eager to hear where he takes you. Then I can make Matt take me there too."

"I'd invite you to go with us…"

"Oh, you would not! And if you did, I'd never intrude. Things are progressing nicely, and I don't want to get in the way. Before we know it, I'll have you as a neighbor."

"I don't know about that," Rachel protested. "This place is gorgeous, and I'm having the best time. I'm falling hard for your neighbor. But I don't know if I can give up my career, the city…my whole *life*."

"It is an adjustment. There were some late winter days that I thought I'd tear my hair out. And there are some weeks of work, like during calving season, when I think I'll die, I'm so tired. But I have to tell you, Rachel, that I know of no finer men than Matthew and Dirk, and no better place to live. This place, this valley, makes me want to celebrate every day of life I've been given."

"Yeah, but what about interaction with new people, new faces? Let's be honest here. Your world is small now, and you've accepted that. It attracts me at the moment, but would I resent it in a year? Two years? Ten years? What would that do to Dirk and me then?"

Beth sighed. "These people are my family, not strangers on the street. My interaction with them means something."

"I know, Beth. I really do. But I can't see giving up everything I've worked so hard for to become the 'little woman' on a ranch."

"Come on, Rachel, that's not fair. You know Dirk would never shove you into a corner—" She stopped herself. "We're getting ahead of ourselves. You and Dirk may not be able to cut it long-term, but you can't start shutting the door now. Don't slam it in his face just because you're starting to get scared about losing all your hard-earned security."

Rachel stared out the picture window and absorbed her friend's words. She caught herself thinking about how sweet it would be to never leave Dirk, how wonderful it would be to live near Beth again, how nice it would be to settle into this valley and call it home.

She dismissed her thoughts, alarmed that she had let her guard down, and stood up abruptly. "I leave Sunday after church. I can't let myself dream like this, Beth. It will hurt too much when I go."

"I won't try to convince you, Rachel. That's between you and God. You have to come to peace with the idea first, and the rest will…work out, one way or another."

"Sounds easy."

"Should be. It's not."

"That's what I was afraid you'd say."

Rachel left Beth to her reading and went to open all the windows as the sun rose higher in the sky, heating up the house even more. The day was certain to be a scorcher. Everything was dead still, and waves of heat rose from the dirt road, making the barn look like an apparition. Weeks of sunshine had taken their toll, and the grass was starting to turn brown. Rachel asked if they should turn on the sprinklers. Beth laughed.

"I'm lucky to have grass up here at all," she said. "Matt griped about having to tend over three thousand acres of fields and then come home to mow the front lawn, but it's my last grip on civilization. Matt gave in on the grass, but you have to winterize sprinklers here—and that was a bit too much. It's the garden hose, honey, or nothing at all."

Rachel laughed and went out the door, resolutely determined to find the hose. She waved at Beth through the living room window, turned the corner, and walked right into Alex's arms.

Her heart stopped. She turned to run, but he grabbed her before she could escape and covered her mouth so she could not scream. "Been waitin' on you, Rachel. Lookin' for me?"

He emanated evil. The recognition of it turned Rachel's stomach, and she fought her body's urge to pass out. He dragged her backward a few feet and whispered into her ear, his breath reeking of alcohol. "Haven't been able to see you for a few days, darlin'. Too many people out and about, and you've been quite busy with your boyfriend. I don't think I like your seein' anybody else."

Rachel tried to get her footing so she could fight back, but to little avail. Alex was moving quickly.

"Nope. Don't like you with anybody else. Don't think I'll ever let it happen again."

CHAPTER TEN

*W*atching the front lawn from indoors, Beth wondered where Rachel could be. The hose was just around the corner. *How could she miss it?* Beth rose and walked out on the front porch, calling for Rachel. When her friend didn't answer, she gingerly stepped off the porch, wincing in pain and knowing Rachel would scold her when she saw her up and about. She turned the corner and saw them in the distance—Alex dragging Rachel backward into the woods, her feet raising clouds of dust. Beth screamed loudly and ran after them, but her body hindered her from moving too fast. She doubled over in pain. "Matt!" she screamed. "Anybody! Help! Alex, stop! Stop!"

Alex didn't answer her, but at least he knew he hadn't escaped unseen. *Help will come soon,* Beth thought. "Jake! Matt!" Beth yelled. Wincing again, she moved as fast as she could to the porch to the triangle that was used to call men for a meal or in an emergency.

But most of the men were out in the fields. The one man who remained ran out of the barn just in time to see Rachel dragged on top of Alex's horse, but they were too far away to apprehend. He ran to Beth as she fainted on the porch step.

Matt was working on a combine engine when his radio crackled to life. "Boss! Boss! We've got an emergency here at the house. Rachel's been kidnapped, and your wife passed out!"

Matt looked over at Jake—who was in the cab of an identical combine twelve yards away—and grimly spoke into the radio. "Call Doc Harmon and get the sheriff. Tell him where you last saw Rachel. Was it Jordan?"

"Yes, boss."

"Call Dirk, too." He switched off his radio and immediately began pulling the men together from the hay wagon and baler. "You five, jump into my truck and come with me. The rest of you get the other men and follow us back to the Dub M as fast as possible. We've got a man to catch! Let's move!"

Alex rode with Rachel struggling in front of him, his grimy hand wound tightly in her hair. About a mile from the Double M, he pulled her off the horse to stand with him. He smelled as if he had not bathed for days, and Rachel guessed that he had spent his time spying and hiding around the Double M.

Grabbing a rope from his lathered horse's saddle, Alex bound Rachel's wrists behind her and gagged her to stifle her repeated cries for help. He pulled her close for a moment, staring into her eyes. She met his gaze defiantly, determined not to let him intimidate her, but it was difficult, since he frightened her so.

His eyes were hard, mean, without a hint of compassion. They were sunken and yellow, and dark circles emphasized his weariness. There was a trace of lust, of desire, but none of humanity.

"You're wonderin' why I brought you up here. Well, you'll find out soon enough. The important thing is that we're together."

You're crazy! She would have yelled it if she hadn't been gagged. *He's somehow decided he's got to have me, one way or another.* She shivered involuntarily, unwilling to think about specifics. *Just survive this encounter and it will all be over*, Rachel told herself. Someone had to lose this cat-and-mouse game he had played for the last ten days, and it wasn't going to be her.

Alex mounted his horse, careful not to let Rachel get more than a few inches away from him. He grabbed her under the arms and hoisted her up in front of him once more, then set off on a barely visible trail. Rachel listened for help from her friends but heard nothing behind them.

Alex laughed loudly, and his arms tightened around her to grip the reins.

Rachel prayed as never before, begging God to intervene.

By the time the ranch hand at the Double M reached Dirk by short-wave radio and Dirk met Matt and the sheriff at the Morgans', thirty crucial minutes had passed. Dirk was furious at himself for leaving Rachel alone, or at least without one of his men on guard. He never thought Alex would dare to kidnap her in broad daylight, right outside the main house. Feeling physically ill, he tried to focus on the task at hand: Find them, and find them quickly.

Beth had revived soon after Alex rode off with Rachel, and she had directed Doc Harmon to leave her alone. "I have work to do," she said with uncharacteristic crispness, which no one chose to challenge. Mary had arrived with Dirk, and Beth asked her to collect some food for the men to take with them. As the sheriff organized the posse, Beth tried to calm Dirk a bit and keep him from tearing off after Alex and Rachel without assistance. She gave one deputy a description of what Alex and Rachel were wearing and, after deciding the search posse was well under way, called Doc Harmon back and allowed him to examine her.

Matt observed his wife for a moment, recognizing how blessed he had been to find her. When he looked at Dirk's anxious face, he knew he had to help him find Rachel. *If Dirk feels a fraction of what I feel for Beth, the man has to be in agony.* Matt watched his friend pace back and forth, impatiently listening to Sheriff Taylor's plan. Twelve men circled around a map, and each man had five others waiting outside to help cover a section of the mountainside. The goal was to snare Alex in a tight loop. After all were clear on the plan, they prepared to go.

"Under no conditions do you shoot at them," Dirk growled. "If you see them, fire twice in the air, and we'll come after you."

Mary stood outside, distributing bread and home-smoked jerky to the men and making sure their canteens were filled. The horses pranced and whinnied, aware of the tension in the air. In moments, the entire posse rode out, a picture that reminded Beth of an old western movie. She wished it were a movie so she could walk out. Instead she got down on her knees, and Mary joined her in prayer.

Alex and Rachel had traveled many miles in a semicircle when they hit the Kootenai River. Rachel's heart raced as she recognized that they were only a few miles upstream from Dirk's ranch. They entered the water's edge and started south toward Timberline and, ultimately, the Double M. Rachel could clearly see Alex's plan: double back, making the trackers think they had taken the wrong trail. Alex had not spoken to her in hours, and her body begged for a break from the rough ride.

As if reading her mind, Alex led the horse out of the river at last, explaining that he needed to relieve himself and fill his canteen. He dismounted and dragged her to a nearby tree where he tied her. She started working on the rope that bound her hands, but Alex came back too soon. Moments later, he untied and ungagged her himself. Her mouth was parched, and they were both soaked from the heat. She knelt by the water without a word, cupped her hands for a drink and another and another, then splashed her face as he sat on a rock and watched her. "I'll take you to a place where you can drink the freshest water in the valley."

"What if I don't care to go?" she asked, wiping a drip from her brow.

"Not an option. It may take you awhile to like me. But you wait, you'll be begging to go everywhere with me before you know it."

"Alex, how many times do I have to tell you? I'm not interested in you, and kidnapping me is not the answer." She stood to her full height and stared up at him. She ignored her aching muscles. "In fact, I'll make sure they send you to jail for a very long time for this escapade."

"You may as well kill that plan." He leaned closer, the muscles along his jaw tensing repeatedly while he stared at her for a long, hard moment. "You'll learn to love me, or you won't live to love at all."

She switched tactics in the face of his threat. Lowering her voice, she asked softly, "What happened, Alex? What could make you so crazy that you had to do this?"

He ignored her questions. "Time to get goin'. They'll be comin' around in not too long, and I don't want them interfering in our little honeymoon." His voice was dazed, his manner odd.

Rachel took a deep breath. She knew he was mentally unstable, but just how far gone was he? Delusional? Manic? Schizophrenic? She licked her lips, forcing courage and a nonthreatening tone into her voice. "I'm... We're not married, Alex."

"I know that! You think that I'm a nut case, don't you? A real nut job." He let out a shallow laugh, and then his brow furrowed. "Start cleaning up your attitude." He gripped her arms and shook her hard. Sweat dripped down his unshaven face. Instinctively, she did not protest. "All I want is a little respect. A woman who will treat me nice. *You* to treat me nice. You're mine now." Silently she watched him bind her wrists again, this time in front of her. "We have some hard riding to do this evening," he mumbled in explanation. "You'll need to hold on to the horn."

By eight o'clock, the men were growing discouraged and Dirk was frantic. "We have to find them before nightfall," he said to Matt as they met briefly at the river to discuss the search. "They could gain miles on us if we don't."

"I don't know, Dirk. I think Alex will hole up until sunrise and then move again. These woods are pretty dense. He'll lose his position if he moves tonight."

"I know it. I just don't want to bet on anything Jordan will do anymore. And I don't want him alone with her!"

The county police helicopter flew over them in a low run, encouraging both men. The chopper had arrived an hour earlier, and they were certain it was their best bet in scouring the mountainside for Rachel and her captor.

The first time the helicopter passed over them, Alex was fortunate enough to be near a cliff overhang. With a quick movement, he eased the horse underneath, and Rachel ducked low to avoid being swept off. Alex swore at this new development in the chase. They stayed there for five minutes, then moved out once more, stretching after being cramped in the tight space. Their path took them at an upward angle, and Alex's exhausted horse could barely move as the shadows deepened. Terrified at the thought of being alone with Alex all night, Rachel devised a desperate plan.

She and Alex could hear the chopper frequently, but it took another thirty minutes before it came directly overhead again, this time with searchlights beaming through the last twilight hours. As Alex frantically looked about in search of a place to hide, Rachel looked for an escape route. If she could just get to a clearing… Seeing no other choice, she tumbled off the horse and into the ravine that they had steadily climbed.

The momentum of her fall fueled her descent, and she was unable to stop without the use of her hands, which remained firmly bound. Alex shouted and swore, but Rachel ignored him. She rolled down the chasm, somersaulting and flipping in her uncontrolled fall. With grunts and cries she hit boulders and logs on the ground, creating a small landslide.

Alex abandoned his horse in pursuit of Rachel, recognizing the potential danger of running the mare down the path they had ascended. He repeatedly swore, and his eyes blurred with hatred toward this woman who had dared to run from him. He would catch her…he would catch her. Nothing could stop him. He'd take her by the hair and bring her to her knees…

The helicopter circled again, this time even lower. They'd been spotted. Gritting his teeth, he looked down the ravine until he located the girl, skidding down the rocks. "Rachel!" he bellowed. "I'm comin'! That wasn't nice of you, darlin'! We're gonna have to have a little talk…"

～

Rachel came to a rough landing with a groan. Shaking her head, she looked upward through the trees and heard her pursuer crashing down behind her. Each cracked tree branch, each rustling leaf, each groaning limb under his feet echoed in her ears. She could not allow him to catch her again.

With pain that robbed her of breath, Rachel stumbled down the ravine. She ungagged her mouth by catching the cloth on a tree branch and used her teeth to work on the knots that bound her wrists. In the darkness the chopper was circling with a spotlight, but too high up. They'd obviously lost them, she decided, fighting off panic. Maybe she could circle around, go back to them. But first she had to get rid of her pursuer. She shuddered at the thought of Alex's fury if he apprehended her again.

The chase was coming down to herself, Alex, and God. *Please, Father, show me the way.* A whimper of fear left her lips, and she immediately clamped her mouth shut, afraid he might've heard her. He was out of sight for the moment, but she knew he was coming fast and hard.

Keep moving…must keep moving. And as quietly as possible.

～

The radio at Dirk's side crackled to life. The chopper pilot informed the deputized members of the posse of Alex and Rachel's position, and the men began to tighten the circle around them. Dirk's crew was closest. His heart raced. *I'll never let her go. If I get her back in my arms, I'll keep her safe forever.* At that moment the chopper pilot announced he had lost sight of Alex and Rachel.

"Wait!" Dirk said, raising his hand to Matt and two others. All four stopped. "I thought I heard her," he explained in a whisper. Was it his imagination? Or had Rachel called out to him? She felt close, somehow, like he could feel her in an extrasensory way. He sighed and shook his head. He was losing it. He nodded, and Matt continued onward.

The night was pitch-black with no hope of a moon. The helicopter was almost out of fuel and heading back to town for the night. Dirk was nearing despair as he fought the dense underbrush and crush of trees to move toward Rachel's last known location.

"Dirk," Matt said under his breath. "The guys. It's dark, and late. We're not doing much good—"

"They can do what they want," Dirk growled. "I'm staying."

"The chopper's lost them—," a man tried.

"And I'll find them! Go! Go if you need to. There's a woman out there that's counting on me, and I will not let her down."

All four men paused for a tense moment, and then two turned their horses for home. There was no need for words. They thought the chase was hopeless, that Alex had escaped. Dirk looked up to the sky, longing for moonlight. *Father!* he cried out in prayer. *Help me! I can't leave her alone out here!* He ducked his head, fighting sudden, embarrassing tears.

Matt clapped him on the shoulder. "Come on, man. That ravine is probably just a quarter mile away. We'll find her." He headed out without another word.

Gratefully, wordlessly, Dirk followed behind.

⁓

Rachel paused to listen for Alex's position: He was gaining on her. Frantic, she crashed through the branches without regard for her skin. After a few steps, she heard water in the distance and noted that the ground was leveling off. She was nearing the valley floor, close to the ranches. She was near Dirk. But exactly how near? It was impossible to tell, any directional choice a blind guess. Alex was close, too close. Could she reach safety before he reached her?

Alex let out an unearthly yell from fifty feet behind her, and Rachel took off in the direction of the water, desperately seeking open skies and a clue to her location. When she found an opening, she abruptly stopped, wildly swinging her hands to avoid falling. She was on a cliff, twenty feet above the Kootenai River.

Trapped.

Dirk and Matt heard Alex's scream. It had been a cry of animalistic fury, a sound that sent shivers down their spines.

"Was that—," Matt began.

"Let's go," Dirk hissed as he led the way through the brush with his flashlight, never pausing. It was Jordan all right, even though he sounded inhuman, ferocious in his search for Rachel. Dirk prayed he hadn't yet had his hands on her, that she had been successful in hiding, fast on her feet while running. *Lord God, protect her.* The man in pursuit of Rachel was clearly sick—capable of hurting her, even killing her. Dirk worked to swallow, his mouth dry. *Father God, I've just found her—keep her safe. Please, God, please, God, please, God,* he petitioned in time with his horse's gait.

This was a nightmare. The valley was largely void of crime. Kidnapping was unheard of—the stuff of *Dateline,* not the local news. *Oh, Rachel. How am I going to get us out of this?*

Rachel struggled to catch her breath as she waited for Alex to show himself. He came out of the forest cruelly laughing, a confident hunter of easy prey. His eyes were fixed on her, and she could feel their heat, even in the cool mountain darkness. He swore at her, calling her hateful, foul names.

"I wanted to treat you well. All you had to do was be nice." Alex took slow, deliberate steps toward her. "But you found that so impossible. You didn't even give me a chance. You'll pay for the wrongs you've done me. You're no better than my ma who left or my stepmother who beat me or the girl who stood me up at the altar. You're all alike."

Rachel could feel his loathing, knew there was no negotiation, no reasoning to be done. Cold sweat covered her body. She saw no other choice.

Turning, she jumped over the cliff's edge and into the water below her, praying that she wouldn't hit anything on the way down. She plunged through the water and plummeted downward nearly twelve feet before coming up to break the surface. Her lungs were bursting for air. Even as the current pulled her downstream, she heard gunfire from above. Alex was shooting at her.

Dirk and Matt yelled from about twenty yards away, hoping to distract Jordan's attention from Rachel, and he calmly turned and shot at them. Both ducked and rolled off their horses, but the firing stopped. All was silent. With their own guns drawn, they cautiously moved forward, bending below branches, pushing aside brush. Dirk resisted the desire to call out to Rachel, to know if she was dead or alive, not wanting to give Alex a chance to shoot at him at such close range.

It was impossible to see in the inky darkness. But as the clearing opened before them and the river became more audible, it appeared that either Jordan and Rachel had moved on or were injured. Ignoring Matt's cautionary hand on his shoulder, Dirk rushed forward. "Rachel, Rachel!" he called, growing more bold and more frightened at the same time. What if Alex had shot and left her for dead in the woods? "Rachel!" he called desperately. "Rachel!"

Rachel shivered and winced as she bounced off several smooth boulders in the river's main current. After five minutes of being pulled downriver, she realized she could not stay in the icy water much longer. Still, she knew it was her best escape route, and the longer she stayed in it, the farther she got from Alex. *If he didn't come in after me. Just a little farther, Rachel. You can do it. You'll be okay. You're gonna be all right.* She gritted her teeth and positioned her feet in front of her to protect against boulders as she was carried downstream.

It hit them at the same time. "They both went in!" Matt said to Dirk. It was too late to descend into the river after them. Their best bet would be to ride to the river's edge, cover both sides, and pray they would come across Rachel before Alex did. Their chances were not good. Crucial minutes had passed. Alex could be a good half-mile away from them if he was in the strongest currents. They prayed Rachel was even farther ahead, that she wouldn't get out of the water and be discovered again by Alex.

Rachel was about to swim for shore when she spotted a bridge that she recognized as being near the south end of Timberline. She and Dirk had paused beside it on one of their rides, and he had pointed out an eddy and pool similar to the one she and Beth had discovered on their picnic. She swam to the far left, hoping to grasp one of the last bridge pilings and ascertain whether or not Alex was following her. She hit the buttress with a groan and grasped its slippery exterior. *No good. Too conspicuous.* She abandoned herself to the current that swept her into the strong eddy.

The eddy swept her back upstream, and for a moment she worried that she might never escape its force. As she reached the farthest point downstream again, she reached for an exposed root on the bank and held on tightly. The current pulled at her body as she considered her wisest move. If she hid, Alex might pass her, still searching. If she made a break for it, he might spot her even though it was so dark. Her heart told her to stay in the water.

She hugged the riverbank and tried to stay absolutely still, not wanting to reflect any light that might catch Alex's attention. He would be cold too and expecting Rachel to get out of the water anytime. She shivered uncontrollably and struggled to keep still. She imagined he would hear her heart pounding or her teeth clattering. Again, she turned to prayer.

Then she spotted him, his head and shoulders bobbing above the water, already slightly downstream. *Steady.* She held her breath and waited for him to pass by. *Steady.*

Dirk and Matt made good headway once they were out on the banks and able to see the dim outline of the river's path. When they reached the bridge, Matt crossed over the water and joined Dirk to discuss their search.

"They have to be frozen if they're still in there," Matt said.

"I don't think they are," Dirk answered.

"Do you think we missed them?"

"Who knows? What a terrible night to have no moon." He gazed over at the pool where he and Rachel had talked lazily and enjoyed their sunny afternoon ride earlier in the week. How he wished he could see her there now! "Let me have your flashlight, Matt."

"Why?" Matt handed it to him. He watched his friend shine it on a small pool and a muddy bank just below. Footholds had been dug out of the bank in a rough staircase fashion. They rode closer and dismounted. "Rachel?" Matt whispered loudly, wondering about the size.

"Judging from previous tracks, Alex had on work boots. It has to be her."

Alex decided she had either drowned or escaped him in the last mile. He was freezing, and he knew she certainly could not take the cold more than he could. He labored to the bank and emptied his heavy boots of water. Grimly he wrung out the rest of his clothes and began to move again. He was no longer cold, and he wasn't tired. Nothing could stop him. It was the most exhilarating night of his life. He was superhuman, and he would find Rachel soon. He would show her. She would know the man she had so callously dismissed. She would *know* him. And then she would die.

Rachel paused by a tree and knelt. She shivered uncontrollably, and her vision was disoriented. She prayed she was moving in the right direction, aware that her brain refused to act as she wanted it to. *If I could just sleep for a while.*

Her heart cried out that it was the last thing she should do, but she could not help herself. Fatigue overwhelmed her, and she passed out in a heap beside a tree, dreaming that it was a fortress that protected her.

CHAPTER ELEVEN

*D*irk tracked Rachel easily, spotting her footprints in the damp ground beside the river. Her steps were uneven and haphazard, and he soon realized that she was either injured or desperately tired. "May be hypothermic," Matt said softly, as he joined his friend and examined the tracks.

Dirk said nothing but urged his tired horse to move even faster. They found her in minutes. Dirk dismounted and ran to her, yelling.

Sixty yards away, Alex heard his call and froze, like a lion pausing to size up his prey. He quietly made his way to them, but Dirk and Matt were oblivious to his presence as they concentrated on Rachel.

"She's frozen!" Dirk said as he encircled her in his arms. She was unconscious, and damp hair clung to her head. Her clothes were soaking wet, and the two men wrapped her in Dirk's coat. Looking around for something else, Matt unsaddled his horse and tossed Dirk the blanket underneath, which Dirk then wrapped around her legs.

The two men cradled her between them, trying to pass her as much of their own body warmth as possible.

"I bet you've always wanted to have both of us this close," Matt joked to his friend.

"You weren't part of the vision, bud," Dirk retorted.

Gradually Rachel's shivering ceased, but she remained unconscious.

Matt looked over her head at Dirk. "I need to get us some help." He moved to his horse, grabbed his shotgun from its saddle holster, and fired two shots in the air.

"They'll know we've found her," he said. "But it'll take a little time to get our exact location. We're awfully close to Timberline. Our best bet may be to go for the phone."

Dirk agreed with a nod but kept his attention focused on Rachel. She was suffering from more than hypothermia—possibly broken bones and internal bleeding. "Go," he said gruffly to Matt.

Matt returned with another blanket and Dirk's pistol from the saddle holster and then helped Dirk readjust Rachel in his arms. He mounted his horse. "I'll be back soon," he promised. With that, he was off.

With satisfaction, Alex watched his adversaries split up, leaving only Dirk to fight. He felt strong and virile. He would show both Rachel and Dirk that they could not mess with him and live to tell about it. *I'll get what I want this time.*

Dirk had no chance to reach for his pistol. Alex had come too close without detection. As soon as he knew he saw him, Dirk moved to lay Rachel down, hoping to shield her with his body if necessary, and prepared to fight. She stirred, moaning. Dirk squeezed her arm in warning, hoping she would regain consciousness, hoping she might be able to escape.

"Get away from her," Jordan growled, waving at them with Dirk's own rifle, which he had grabbed from the saddlebag.

"Easy, man," Dirk said with his hands up. "We don't want you. We just want to get Rachel home safely."

Alex lifted the rifle and pointed it at Dirk's chest. He kicked the pistol into the brush. "You should have stayed out of this from the beginning. I guess I'll have to kill you. Rachel is my concern, not yours. And you won't stay out of our way."

"What good will it do to kill me?"

"You'll be out of my hair and leave us alone."

Dirk glanced back at Rachel and nodded his head at her. "Does that look like a woman dying to spend time with you?"

"She *will* die. But first, we have some business to attend to. Now load her on that horse."

"You've got to be kidding. You think I'll help you escape?"

"You have no choice. Do it, or I'll kill her in front of you and then finish you off too. Big rancher who thinks I can't do anything. Guess you finally see just what I'm made of."

"Guess I do. Too bad I don't like what I see."

"Just load her up, big mouth."

Dirk gathered Rachel in his arms and saw her peek at him through squinting eyes. He placed her, slumped forward, on Caleb's saddle and looked back at Alex. Stealthily he slipped one of Rachel's feet into a stirrup and moved to the other side of the horse. "I'll need some rope to make sure she doesn't fall off."

When Jordan looked to Matt's saddle for spare rope, Dirk slapped the horse's rump and yelled, "Go, Rachel, go!"

Rachel opened her eyes and kicked the horse's sides, urging it quickly forward. Alex yelled and ran after her, but Dirk tackled him to the ground. Knowing she could not help even if she stayed, Rachel leaned low on her horse and rode as fast as she could toward what she hoped was Timberline.

Behind her, Dirk and Alex continued their struggle.

The gun had gone flying over Alex's shoulder, and both men struggled to get to it first. Alex reached for it while Dirk tightened his fingers around Alex's throat, trying to render him unconscious but not kill him. With one last desperate move, Alex closed his fingers around the barrel and slammed the gun against Dirk's head. Dirk rolled backward, his hand pressing the week-old wound, which had begun bleeding profusely again.

Realizing that if he fired the weapon, Matt would return to defend Dirk, Alex grabbed a heavy branch instead and hit Dirk in the back of the head with all his might. He smiled smugly as his adversary fell forward and lay still. Then he set off in a dead run toward Timberline, the direction in which Rachel had gone. He left the forest's edge. The dawning hours had arrived, sending brilliant scarlet hues to the mountain skies, announcing the sun's imminent arrival. Announcing his arrival.

Timberline was in sight. Outside were Rachel's and Matthew's horses. He checked the rifle's ammunition. *Full up. That's good.* He cocked the weapon. *I'm coming, Rachel. I'm coming for you. Can you feel me near?*

He felt no pain, no weariness as he left the woods and jogged along next to Timberline's barbed-wire fence. *I am the man,* he told himself. Tanner was out of the way, and Rachel was soon to be his again. *I'm coming, Rachel. I'm coming.*

⌒

When Rachel reached Dirk's ranch house, she almost wept with relief. She slipped off the tall horse and dragged herself up the porch steps, gasping in pain. Opening the door, she called out, feeling hysterical. "Mary? *Mary?*" But she was too weak, and there was little volume to her voice. No one answered.

She heard a low voice in the kitchen and stumbled toward the room, fighting the urge to crawl. Dirk was out there with Alex. He might be injured. He might need help…

Matthew stood at the phone, relaying information to the sheriff through Beth, giving her directions to where he had left Dirk and Rachel ten minutes before. He turned to see Rachel just as she collapsed in the doorway.

Matt rushed to her and was just rising with her in his arms when he caught sight of the man outside by his horse. He ducked as the first shot tore through the kitchen window. Knowing he had to find a hiding place if he was to gain an advantage, he sidled into the back hallway just as Alex burst through the front door.

The rescuers moved out at once, driving or riding horses in preparation for another back country chase. The helicopter spotted Dirk's still form in a small clearing near the ranch. The pilot circled low and reported his location to Jake Rierdon, who was leading the nearest search party. They were in a truck on the highway, en route to base camp with fresh horses, and could reach the woods near Timberline before those across the river on horseback.

Jake and two other men came across Dirk first. He leaned over Dirk, who tried to speak. "Rachel… Jordan's right behind—"

"We know. The police are heading to Timberline right now. Rachel's with Matt."

"I should be there," he said, trying to rise. But it was obvious to all of them that he wasn't going anywhere.

"Be quiet, Dirk. She'll be fine. You have to concentrate on yourself right now. Can you move your hands and feet?" Jake asked. "Do you think you have any spinal injuries?"

"Nah. Just a couple of blows to this hard head of mine."

"I'll say." Jake wiped blood away from his face, relieved to see that the wound looked fairly superficial.

One of the other men came up with a torn T-shirt and wound it around Dirk's head, effectively slowing the flow of blood. The other man spread a blanket on the ground. Then the three lifted Dirk into the makeshift stretcher. The movement and loss of blood was too much. He groaned as the men rose and gingerly walked toward the truck, careful not to jostle their patient more than necessary.

Dirk's last conscious thought was of Rachel.

Matt held his breath as Rachel moved and moaned softly in his arms. They hid in the laundry room next to the bedroom Alex had just entered. Knowing that he would turn the corner any second and spot them, Matt decided to make a break for the back door, but he would have to leave Rachel. The back door creaked loudly; he had given Dirk a bad time about it two weeks before. "A little WD-40 would take care of that in seconds." He laid Rachel across the washing machine and dryer and closed the door halfway. He was going to have to run with everything he had in him—in hopes of distracting Alex from looking in the laundry room—and yet keep himself alive. *I love you, Beth,* he said silently, as if he could will the words across the miles and into her heart. He looked back at Rachel. *It's our only chance.*

He turned and ran down the hallway, barreling forward as he once had as a high-school football player.

Alex whirled as he heard the back door squeak in protest.

The helicopter roared low overhead.

Matt barely reached the safety of the stables as Alex ran outside the house. The gunman's attention was immediately drawn to the police above him as they yelled through their loudspeakers, demanding that he drop his weapon. Instead, Alex raised the rifle to his shoulder, took aim, and fired. The first bullet nicked a door and cracked a window.

As Alex aimed again, the deputy on board fired.

A sharpshooter at the academy, he needed only one shot to stop Alex from ever hurting anyone again.

Beth and Mary quietly watched as Doctor Harmon completed Rachel's examination. He wrapped her badly sprained wrist in an Ace elastic bandage and bound three broken ribs, then gave her a light sedative to keep her from tossing and aggravating her wounds. "She's dehydrated and needs a couple weeks of rest, but she'll be fine," he said.

She awoke an hour later in a guest room at Timberline. Frightened by the silence, Rachel rose, wincing, to find out what had happened.

Dirk was sitting in the living room, his head bound in gauze. Matt stood beside him. Both broke into huge smiles at the sight of Rachel. She was battered and bruised, her hair a mass of tangles. "Hello, gorgeous," Dirk said, as he struggled to rise, but failed.

She laughed and stumbled over to him, sinking between his knees and hugging his chest in relief. She gasped at the pain of it but could do nothing else. He was alive! Alive!

His head throbbed as he leaned over to hold her, but there was no way he would let go. "Thank God that you're okay. Rachel, I'm so sorry!"

"Oh, Dirk, don't be sorry. You did everything you could. That man was crazy. And I'm so glad that you're all right." Her eyes suddenly were fearful. "Did they get him? Is he in jail?"

"A deputy killed him after he tried to shoot down the helicopter. He's gone, Rachel."

Her relief was obvious. He kissed her on the forehead and released her as Beth and Mary gently pulled her to her feet. They led her upstairs and into a warm bath.

"Doc Harmon says you have a sprained wrist and three broken ribs," Beth told her.

"And Dirk? That bandage—"

"Makes it look worse than it is, thanks be to God," Mary said. "Concussion and twenty stitches. He'll be right as rain in a few days. Everyone just needs some rest around here," she continued, but Rachel did not stir. She was already falling back asleep, right there in the tub.

SATURDAY, JULY 31

When Rachel awoke fifteen hours later, she was stiff, sore, and still very weary. She recognized that she was not at the Double M and sleepily remembered that she was at Timberline. Dirk peeked in on her and then entered when he saw her weakly smile. Mary followed with a tray loaded with food. She set it down on a table beside Rachel's bed and gently pushed the hair away from her patient's eyes. "How are you feeling, dear?"

"A lot better than yesterday."

"I bet," Dirk said. Mary moved away, and Dirk sat on the bed's edge, grimacing at the pain in his head.

"So, tell me about your wounds," Rachel said with concern.

"He hit me a couple of times," he said, pointing to the front and back of his head. "But I'm a tough egg to crack."

"I am so glad you're okay, love."

"And I, you," he said softly. "It turned me inside out when he went chasing after you and I couldn't help."

"I guess it had to come down to me and Alex and God."

"It sure did." He got up, went to the other side of the bed, and climbed cautiously on top of the covers, careful not to jostle her. "I love you so much, Rachel Johanssen." He held her hand silently, and soon they both dozed off again, leaving Mary's food untouched.

Rachel awoke that afternoon and found Dirk studying her closely. "Hungry?" he asked.

"Starved. But more than that, parched."

He got to his feet and went over to Mary's tray. In half an hour, they had eaten everything on it and had drunk all the tea and water.

"We made short work of that," she said. Feeling better, she began to think of her world outside of that room and Dirk. "How are Matt and Beth?" she asked anxiously.

"Both are feeling better all the time."

"We're like a camp of walking wounded. Is it always so exciting around here?"

"Not always," he said. "In fact, I hope I never experience excitement of this sort again." He tenderly cupped her cheek in his hand.

She lowered her eyes from his. "What day is it, Dirk?"

He dropped his hand. "It's Saturday."

"Saturday...I have to leave tomorrow."

"You're in no condition to leave," he said a bit angrily, striding to the window and gazing out.

"Maybe you're right. But even if it's not tomorrow, I have to leave Monday. Or Tuesday. We've been dreading this for a week, and now it's here. We can't avoid it." She paused, staring at the plaid duvet cover. "I'm leaving and you're staying."

"You don't have to leave."

She sighed and grabbed a handful of the sheets, twisting them tightly. "I do. I can't just walk away from my life after a two-week vacation. Besides, it's dangerous here," she quipped, trying to lighten the moment. "I need to get back to the safety of the city. You know, the gangs and the robbers and the carjackings and..."

He looked at her until she met his eyes, and his gaze made her heart pound, her words fade away. The sun streamed in the window behind him, highlighting his strong jaw line and making his wavy brown hair shine. "Please don't go away, Rachel."

"I have to," she mumbled, looking at the sheet.

He walked over to her bed and knelt beside it. He took her hand gently. "Rachel Johanssen, you are the most beautiful woman I've ever met, inside and outside. I want you to be my wife. I promise to do my best to keep you safe, and I'll love you forever."

Tears rolled down her cheeks. "I can't, Dirk."

He rose angrily. "Why not?"

"We can't just get married after two wild weeks of romance and adventure. This isn't real life, Dirk. How can we even guess at how we'll do in five, ten years? I'm not ready to leave my home on a gamble, and I don't see you ever moving there."

He opened his mouth to say something but stopped. He was visibly upset and frustrated with her, helpless against her logic. He shook his head, stared out the window, and then walked out of the room.

That evening Beth called, and Mary brought Rachel a mobile telephone. Mary said nothing about Rachel's tear-stained face and puffy eyes, probably connecting them to Dirk's dark mood.

Rachel quietly asked Beth to come and pick her up, saying she wanted to stay at the Double M on her last night in the valley. Beth arrived soon afterward, quiet in the face of her friend's obvious grief. Both noticed that Dirk was not around as Rachel hugged Mary warmly and thanked her for all her help.

Dirk stood in the early evening shadows. He watched her from behind a barn window as she glanced around one last time, then quietly got in Beth's car and drove away.

Mary knew where he was. She strode to the barn and found him sitting in a dejected heap, staring at the fading sunlight that shone through the window above him. His handsome face was partially hidden in the dim light. "You're just going to let her go like that?"

"I asked her to marry me. She said she couldn't."

"So you're giving up?"

"What do you want me to do?" he asked, angrily knocking a fist against a timber. Mary knew he was furious with himself, not her. "What do you want me to do?" he repeated, much softer, as if in a whispered plea to God.

"Dirk Tanner, your whole life long I've never seen you back away from a fight. That girl's been through a lot lately, but she loves you!

And you're farther gone than I've ever seen. More in love with Rachel than you ever were with Debra."

"Tragic, isn't it?" His voice dripped sarcasm.

"It is if you let her get on that plane tomorrow."

"I have to let her go, Mary. Don't you see? She's overwhelmed. She doesn't get it yet; it's too close. It kills me, but I have to let her go."

CHAPTER TWELVE

*A*lthough Rachel felt a lot better, she was still stiff and bruised. As she entered the kitchen and saw Beth, she pasted on a smile and said, "Well, I must say that a sunny island beach would have been much more relaxing than the last two weeks here."

Beth smiled back at her. "But then you wouldn't have met Dirk."

"Or Alex." Rachel raised her hands. "Please. Let's not talk about it. In spite of everything, it's been good to be here. I'm glad I came." She raised an eyebrow. "And that's saying a lot, considering!"

"Sure you can't stay for a while longer?" Beth asked hopefully. "I promise you'd have a very quiet, restful time—I'd even let you off kitchen duty—and maybe you and Dirk could find some meeting ground."

"That's not the point, Beth. Dirk's been wonderful. I just need to go home and get back to a normal life. Reality. I need space to think. Time to heal, physically and emotionally."

"I understand. Can you at least get a few more days off to recuperate? Here, or in the city?"

"I don't think that will work either. The guys at work are probably tearing their hair out by now. I'm feeling better. I'll just keep my days shorter this week."

"Okay, friend. If you think it's right. What time's your flight, again?"

"Nine."

"We'll drop you off and go to the second service at church."

"I wish I had another opportunity to worship there. This vacation has made a real difference in how I see God, and that church was the spark."

"It's a special place," Beth agreed. "Wish you could become a fellow parishioner…"

"Enough, Elizabeth. Enough."

Matt loaded Rachel's luggage into their truck and drove her and Beth out to the tiny airport. Rachel stared outside the window, wanting to memorize every contour of the land so she wouldn't forget. How she had changed in two short weeks! Her appreciation of the valley had become intense, and it would always be special to her. She grieved that she had not been able to say good-bye to Dirk and fought back the tears. *Matt and Beth have been through enough waterworks.* She could wait until she was on the plane to break.

They drove in silence until Matt turned off the highway and into the airport parking lot. It was a blustery day and cooler than it had been. Fluffy clouds floated over them, growing in weight and moisture as they traveled toward the mountains. Rachel breathed in the fresh, clean air, wanting to remember the smell.

Matthew picked up her luggage, and Beth linked arms with Rachel, quietly moving her toward the terminal. Just before they entered, Dirk called her name from behind.

She knew his voice and turned with relief, fighting the urge to run to him. He took her in his arms and kissed her tenderly. "Go if you need to, Rachel. But know that I love you. Promise me you'll remember that."

The Morgans discreetly moved inside the terminal to wait.

"I know you love me, Dirk. And I love you. If only we had more time! I'm just so confused. I don't want to leave you," she said, laying her face against his chest.

"I don't want you to go."

They stood together, miserable, until her flight was announced. Wearily she tore herself from him and looked up to meet his gaze. "Thank you for coming to say good-bye, Dirk. I would never have gotten over it."

"I had to be here. Good-bye, love." Gently he held her face in his hands and ever so softly kissed her cheeks, eyelids, and finally her lips.

With tears streaming down her face, she turned away, entered the terminal, took her bags from the Morgans, and silently handed them to the airline agent along with her ticket. Hugging Matt and Beth hard, she left without a word, crying again as she walked up the steps to the airplane. Every movement forward was almost physically painful, and her heart screamed at her to stop, to turn back. But she pressed on.

And as her plane sailed into the bright blue sky, Dirk stood by his Jeep and cried silently until it disappeared from sight.

WEDNESDAY, AUGUST 25

Rachel jumped from the cable car and faced the wind blowing off the bay. For just a moment, the brisk air felt as it had the day she left the Elk Horn Valley. As she did countless times a day, Rachel paused to remember. If she concentrated hard enough, she could smell Dirk's cologne and feel his powerful arms around her. Suddenly aware that she was attracting the attention of passersby, she urged herself to move forward, feeling as though she were tearing herself away from Dirk once again.

They had not spoken since she had returned home. Despite the fact that Rachel had thrown herself back into her work and had begun "church shopping," not five minutes passed without a thought of him. A new man at work was paying her special attention these days, but in her heart, she knew he didn't measure up to Dirk. She ignored his advances and dreamed every night of the man in Montana.

She knew that she was in love and that it was not just a passing thing. But she could not bring herself to call him. Each night she sat by her phone, struggling with the desire to dial his number, to hear his voice, but in the end always decided not to do so. She would crawl into bed weary from the battle that raged inside her. She knew Dirk was waiting for her to make a decision, that he was allowing her the space and time she needed to figure things out.

The sad fact was that she only grew more confused as time passed. She wanted to call, but she also did not want to look as though she was running to him. She struggled with both pride and fear. Pride in her own work. Pride in her ability to make decisions. Pride in her way of life. To call him meant she had to let it all go.

Rachel walked outside for lunch and looked up at the tall buildings that surrounded her, feeling tiny and anonymous. On a whim, she wandered into an open cathedral, sat down in a pew, and stared at the cross and the beautiful stained-glass windows. In the quiet, she felt protected. Just as she had in Dirk's chapel. Her thoughts began to gain focus.

She loved her work. Her career looked bright. But suddenly it didn't seem enough. She wanted more. She wanted a husband. She wanted glorious, wide-open spaces, not the glare of the inner city.

After praying for a while, she simply sat and soaked in the peaceful serenity. Her decision seemed suddenly clear. Rachel stood and walked back out into the heart of San Francisco. *You have to make a gutsy decision, Rachel. You have to risk if you want to gain. And Dirk is worth the risk.* She strode quickly back to work.

Her secretary looked at her sternly, as if to show disapproval of Rachel's two-hour break. Rachel ignored the woman and walked straight back to her boss's office. She knocked and peeked in the door. "Susan?" she asked.

Susan waved her in while talking on a speakerphone to one client, and two other lights blinked on hold. Rachel sat and waited, wavering over her decision. After fifteen minutes, Susan was finally finished with all three callers. "Don't even *think* about getting more than one phone line in your office, Rachel." Susan had the habit of speaking dramatically and fast.

"That's kind of what I wanted to talk to you about."

"So talk, my dear woman, talk! Does this have something to do with whatever's wrong with you? Yes, I've noticed you haven't been doing your usual fabulous work. That's not to say it hasn't been decent. It's just not quite *there*, you know—since you got back from Alaska or wherever you went. Whatever is going on?"

"I hope you won't hate me but, Susan, I need to leave. When I was in *Montana*, I met a man. Quite a wonderful man, actually. I'm risking everything. I'm going back to the Elk Horn Valley, if he'll have me. I love my job, but I have to do this for myself." She waited for her boss's response.

Susan leaned back. A phone buzzed, and she asked the receptionist to take a message. "I suppose you've thought this through?"

Rachel nodded apologetically.

"You've thought of the income you'll be losing?"

"Yes."

"You've thought of the pension, the health benefits?"

"Yes."

"You're ready to give up the black-tie parties, the occasional opera...the shopping?"

Rachel smiled. "All of it. Believe me, I've thought of everything in an effort to beat my obsession for this man."

Susan pursed her lips and studied Rachel. "Sounds like your mind's made up."

Rachel took a deep breath. "It is."

"Well, how can I compete with love? Who would've ever thought that Rachel Johanssen would find romance in the middle of nowhere? Here I thought you were going someplace safe, not someplace that would steal you away. You're sure it's worth the risk?"

"If I don't try it, I'll never forgive myself. What if he's what I think he is, Susan?"

Susan threw her hands in the air dramatically and smiled. "You owe me big for this one, darling. Go check it out. If it doesn't work, come back. There'll always be a job waiting here for you, and I like the idea of your being indebted to me."

"Oh, Susan, thanks for being so wonderful! I'll miss working with you. One last thing... I wanted to give you two weeks' notice, but now that I've decided, I can't bear the thought of waiting. I want to tell Dirk in person."

"I need you to brief some other associates on your accounts

before you leave. Finish the week out, and then fly off to *Montana*. Doesn't it take time to charter one of those bush planes anyway?"

"It's not quite that remote." Rachel grinned, remembering her previous impression of the small airline. "I'll try to survive a few more days. I don't want to leave you stranded, but I also know that since I've made a decision, I won't be much good here."

"Get your work done, and get out of here. I do enjoy a good love story, now and again!"

Rachel walked out of Susan's office beaming and went to her desk to start prioritizing her accounts. In the morning, she would begin doling them out.

As she rode the cable car out of the center of town that evening, Rachel dreamed of calling Dirk. She agonized over the fact that she had left him and not called for weeks. Perhaps he would be so angry he wouldn't want to talk. He had seemed to accept her needs, but there was no way to know how the last weeks had affected him. Preoccupied, she almost ran into a pedestrian when she hopped off the cable car. She walked three blocks to her apartment building and opened the century-old, glass-and-wooden door with an over-size key.

She entered the hallway and smiled as she walked up the three flights of stairs to her flat. On each step lay a red rose, perfect in shape and color. She picked up each as she walked, her heart skipping a beat as she wondered if Dirk could possibly have left them for her. *Calm down. It's probably that guy at work.* By the time she reached the top, she had collected forty-eight red roses, and a white one was taped to her door. Attached was a note that read: "Roses are red, roses are white, meet me at the Golden Gate Stables at six tonight. Dirk."

Her heart sailed as she sank to her knees, laughing and crying tears of joy. *Dirk's here! He's come for me! He still wants me!*

She placed the roses in a huge crystal vase filled with water, then showered and dressed warmly. Even in late summer, Golden Gate Park was cold at night. She was ready to go within an hour and called a cab.

Arriving at the stables, she reached over the seat and threw a twenty-dollar bill at the cab driver, aware that she was leaving a sizable tip and not caring. Trying not to run, she walked toward the main office, looking around for Dirk.

A small bell over the door rang as she opened it, and a kindly looking woman entered the room from the back. She looked Rachel over with a smile. "Ms. Johanssen?"

"Yes, that's me," Rachel said, hoping Dirk hadn't called to say he was late.

"Mr. Tanner has arranged for both of your horses. You'll find your mare, Salome, in stall five all saddled up and ready to go. Here's a map of the park. You're to meet him here." She pointed to a red *X* and smiled at Rachel conspiratorially. She was in on the secret and enjoying it immensely.

The sun was low in the sky as Rachel rode her horse along the rock path to where Dirk awaited her. Her heart pounded as Salome strode to the high point of the park: the bluffs overlooking the ocean.

Dirk stood with his back to a sunset of glorious oranges and reds, the wind blowing his hair forward. Another horse idly stood nearby, tied loosely to a rugged Pacific oak. Never taking his eyes off her, Dirk walked toward Rachel to help her dismount. They embraced without saying a word, tears streaming down their faces. After several minutes he released her, but when she started to ask him questions he hushed her quickly with a long, deep kiss.

Taking her hand, he led her to a tree that had a red rose tied to it. She smiled up at him, and he held her as she tore a note from the flower and read it aloud.

> Twice or thrice had I loved thee,
> Before I knew thy face or name.
> So in a voice, so in a shapeless flame,
> Angels affect us oft, and worshipped be.
>
> —John Donne

Dirk untied the rose, handed it to her, then led her to the next tree. This time he untied the rose and read to her the contents of the note.

> Come live with me, and be my love,
> And we will all the pleasures prove,
> That valleys, groves, hills and fields,
> Woods or steepy mountain yields.
>
> —Christopher Marlowe

He led her to the next tree. She took her turn and read the note as he untied the flower for her.

> Then the LORD God made a woman from the rib
> he had taken out of the man, and he brought her
> to the man. The man said, "This is now bone of
> my bones and flesh of my flesh; she shall be called
> 'woman,' for she was taken out of man."
>
> —Genesis

Rachel looked up from the note to meet Dirk's gaze. His voice was low and gravelly when he spoke. "Rachel, the day you left I felt like a rib was torn out of me. I knew then that we should be together, but I held off, giving you time to think. I don't want to rush you, but I plan on pursuing you till the day I die, even if you keep refusing me. I'm so crazy about you I'd even move out here to be near you."

She said nothing but merely smiled at him as he led her to the final tree. An enormous white rose was tied to it. He tore the note off but did not read from the paper. Instead he recited the verse from memory as he knelt on one knee before her.

" 'Love is patient, love is kind. It does not envy, it does not boast, it is not proud. It is not rude, it is not self-seeking, it is not easily angered, it keeps no record of wrongs. Love does not delight in evil but rejoices with the truth. It always protects, always trusts, always hopes, always perseveres.'

"Rachel, I love you. Those verses from Corinthians will help us form the kind of love that we can share for the rest of our lives." He reached up to the rose and untied it. From within the white bud he pulled out an engagement ring with a large square diamond and several emeralds on either side, set in platinum. Still kneeling, he said, "Rachel Johanssen, will you marry me?"

She looked down at his earnest face and then out to the setting sun. Her heart was full, and she could think of nothing she would rather do than spend the rest of her life with this man. It was crazy...too fast...too romantic. But so, so right. Their love was invincible. Her heart told her that this was good, that this was true, and she made her decision.

"Yes, Dirk, yes."

Emily

CHAPTER ONE

*T*he thin, blond seven-year-old watched the continuous action around her with doleful eyes. *Maybe Mommy isn't coming back either.* Her brow wrinkled in fear at the thought. After all, her father, big and handsome, had knelt in front of her and promised that he would be back "in a few days." That was many months ago. Tears threatened, but she held them back.

She fervently prayed that her mother would be all right, as the kindly nun had directed her to do. After all, they were in a hospital called "Saint Catherine," her mother's own given name. *That means God will really hear me.* The thought comforted her.

Emily opened her eyes and continued to watch, her small back straight, her gaze never wavering. When the nun who had deposited her in the waiting room strode purposefully down the hall, Emily whispered, "Where's Mommy?" But the woman in the habit did not hear her.

Emily slipped out of her seat and peered down the corridor. She walked toward the nurses' station but paused midway down the hall. Ahead was the large desk. The nurses on night duty had an eerie look as the fluorescent lights under the counter lit their faces from the chin upward. She did not recognize any of the women, and she was afraid to approach them. Defeated, she walked back to the waiting room, her tiny shoulders slumped and her brow furrowed.

Hours later Sister Maria grabbed her coat and walked down the hall toward the parking lot, rubbing her neck in exhaustion. As she passed the waiting room, she spotted the tiny girl, curled up on the lime green vinyl cushions, asleep. With a frown, the woman returned to the nurses' station.

"What's the matter?" the nun on duty questioned. "Haven't you had enough for one day?"

"I think we have a problem. I need you to check on that trauma victim we got in this morning. The one with multiple head wounds. I think her name was Walters or something."

Seeing her coworker's serious gaze, Sister Joanie looked quickly through the charts. "Walker. Catherine Walker. Admitted to ICU at 7:30 A.M. and died from multiple head injuries at 10:43 A.M. Looks like it was so bad there was nothing they could do but pray."

"Was she married?"

"DMV has one listed, but we never could track him down. It looks like she was on her own."

"Not quite. I heard something about a little girl this morning, and I think she is still here. Better put in an emergency call to Child Welfare." Sister Maria returned to the waiting room after stopping to get a glass of water and a candy bar for the child. *The doctors are supposed to tell next of kin*, she thought angrily. Obviously this little girl had slipped through the cracks.

"Child," she whispered, gently touching the girl's shoulders as she sat down beside her. Emily was instantly awake, probably imagining the hand to be her mother's. She frowned as she recognized the nun, refusing the candy bar but accepting the glass of water.

"What's your name, child?"

"Emily."

"Emily what?"

"Emily Walker," she whispered, fear in her big eyes.

The nurse knew her own eyes probably conveyed what her heavy heart had to share.

"Emily, we've been trying to call your father. Is he away at work?"

"Daddy's gone."

"Oh, I see. Is there some place we can reach him?"

"I don't know. But you don't have to. Mommy always says we're jus' fine by ourselves."

"Oh." Sister Maria searched for the right words to break the news. She agonized for Emily, not wanting to bring her any more hurt. *Father, please help this child.* Silently, she continued to pray as she sat with her arm around the little girl, waiting for the arrival of the Child Welfare agent. *Help her to get through this nightmare, and be with her always. Make her your own. Let her find a quiet refuge in you.*

Twenty minutes later, a tall blond woman with straight, evenly cropped hair walked into the waiting room, breaking up their quiet vigil. Seeing Sister Maria with the small girl, the woman walked over and knelt before them.

"Are you Catherine Walker's daughter?" she asked the child softly.

Emily frowned, obviously uncertain as to whether she should answer the stranger. The nun nodded her encouragement.

Emily looked back at the tall blond woman and nodded too.

The woman gave her a weak smile. "My name is Kim," she said. "We've been trying to track down your daddy. Do you know where he is?"

"No." Emily's lower lip quivered.

"You need to come with me, honey. We're going to try to find him. We'll get you into bed and start right away tomorrow morning."

Frightened by the prospect of being taken away from her mother, Emily dared to ask the question she'd been holding inside. "Where's my mommy?"

Kim looked at Sister Maria. "No one has talked to this child yet?"

The nun shook her head sadly, then turned toward Emily and knelt before her. "Emily, your mommy died this morning. We tried to help her, but she was hurt too badly. I'm sorry, honey...so sorry. I know it hurts that she is gone. But I promise, she is in a much better place."

"God didn't hear me," the tiny girl said forlornly. Her eyes registered her pain as tears again flowed down her cheeks.

"God heard you, Emily. He'll take good care of your mother, and he'll watch over you." Sister Maria fought to keep her voice strong and reassuring.

Emily was obviously not convinced.

"You have to go with this lady, Emily. She'll make sure you have a place to go. You'll be fine."

Emily turned her gaze from the nun and pushed herself off the couch to stand beside the agent. She took the hand the stranger offered and walked with her into the dark, icy-cold night.

CHAPTER TWO

ELK HORN VALLEY, MONTANA
SUNDAY, JANUARY 16, 2001

As Dirk and Rachel drove home from church with their new foreman, Jake Rierdon, fierce winds kicked up clouds of snow from the mountainous drifts that lined the highway. Swirling flurries and dark, overcast skies limited visibility to several feet.

"Man, I haven't seen it this bad in years," Dirk said, squinting to see the road better.

"Keep your eyes peeled for deer," Jake warned. "I've been seeing a ton of 'em around here." With the continuing harsh weather, starving animals were venturing farther down in the valley to find food. Their hunger made them less cautious than normal about highways and cars.

"Look out!" Jake shouted as the beacon of the Ford's headlights caught a sudden movement at the side of the road. Rachel gripped her husband's leg, and Dirk swerved to miss the form.

"That wasn't a deer!" Rachel said. "Someone's out there!" Dirk pulled over, then paused to button up his fleece-lined coat and pull on his gloves. Jake was already out of the truck and fighting his way back through the winds and drifting snow toward the mysterious figure.

Rachel shut the doors quickly behind them, shivering from her brief encounter with the elements. She cupped her hands directly over the heater vents and looked over her shoulder to try to catch sight of the men, but they had already disappeared into the wall of swirling snow. "Please, God, keep them safe," she whispered.

Men got lost on nights like this, not five feet from their houses.

Dirk and Jake trudged back through the blinding storm, shouting into the wind and searching desperately for the figure they had passed. After several long minutes that turned up nothing, Dirk shook his head and called to his companion. "There's no one out here! We must have made a mistake. Come on! We'd better head back before we get frostbite."

Jake reluctantly turned around but continued to scan the snow-drifts on the way to the truck. Finally he caught sight of a form to the right, down the slope of the highway and in a ditch. "There!" he yelled over the wind, and Dirk followed his lead, wading through thigh-high snow.

They could see that the woman was in trouble from her blue lips and white face. She had been out in the elements for quite a while. Without hesitating, Jake crouched and easily lifted the stranger in his arms. Dirk led the way back up the embankment, carefully making footholds in the snow for his friend.

Watching from the window, Rachel saw them making their way back toward the truck. She jumped out and helped Jake get in the backseat of the King Cab with the young woman in his arms. Then she grabbed the cell phone and radioed Doc Harmon as Dirk threw the truck into gear. The doctor's home was close to their ranch, and it was agreed that he could reach it more quickly than the clinic in town. As they headed for home, Jake carefully obeyed the physician's instructions. He removed the woman's thin gloves, noticing how tiny her hands were within his own, and placed her icy fingers inside his coat, against the warmth of his shirt.

"She's soaking wet," Jake said. Instinctively, he removed her wet shoes and coat. Underneath, she wore a wet turtleneck and jeans over a couple of other layers. "Her arms are as cold as ice!" He shivered as he drew her close and willed his body heat into her own. *Please, God,* he prayed, *don't let her die.*

They pulled off the highway and soon arrived at the huge log house that was at the center of Timberline Ranch. Jake got out of the truck and rushed the woman inside past the wondering gaze of Timberline's housekeeper.

"Come on, Mary," he urged her. "We'll need you right away." He took the stranger to an upstairs guest room that characteristically drew more heat than any other in the house. As he wrapped the woman in a down comforter, he asked Mary to draw her a bath of over 104 degrees, but less than 108, per Doc Harmon's instructions.

He drew the tiny woman into his arms, careful to keep her covered with the comforter. Her pulse was so slow it scared him, and he willed her to keep breathing.

Moments later Rachel rushed into the room, dry clothing in her arms. "Okay, is the bath ready? Mary and I had better get her into that tub. It's going to be painful, but we have to warm her up fast." Jake nodded and relinquished the woman to Rachel.

After he left the room, Mary and Rachel undressed the unconscious woman to her underwear, peeling off layers of filthy and worn clothing. "I don't know where you've been, sister," Rachel said under her breath, "but it's been a long and dirty road, huh?" As they eased her into the water, their patient moaned from the pain but remained unconscious. Mary brought a thermometer from another bathroom and held it under the woman's tongue.

"Ninety-five degrees," Mary said grimly a minute later. Doc Harmon heard her pronouncement as he entered the bathroom.

"She's lucky you found her when you did." The doctor set down his black bag and moved over to his patient to lift her eyelids and check her pupils. "Get much lower, and she would've been a candidate for coma or cardiac arrest." He examined the woman's body, noticing the odd scars that covered her. "Either of you recognize her?" he asked. Both women shook their heads.

Doc Harmon continued his examination, taking the woman's vital signs and looking closely at her hands and feet. Rachel grabbed a cloth and washed off the young woman's face. She was quite attractive underneath the layer of dirt, with smooth skin and refined features. Rachel guessed that her hair would be a very fair blond, once it was clean.

The doctor leaned over Rachel's shoulder and looked at his patient. "Pretty young gal, isn't she?" he commented, not expecting an answer. "She has multiple contusions, hypothermia, and a little frostbite. She also appears malnourished. She really shouldn't be moved for a day or two. Okay with you if she stays here?"

"That's fine," Rachel said.

The doctor checked the woman's temperature again. "She's up to ninety-seven degrees. Let's dry her off and get her into bed. Do you have a long-sleeved nightshirt we can put her in?"

"Right here. She'll be swimming in this, but we can try it."

"Better yours than Dirk's," he said with amusement.

⌒

Once she and Mary had the woman dressed, Rachel called Jake into the bathroom. He easily picked up the woman in his arms, carried her over to the bed, and gently placed her under the mounds of blankets, covering all except her dainty mouth and nose. *She's so fragile,* he thought. *And so pretty.*

Doc Harmon set up an IV bottle and, despite some difficulty in locating a vein, inserted a needle into her arm. Then he gently covered her again, studying her face as if he could guess at what brought her to the valley.

"This woman needs plenty of rest, warmth, and good food," he said. "We'll know more about the frostbite in a few days. I'll arrange to have her moved to the county hospital as soon as the weather clears."

"She's welcome to stay as long as she needs to," Rachel said firmly.

"Well, that's kind of you, Rachel." The doctor rose and shook Dirk's hand. "I'd stay and wait for her to wake up, but Sherry Johnson is going to give birth in a few hours, and I need to get to the hospital to greet her new baby. In this storm, it'll probably take me that long to get there. I'll come back tonight to see how she's doing. Keep a close eye on her. No electric heaters; frozen skin burns easily. Know her name?"

"We don't know anything about her," Dirk answered.

"No ID?"

"She didn't have any license or money on her. I think she must be homeless and broke," Rachel said, looking at the woman with compassion.

"Suddenly a detective, huh?" Dirk asked her.

"No. Just my best guess. When you work a few times in the San Francisco shelters, you learn to pick up the clues."

Jake peeked over the mound of blankets at the sleeping woman and whispered, "You think this girl's homeless?"

"I'd say that *girl* is a young woman in her twenties," the doctor corrected him, and with that, he left.

Jake took a step back at the news, seeing the woman for the first time as a peer. "In her twenties?" he wondered aloud. He looked at Rachel. "But she's so small—I thought she was just a kid!"

"She's very thin," Rachel agreed. "Probably hasn't had a decent meal in ages. But I bet she's not much younger than you."

Jake's heart went out to the woman. *How could she be all alone?* "What do you think she was doing out there?" he asked.

"Who knows?" Rachel responded. "We'll have to wait and ask her when she wakes up." She dragged a big, cushy chair from the corner of the room to the bedside. "One of you take first watch while I make us some dinner."

"I'll do it," Jake said quickly. Dirk never had a chance to volunteer.

Dirk and Rachel stood in the kitchen, fixing sandwiches and hot tea for themselves, Mary, and Jake. The ranch hands had Sundays off. It was the one day of the week when they fended for themselves in their own mess hall.

"Jake seems quite taken with the girl," Dirk mused as he sliced leftover roast beef for Rachel to pile on thick chunks of bread.

"She's a mystery woman. Irresistible for men. Especially when a woman that cute is involved. They bring out the fierce protector in you big, burly, brawny guys." Rachel smiled as she taunted her husband.

"So you're saying we big, burly, brawny guys actually like seeing women in trouble?" Dirk asked, taking his wife into his arms.

"No," Rachel relented with a smile. "Tough situations just make the testosterone surge through your bodies a bit more. Actually, you're quite helpless in the face of it." She swiped the tip of Dirk's nose with mayonnaise, grabbed the plate of sandwiches, and walked into the dining room.

Dirk shook his head, grinning, still feeling like a honeymooner after five months of marriage. Rachel deposited the sandwiches on the dining room table and headed upstairs with another for Jake.

Rachel smiled as she entered the guest room. She paused at the sight of Jake earnestly leaning toward the stranger's face, as if searching it for clues to her thoughts, her memories. *I haven't seen a man so intrigued since...well, since Dirk stared at me for the first time.*

Jake blushed as he looked into Rachel's knowing eyes. "Interested, that's all," he mumbled.

Rachel nodded and grinned. "I can take over guard duty after dinner."

"Sure, Rachel," he said with a hint of disappointment. "Sure." He looked back at the woman's face, his sandwich already forgotten on his lap.

Forty-eight hours later Emily Walker awoke to an empty room. With groggy movements, she stretched under the covers before opening her eyes. As her vision cleared, her mind registered increasing panic as she took in her strange surroundings. Looking around, she knew she was not in a hospital. Scarier still was the IV needle in her arm.

Emily pulled back the plaid comforter and discovered that she wore a large flannel nightshirt, definitely not her own. She looked around for her jeans, shirt, and jacket and breathed a sigh of relief when she discovered them across the room on the hearth, neatly folded and laundered.

She didn't like being in a home she did not recognize, particularly when she didn't know how she'd gotten there in the first place. Her first instinct was to run, and she obeyed instincts. It was how she had survived.

Taking a deep breath, Emily yanked the IV needle from her arm and wrapped a nearby towel around the bleeding wound. She stumbled as she stepped out of the bed, wincing at the pain in her feet and falling heavily to the hardwood floor. With determination she picked herself up, crawled to the hearth, and dressed as quickly as she could.

Downstairs, Rachel paused in her reading when she heard the thump. Anxious that their guest had awakened without anyone to greet her, Rachel made her way out of the library to check.

The woman was just pulling torn sneakers over her black-and-blue toes when Rachel entered the room. The first thing Rachel saw was the blood on the white hand towel. "Are you hurt?" she asked. As she rushed toward the woman, her guest instinctively cowered.

Seeing her reaction, Rachel stopped. The woman's response reminded Rachel of an abused dog that she had adopted as a child from the local shelter. Even after he was safe, he had obeyed old reflexes and flinched when she bent down to pet him. It had taken years to gain his trust.

Rachel took a deep breath and lowered her voice to a soothing level. "I'm Rachel Tanner, and this is my house. We found you out on the highway two days ago, nearly frozen to death, and brought you home. It was such a fierce storm, we couldn't get you to the county hospital or the local clinic. I'm afraid this was the best we could do." Rachel paused, feeling awkward and hoping the woman would respond.

She didn't. Instead, seeing that Rachel was not going to strike her, she sat up, proudly lifted her head, and looked at her hostess. She rose gracefully but was unable to walk without reaching out to steady herself against the wall.

Rachel moved to help her, but Emily shied away from her touch. She grabbed her old jacket from the hearth, noting that it too had been cleaned. Each step caused her to wince, but she settled into a rhythm: step, wince, straighten shoulders and head, step, wince, straighten. For years, Emily had relied upon the inner rhythms she had established for herself: Run away from danger, walk away from hurt, breathe steadily while stealing food.

As Emily left the room and paused at the top of the grand staircase, Rachel ran in front of her and tried one more time to keep her from going. Was that concern in her eyes? Fear?

"Give me a chance. You're in no shape to walk out of here. Your feet have to be screaming at you to stop. I'll take you to the hospital right now if you don't feel safe. I'll drive you wherever you want to go. Is there somebody you want to call?"

Rachel backed down the stairs as the woman paused on each step to gain her balance and defy the pain. Rachel saw her skin grow whiter and whiter and anticipated what was coming.

When she crumpled in a heap a step above her, Rachel caught her easily. She guessed the woman must weigh less than a hundred pounds, but moving her was harder than she had anticipated. She yelled for Jake, who was shoveling snow just outside the front door. Hearing her voice, he ran up the porch steps and opened the door.

"Rachel?" he asked tentatively as he peeked in. Catching sight of the two women, he ran inside, leaving the door ajar. "What happened?" he asked as he picked up the limp form in his arms and looked at Rachel accusingly.

"Oh, knock it off," Rachel said. "What do you think I was doing, pushing her out of here? She was running like a scared rabbit."

Jake's face softened. "Sorry. Guess I'm feeling a bit protective." He looked at the woman in his arms. "Back upstairs?"

"Yeah. Let's take her on up and reinstitute guard duty. I want to talk to her before she has a chance to run away next time. I'll take first shift. You had better call Doc Harmon. As you can see, she grew tired of the IV."

CHAPTER THREE

*D*oc Harmon arrived shortly after Jake's call and stitched up the wound caused by the hastily ripped out IV needle. "She really didn't need it anymore," he said. "I could have removed it this morning anyway. That arm should heal up all right now. She probably fainted from moving too fast and too far after being in bed for days."

"What can we do?" Rachel asked.

"I've given her a light sedative. When she wakes up, it might slow her down enough to give you a chance to reason with her. Tell her I'll come immediately and take her to the hospital. Just don't let her leave without seeing me first."

"I tried to reason with her," Rachel said. "She wasn't stopping to hear a word. She just wanted out. I feel so bad for her."

"If she gives you half a chance," Jake said, "I bet she'll figure out that Timberline was the best thing that ever happened to her."

"Don't you mean that if she gives *you* half a chance, she'll find the best thing that's ever happened to her?" Dirk teased. Jake glowered at his friend but made no comment.

"We're willing to put her up here for a while if she wants to stay," Rachel said as she stared at the woman. "But I am not going to push her. I suspect she's been pushed around too much in her life."

Emily awoke again, but this time her eyelids felt heavy and her mind calm as she took in her surroundings. Her eyes came to rest upon a woman sitting in the corner. Rachel glanced up from her book.

"Ah, you're awake again. You sure scared me when you fainted on the stairs. Can we start over?"

Emily took a deep breath. "Maybe," she whispered.

"Good." Rachel said brightly. "As I said before, my name is Rachel Tanner, and I'm your hostess, for what it's worth. You're at Timberline Ranch. I'm new here too. Arrived five months ago as a new bride from California. My husband's name is Dirk. Am I talking too fast?"

Emily shook her head.

"I would imagine you know you're in Montana. Did you know you're in the Elk Horn Valley?"

Emily shook her head again.

"Look, I don't know anything about your situation. And I don't want to pry. But I figure it must be some pretty hard luck that caused you to be out in that snowstorm, and I'm guessing you don't have anywhere special to call home. The fact is, I could really use an extra hand around here. So if you'd like to stay and work awhile after you recover, my husband and I would love for you to stay—even if it's just until you get back on your feet. A day, a month, a year—whatever is right for you."

Emily was overwhelmed by what her hostess was saying. *Stay? Why is she being so nice? What's the catch?*

Rachel continued. "You don't have to answer now. Just let yourself rest for a while, kick the idea around, and see what you think. What's your name?"

She studied Rachel, carefully considering her options. The woman seemed honest. Earnest in her desire to help. And if she could find work instead of taking charity again— "Emily," she said softly. "Emily Walker."

That night at supper Rachel could see in the men's eyes questions about the woman upstairs, but none dared to ask them aloud. They were all good men, and Rachel decided it was best to be up front with them.

Over dessert, she made an announcement. "I'm sure you all know that we have a guest staying with us. Her name is Emily Walker, and we found her half frozen by the road on Sunday. This woman has been through the wringer, and I want you all to treat her like a fine china teacup. Give her your ultimate respect and care, and don't make any sudden movements around her. She has some healing to do, inside and out."

The men all nodded solemnly, taking on this new responsibility like a bunch of proud, serious uncles. "How long will she stay?" a slim man named Jeffrey asked.

"It's up to her," Rachel answered.

Rachel watched the men carefully, afraid that some would not like the idea of another strange woman in their midst; after all, they'd just gotten used to her. She was relieved to see their respectful reactions. Dirk had handpicked his ranch staff, and it showed. Their newest hire was a wizened, English-born, fifty-year-old man named Anton, who had an odd manner of speaking. The boys had quickly dubbed him "Que," referring to the quotes he regularly used in conversation.

"'But unto you that fear my name shall the Sun of righteousness arise with healing in his wings,'" Que said solemnly. "This young woman will find healing here," he said to Rachel with a prophetic tone.

Jake agreed. "If she's going to get better anywhere, Timberline is the place."

Rachel smiled around the table at the men. "Let's hope so, boys. Let's hope so."

After supper Rachel and Dirk went into the living room and sat down on the couch together. Jake came in and sat across from them on an overstuffed leather chair. Something was obviously on his mind. "Do you think Emily is ready to meet anyone?" He cut right to the heart of the matter. "That is...I mean, me."

Rachel answered firmly but with compassion. "Oh, Jake, I don't think so. She's so gun-shy. Let her get used to me first. Then we'll ease into the introductions. My feeling is that Emily hasn't had much contact with good men like you and the others on the ranch. It will take some time."

Jake nodded with a look of disappointment and placed his hat on his head. "I suppose you're right. Whatever is best for her. Good night, then." He walked out the front door, closing it gently behind him.

"Whew! He hasn't even met the woman properly, and he already has it bad." Dirk smiled at his wife. "I know how the poor guy feels. Remember when I burst in on you in Beth's kitchen last summer? I was head over heels in love with you before we'd been introduced."

"Oh, Dirk," Rachel said, her eyes tearing up with joy. "I love you." She kissed her husband softly, then brushed a soft brown curl out of his face and gazed into his dark chocolate eyes.

"Well...?" he said.

"Well what?"

"Now it's your turn."

"My turn for what?"

"To tell me how I was so handsome and dashing that you almost fainted when I first walked in."

"Oh...that." Her expression changed to one of puzzlement. "Wait a minute, is that how it happened?"

"You know very well that you didn't have a chance after meeting me, Mrs. Tanner."

"You think I was won over that easily, huh?"

"Who said yes to my offer of marriage not six weeks after meeting me?"

"I suppose that must've been me," Rachel said with a smile, remembering Dirk's proposal in the park outside of San Francisco. She leaned closer and kissed him. "Yep. I remember those lips. I must've swooned when you kissed me. I would've said yes to anything."

"Anything?" he asked, wiggling his eyebrows mischievously.

WEDNESDAY, JANUARY 19

Emily awoke to the sounds of running water. "Good morning!" Rachel said brightly as she emerged from the steamy bathroom. "I know that a nice hot bath with some good-smelling herbs can do wonders for me. How 'bout it? I drew one for you."

"That would be nice," Emily said. *Why is this woman being so kind to me?*

"Nice? It will feel marvelous! I stopped at this fabulous bath shop in San Francisco before I left civilization and picked up a basket of salts and soaps. Living on the ranch, a girl just needs to take some time out to *feel* like a girl. I recommend the sea-foam bath oil and the mint soap."

Emily sat up and, with Rachel's help, made her way to the

bathroom. Leaning on the sink, she thanked her hostess and closed the door firmly, locking the door behind her.

"Doc Harmon will be here in two hours to talk with you about your frostbite, Emily," Rachel said through the door. "I'll be back in a while in case you need help when you're done."

Emily didn't respond. Instead, she disrobed and slid into the warm, healing waters and felt the tension leave her body. It seemed ages since she had had a normal conversation with anyone, and even Rachel was unable to make her feel at ease. She felt walled off from the world, too badly damaged to have a normal life again.

The old-fashioned tub was deep and sturdy on its feet, and it allowed her to settle in up to her neck. The heated blue-green water did indeed make her think of sea foam, and she smiled at the luxury. Not since she was little had she enjoyed something like a bubble bath. She felt grateful toward Rachel for treating her kindly. *Can I really consider staying here? Do they seriously need help, or are they just trying to be charitable? That would grow old.* Her thoughts whirled, and she struggled to relax.

Emily washed away the grime from her body and hair, relishing the foreign feeling of cleanliness. She pushed away ugly memories of filth and despair and tried to concentrate on the good around her. After a while she got out of the tub and pulled the chain. She watched, entranced, as she imagined the traces of her old life draining away with the dirty water. *Maybe I really can stop running. Maybe these people do need some extra help. Maybe...I can finally find some peace.* Her heart urged her to rest, to give the place an honest try.

As the drain noisily slurped the last few ounces of water, Rachel knocked softly on the door. "Do you need any help, Emily? Doc Harmon will be here in a few minutes."

"I'm okay. I'll be out in a minute."

"All right. I left a clean robe out here for you. You were in there so long, you must be shriveled up like a prune. Felt good, huh?"

"Yes." Emily paused, trying to remember how to converse sociably. "Thank you." Even to her, her voice sounded stilted, sad, and alone.

Rachel leaned her head against the door. She took a deep breath and said simply, "You're welcome, Emily." She put some clothing on the foot of the bed then discreetly left the room to give her privacy.

After a few minutes, Rachel called to her from outside the cracked bedroom door. "Emily? Are you ready? I think I hear Doc Harmon in the kitchen with Dirk."

"Yes." Emily finished pulling on her jeans and a shirt that Rachel had loaned her. She picked up a wide wooden brush from a table beside her bed and admired the soft bristles. She felt like a princess as she stroked it through her damp shoulder-length hair. Without emotion she stared into the mirror, searching her face for an answer to a question she could not name. It felt good to be here. But there was still something missing.

Rachel walked up behind Emily, upsetting her train of thought. She jumped.

"Sorry if I spooked you," Rachel apologized. "If you were my sister or my friend Beth, I would've snuck up on purpose to try to scare you. Do you have any sisters?"

"No." Emily looked at the reflection of Rachel in the mirror rather than talking directly to her. She wished she'd had a friend or sister like Rachel long ago.

Rachel picked up the brush and started brushing Emily's hair. "Do you mind?" she asked.

Emily remained silent, unaccustomed and uneasy with the friendly touch but not wanting it to end either. Rachel seemed to take her silence as acquiescence rather than rudeness. "I knew you were a beautiful woman under that layer of dirt," Rachel said to her.

Emily looked at herself in the mirror again. *Beautiful?* She had not thought of herself as attractive in her entire adult life. In fact, she had spent a considerable amount of time hiding any trace of beauty. The road was no place for a pretty, diminutive woman. She had to appear as foreboding as possible at all times. Her eyes glazed over at the memory of times when her rough appearance had not protected her.

"Don't look so surprised," Rachel said, intruding on her thoughts. "I picked that shirt for you 'cause I knew it would bring out your fabulous baby blues. And I always wanted a tiny, feminine frame like yours, rather than this gangly thing."

Emily again examined her hostess in the mirror. "I always wanted to be taller."

Rachel met her eyes in the reflection and smiled. "I guess we'll form a mutual admiration society, huh?" Emily dropped her gaze, uncomfortable with how the eye contact let Rachel in. Rachel patted her shoulder. "You just start thinking of yourself as the pretty woman you are and allow it to be. I don't know why you don't like that part of yourself, but it's a blessing to be created so beautiful. Now let's get Doc to take a look at those frostbitten toes and fingers of yours so the whole creation can be pretty."

As her hostess started to leave the room, Emily called after her. "Rachel?"

"Yes?" Rachel turned from the hallway back to the door.

"Do you *really* need help here at the ranch?"

"Oh, if you'll stay, you'd truly be a godsend. I'm not the best cook. And I am not your champion housecleaner. My talents don't stretch much further than picking up takeout food and calling the local chapter of Merry Maids. Dirk and I agreed that I could set up my own business if traditional ranch work did not suit me, and I'm about to begin telecommuting with my old company on a part-time basis…which tells you how I've adapted to ranch life." She grinned.

"Unfortunately, that leaves our terrific housekeeper, Mary, on her own. She really is incredible, but with the five new ranch hands we've added in the last year, it's just too much work for one person. If you're willing to help in any capacity once you're well, then you've stumbled onto an employment opportunity. It's not charity," she added firmly, obviously sensing that Emily would reject that kind of help. "It's a job."

Emily sat with dignity, her back straight, her chin up. *I can always leave if I don't like it.* "If it really is a help to you, I could stay for a while. I owe you."

Rachel held back a grin. "Believe me, you'll work that debt off soon, my friend."

She left Emily to her own thoughts and smiled from ear to ear all the way down the stairs and into the kitchen, where Dirk stood talking with Mary and Doc Harmon.

Dirk opened up his arms to welcome her, smiling back into her eyes. "What're you so happy about?"

"She's going to stay," she whispered. "At least for a while. She'll work with Mary."

"Is she up to it?" Dirk asked.

"Oh no. Not yet. And I'll continue to give Mary a hand until she is. But I tell you, that woman has a will of iron. I'm guessing she'll be in this kitchen peeling potatoes by the end of the week."

Dirk nodded and turned to their housekeeper, releasing his hold on his wife. "What do you think, Mary?" he asked softly, not wanting Emily to overhear.

"Oh yes!" Mary shushed him with a wave of her dishtowel. "Rachel and I had a long talk about it. I think it would be just fine and dandy to take that little bird under my wing."

Dirk laughed and smiled at the doctor. "See what's going on here, Doc? I have two women running my life and making the big decisions."

Doc Harmon slapped a big hand on his shoulder as they walked out of the kitchen. "Yes, my man, you had better get used to it. With twenty years of marriage under my belt, I can assure you that this is only the beginning." They laughed together, enjoying the camaraderie of feigned persecution.

When the doctor emerged from Emily's room thirty minutes later, the prognosis was encouraging. "She has improved sensitivity in her feet. With any luck, they'll just continue to get better, and she'll be able to walk normally. One of her little fingers is still completely numb, but the rest should return to normal. As for her fatigue and malnutrition, she's recovering quite rapidly, with your care and good food.

"You folks are probably the only good thing that's happened to her in a very long time," the doctor continued. "I'd say if she doesn't perk up in a few weeks, you might consider a visit to a family psychologist in Elk Horn."

"She'll be fine, Doc," Rachel said firmly. "But I'll keep it in mind."

"Such wonderful news!" Mary exclaimed as the doctor departed. "And maybe that little bird will be better at kitchen work than our new bride here," she nudged Rachel.

"Let's hope so," Rachel said smiling. "Or we'll *all* be in trouble."

CHAPTER FOUR

*T*hree days later Emily emerged from her room and began to try her hand at a few small chores around the house.

As Jake climbed the front steps to the porch, he spotted her limping through the snow, her arms overburdened with the load of wood she carried. She wore thick wool socks and Mary's rubber boots to protect her healing toes. Jake paused, transfixed. Rachel's leather coat dwarfed Emily, and the wind blew her blond hair and turned her cheeks a bright pink. Jake felt suddenly dizzy and realized that he wasn't breathing. He forced himself to consciously inhale as he gazed at her. *She is truly a beautiful woman. So delicate, such perfect features.*

Jake watched as she tried to recover a piece of wood that had fallen from her load. When she stooped to pick it up, the others tumbled from her arms. Jake sprang into action. He jumped down the stairs two at a time and was by her side in seconds.

Emily looked up in fear as the big man approached, then recognized him as one of the men Rachel had pointed out to her during the week. *Relax,* she told herself. *It's just one of the ranch hands.*

Jake smiled into her eyes as he bent to help her pick up the wood. "Hi, I'm Jake Rierdon. Let me help you—you've got a big load here."

"I've got it," she said. Without malice, she firmly took from his arms the wood he had picked up and added it to the stack she already held. She stood, carefully balancing her load.

"I just wanted to help," Jake tried to assure her. He gazed down at her, lost in the deep blue of her eyes, the flush of her cheeks, the soft curve of her lips. She stood in front of him, unmoving.

What is it about this man? she wondered. There had been few men in her life with whom she had felt so at ease. She recognized Jake's handsome looks: caring, soft brown eyes, a strong, square jaw line with just a hint of stubble, and soft brown hair that was layered with snow. He stood a good twelve inches taller than she. Men of his height usually put her off right away, but to her surprise Jake did not.

"I can manage, thanks," she said, ending the moment. *Don't owe anything to anyone,* Emily reminded herself. She turned and tromped down the snow-laden walk to the front steps.

As Emily entered the house, she saw Rachel standing at the huge picture window with a cup of coffee and knew that Rachel must have seen her interaction with Jake. She walked over to the huge stone fireplace and released the pile of wood from her aching arms.

"Jake is a remarkable man," Rachel said quietly. She remained at the window, looking at the heavy, swirling snow falling outside.

"I suppose he is," Emily mumbled. She headed toward the kitchen to join Mary.

"He's the one who saved you, Emily," Rachel called after her.

Emily paused in the doorway. "What do you mean?"

"He spotted you on the edge of the highway. When he and Dirk went back to look for you, they couldn't see anyone. Dirk was ready to give up when Jake found you. You were deep in the snow, down the embankment from the highway. He carried you out."

Emily stared for a moment at Rachel and then walked into the kitchen without a word.

A month later the jingling of sleigh bells drew Mary to the kitchen window. She laughed as she spied Dirk and Jake piling blankets into an old carriage on skis.

"What's going on?" Emily asked.

"Oh, they're at it again. They've gone and pulled that ancient sleigh out of the barn. Dirk insists on getting it out at least once every winter. You'll see. He'll demand we all come with him for a ride."

"Uh, I think I'll stay here—"

"You might as well start bundling up those delicate feet of yours now. Dirk won't take no for an answer."

As if on cue, Dirk came bursting through the door.

"Rachel! Mary! Hey, Em! Get on out here!" he hollered. "We're goin' for a ride!"

Rachel came out of her office, puzzled that Dirk would be rounding up the household in the middle of the day. "What in the world…"

He pulled her into his arms. "Bundle up, you green Californian. We're taking the ladies for a sleigh ride."

"Oh, Dirk, I've got so much work to do."

He picked her up, and she laughed at his unexpected move. "Dirk—"

"You heard me. I said bundle up. If you don't, I'll take you out as is."

"All right, all right."

As Dirk put her back down, Rachel looked at the two women

smiling at them from the kitchen doorway. "Come on, gals. Let's get ready for a sleigh ride."

"Rachel, I—," Emily began.

"No way, Em. If I have to go, so do you."

Dirk sat on the front seat beside Rachel, who was bundled beneath brightly colored wool blankets. He held the reins as Jake assisted Emily and Mary into the open sleigh behind them. The ancient carriage mounted atop giant silver skis was beautiful, an antique. "Eighty years ago this old gem carried my grandfather to school on cold winter days." Dirk looked lost in the history of it; Emily knew he had lost his parents in a car accident—maybe it gave him a sense of connection to the family he once had. Their shared loss made Emily feel somehow more at home at Timberline. Understood, in a wordless way.

Mary settled herself on the end of the single bench, leaving Emily little choice as to where she should sit. "Come on, child," Mary said as Emily hesitated beside Jake. "You'll be warmer between us."

Resignedly Emily seated herself and pulled a blanket over her lap. Jake sat down beside her. *Too close,* she thought and nudged toward Mary. He didn't comment on the move away from him but instead smiled benignly and joked with Dirk.

As soon as everyone was settled in, Dirk clucked to the two strong draft horses, Hercules and Thor, and they were off. The bells jingled and the skis groaned as they slid over the crunchy snow. Emily closed her eyes and took in the smells and sounds of her first winter's sleigh ride. Gradually she relaxed.

"Let's sing carols!" Dirk said enthusiastically.

"Christmas was two months ago!" Rachel exclaimed.

"Yeah, well it was too cold to take the old sleigh out for a ride then. I guess we'll just have to make up for it now."

Seeing his determined face, Rachel grinned and began, "Jingle bells, jingle bells…"

The rest joined in, singing loudly to the accompaniment of the sleigh bells.

Emily allowed herself to hum along.

⁓

After two months on the job, Emily knew she was proving herself to be a versatile employee. She was busy at work in the kitchen one morning when Mary walked in, her hands full of freshly washed towels and dishcloths. The older woman put them away in the cupboard and sniffed the air.

"Something smells delicious. What are you making?"

"Oh…well, I told Rachel how much I've enjoyed cooking, and she bought me a new book of recipes. See here? I thought I'd make a roux for a soup base. Maybe corn chowder with cilantro and red pepper?"

Mary walked over to stand beside Emily as she stirred the butter, onion, and flour mixture in a deep cast-iron pot. She squeezed her shoulders. "I'm sure it will taste terrific."

Emily smiled to herself as Mary left to do more laundry. She often experimented with cooking under her older friend's watchful eye and found great pleasure in the creativity. More than that, she found the ranch hands' distinct satisfaction in her meals gratifying. She couldn't remember the last time she had believed that she was giving to others. The sensation made her feel real happiness for the first time in her life. The last two months had been a dizzying experience: meeting an entire ranch staff of thirteen boisterous men, learning the ropes of cooking for an army, and cleaning furiously until the household shone.

Emily began to look at herself in the mirror with a glimmer of hope. She had purpose. She had direction. She could even see for herself a bit of beauty in her war-torn face. And with the arrival of the spring thaw, she felt the traces of her old life—the misery, grime, and illness she had suffered—slowly melting away with the snow. But as much as she hated her old life, she was not yet completely comfortable with the new. The world in which she found herself was rather confusing.

Perhaps most bewildering of all was Jake.

As if reading her thoughts, Jake entered the kitchen at that exact moment to get a glass of water. Most of the ranch hands stayed around the bunkhouse and small mess hall when they were off work. But as foreman of Timberline, Jake had access to the main kitchen and big house—a privilege he had taken full advantage of since Emily's arrival.

Her heart started beating quickly at Jake's appearance, but she barely acknowledged him as she continued to stir.

"Hello, Emily," Jake said softly. "What are you making?"

"Corn chowder."

"I love corn chowder! Haven't had it since I was home." He paused, and when she didn't respond, went on. "Timberline feels more and more like my home. But I was raised in San Francisco. I love chowder with a thick crusty loaf of French bread. Too bad you can't get bread like that here."

She still didn't answer, and he struggled not to push further.

Careful, Jake. Don't overdo it. Gentle…gentle, he reminded himself. *Always gentle around Emily.*

He tore his eyes from her and forced himself to leave, not trusting himself to remain around her for long without making a buffoon of himself.

She watched from the kitchen window as he walked toward the stables.

No matter how she responded, Jake was always there, always smiling, always eager to help. He was careful to maintain his distance, but it was plain that he was growing more fond of her each day. His attraction to her was both frightening and pleasing. *I'm so confused,* she thought. *I don't need any complications in my life right now.* Even so, she found herself turning the cookbook pages for a French bread recipe.

That night at dinner, she placed a steaming loaf on the table and smiled as Jake's eyes lit up. She turned away before he could say anything, busying herself by serving the others from a tureen of soup.

It was the first move she had made toward Jake. He sensed her fear and resolved to keep far enough away that he wouldn't scare her but close enough that he could be right there if she began to let him in. He was terrified of turning her off, or worse, hurting her in some way.

I haven't suffered like she has, he reminded himself. He had grown up in a wealthy household in a prestigious neighborhood with the benefits of his parents' lavish lifestyle.

The pain he suffered was different from Emily's. It resulted from years of living to please parents who could not be pleased. It came from years of guiding his life according to their wishes. Architecture had never been his choice; he always knew his heart called him to something simple and wholesome, something wild and different. He had found himself at Timberline Ranch. And he desperately wanted Emily to find herself there too.

~

Thursday, March 30

Over a month after Emily's first sleigh ride, the Morgans pulled up on their own sleigh of sorts: a giant toboggan. Matt had rigged a rope to pull Beth along behind his horse, and they arrived early in the afternoon on a beautiful spring day.

"Come on!" Beth said, as she burst into the kitchen. "This is the laziest ranching month of the year. Let's go play!"

"You go on," Mary said. "Go collect Dirk and Jake; they'll be game. Rachel might even go. But I'm too old for such foolishness."

"Okay," Beth said, too excited to be put off by Mary's refusal. "How 'bout you, Emily? It would do you some good to get outdoors. Come with us! It's a blast!"

Looking into Beth's happy, rosy face, and remembering the enjoyment of her previous excursion, Emily hated to refuse. Still, she was nervous at the thought of being out with Jake again. "I don't know, Beth. Doc says I should still be careful about letting my feet get cold."

"Don't worry! We'll keep you toasty. If you get cold at all, we'll head home. Go on, get ready! I'll collect Rachel out of her office crypt."

She set off before Emily could say another word.

Why is it so hard to say no to these people? she wondered. Yet she was glad they wanted her along. After making sure Mary didn't mind her leaving for a short time, she left the kitchen to bundle up.

"Remember how last month's sleigh ride lifted your spirits? Go, child! You'll have a good time. There's nothing like a fast run down a snowy hill to get the juices flowing."

Out on a western slope, above the river, Dirk and Rachel claimed the front of the toboggan. Emily climbed on behind them, gingerly clutching Dirk's shoulders. Jake sat behind her, and Matt prepared to push them off. All six of them could have fit on the old nine-foot giant, but Beth declined, determined not to endanger the baby she carried. She was seven months pregnant and would only ride on flat ground behind Matt's horse. "Next year, I'll take you all on," she challenged. "I'll go off a hill much steeper than this wimpy incline."

"Yeah, yeah…you talk big, little momma," Rachel said as she looked with wide eyes down their intended path. "We'll see how brave you are next year."

Matt pushed the moaning toboggan off to a slow start, but the sled quickly gained speed. As they flew down the hill, Rachel shrieked and Emily held her breath. "Look out!" Dirk yelled, too late. They hit a small mogul and flew into the air, breaking up their tight formation. All four came down hard and were sent sprawling in the snow. Emily opened her eyes and found herself nearly on top of Jake, who grinned back at her, his face nearly covered with snow. It took her a second to react.

"Oh, Jake, I'm sorry—"

"No! It's okay! Having a pretty lady land in your lap is just one of the perils of tobogganing."

Emily blushed at his comment and hurried to join Rachel, who was trudging up the hill to where Beth and Matt sat laughing hysterically.

CHAPTER FIVE

*F*rom the protection of the barn's shadows, Jake watched Emily sweep slush off the front porch. She was bundled up in Rachel's old jacket, and her breath created little clouds of fog in the early spring air. Her tiny body swayed to a rhythm in her mind, making her chore appear as a dance.

Que rode into the barn but was ignored, since Emily was in sight. He tied the mare to a post and walked up behind Jake to see what had him so fixated.

"Oh," the older man said with understanding. He clamped Jake firmly on the shoulder in camaraderie. "I know this is hard for you, Jake. It's clear you're trying to give her space, and that can't be easy. But you're thinking of her needs first, and that's an important lesson in real love. As my old friend Sir Walter Scott said, 'We shall never learn to feel and respect our real calling and destiny, unless we have taught ourselves to consider every thing as moonshine, compared with the education of the heart.'"

"I actually feel pain," Jake said, tearing his eyes away from Emily to look into Que's. "I want so much to help her."

"She has to make her own way, Jake," the older man said firmly. "If you get in the way, I guarantee that you'll lose any chance you might have. The bird's been burned, and badly at that. She's just beginning to grow new feathers. Don't stifle or distract her just yet. If it's right, she'll come to you in her own time." Jake turned away to watch Emily sashay back into the house. He pondered Que's advice. It was the most Jake had heard him speak since his arrival, other than lengthy quotes. *In her own time*, he repeated silently. *In her own time.*

The next morning after the crew left for breakfast, Mary shooed Emily out of the house, telling her to go explore. "You've been here for three months, and I'll bet you haven't been farther than the porch steps. Go on, child. Take the morning off. The house is in order. Come back in a few hours and we'll get lunch goin'."

Emily fought off the feeling of being banished, knowing the motherly housekeeper was just trying to help. The truth was, she *hadn't* been much farther than the porch steps. She walked to the living room window and looked outside. It was a glorious spring morning. The blue sky had not a cloud in it, and the temperature had even risen a few degrees.

She heard Rachel in the library, busily brainstorming an ad campaign with her boss in San Francisco. Rachel's bid to work out of her house was going well. She was doing what amounted to part-time work but was devoting forty hours a week to her efforts in order to prove her ability to work long-distance. Emily knew she was helping Rachel to do what she really wanted to do. The knowledge made her feel good…and a little less indebted.

Taking a deep breath, she lifted Rachel's coat from a hook by the door and wrapped it around herself. Its warm folds enveloped her, giving her a sense of security. *Maybe I should go see a little of the ranch.*

She stepped out onto the porch and hugged herself as she shivered in the crisp spring air. She contemplated exploring the barn and stable but quickly ruled out the idea for fear she might stumble across some of the men. *Worse yet, I might run into Jake. And what would I say?*

Moving toward the corrals, she spied Jake with Dirk and two foals. Emily thought about turning away, wanted to turn away, but instead was drawn closer, curious about the baby horses and what the men were discussing.

She was not in much danger of being noticed. Jake was intently explaining to Dirk a new training technique he'd read about, one that prepared a horse from birth to eventually accept a rider.

Emily paused, enjoying the scene. The sky was a brilliant blue, and the sunlight seemed to hold a tinge of summer. She closed her eyes, tilted her face upward to absorb its warmth, and listened to the sounds of the ranch: a distant chain saw on the south fields, horses nickering contentedly, the screen door banging shut... *It is such a busy, happy place.*

She opened her eyes again and watched the men as Dirk calmly approached the nearest foal. He motioned for Jake to hold her while he checked out her teeth and hooves. But as soon as Dirk lifted the tiny horse's mouth, the foal suddenly writhed, throwing Jake off guard and to the ground.

Emily laughed out loud. Her reaction startled her, and she covered her mouth quickly, looking around to see if anyone had noticed. Laughter was foreign to her. Certainly she had observed more of it at Timberline than anywhere else in her life, but until now she had not felt the freedom to laugh herself. Mary warmed Emily's heart when she mothered and fussed over her. Rachel's forthright, sassy manner delighted her. And Dirk's tender love for Rachel often brought a smile to her face. But until now, nobody had made her laugh out loud.

To Emily, the sensation was at once delicious and awful, because she had not been able to control it. Telling herself it was all right, a healthy thing, she quietly disappeared around the back of the house, while Jake brushed himself off and Dirk got control of his own laughter.

Beth Morgan drove up to the house in her red Ford pickup to see Rachel after having taken a two-week vacation to San Francisco. Rachel spotted her and squealed with delight, pulling Mary out of the kitchen with dish and towel in hand. "Beth's back!" Rachel said with a huge smile. She ran out of the house, stopping short as Beth got out of the truck.

"Whoa! You're as big as that truck, woman!"

"Oh, hush up and give me a hug. After a trip to see the folks, I need one."

Rachel leaned over her friend's growing belly and hugged her for a full thirty seconds. "Oh, it's good to see you, Beth! Come inside before you catch a cold. Tell me all the news from the city."

"A cold? It's practically summer out…and I don't need more mothers than the one I've got, thank you very much."

"Mumsy got on your nerves, I take it?" They walked toward the porch steps, arm in arm.

"She wasn't the only one." As they entered the house, Mary came over and gave Beth a big hug.

"You look wonderful!" the older woman raved. She patted Beth's stomach and looked meaningfully at Rachel.

"Oh, now Mary, it's only been seven months since Dirk and I married!" Rachel protested the unspoken message.

"Just the same," Mary said as she hustled off to make some tea, "you're not getting any younger, you know."

Rolling her eyes, Rachel pulled Beth by the hand and sat next to her on the couch. "I don't have to worry about my biological clock. Mary's is ticking for me!"

Emily bit her lip and hurried along the path. She remembered what Dirk had told her weeks earlier: "Go ahead and explore anywhere you like. There's a path behind the house that leads to a chapel up the hill. It's a great place to relax and think." She had climbed quite high and her feet were sore, but she continued on, wanting to see the place for herself.

Emily emerged from a thick blanket of trees and gasped. She stood on a cliff that overlooked the entire valley, and in front of her sat a quaint chapel made of stone. She breathed in brisk air, heavy with the scent of pine, withdrew her icy hand from her jacket pocket, and unlatched the wooden door.

Entering, she observed with pleasure two comfortable chairs and a wood stove, as well as a small altar and cross. *I don't get it. Why have another entire building for this?* She questioned the building's purpose but felt drawn to the peaceful quiet and sanctuary it created.

If it were just warmer, I'd stay a little while. Opening the small wood stove, she saw logs and kindling laid on the grate, ready to ignite. *Who did that? Dirk? Jake?* She lit a match and touched it to the dry tinder, pleased to see it burst into eager flames. *I'll come back tomorrow and lay a fire for the next person.*

As she watched the dancing, growing flames of blue, red, and orange, Emily was struck by the memory of her foster home. She had joined Arthur and Anna Jones when she was twelve years old, after years of living in the county home. Her foster father had been a kind man who loved children. Emily remembered how he had built fires in the hearth of their cozy home to chase away the New England chill.

Arthur Jones had instilled in Emily manners, a love for reading, and the beginnings of trust and love. But four years after Emily joined the family, Anna was diagnosed with Lou Gehrig's disease and became bedridden shortly thereafter. Anna's illness had demanded a lot of Arthur's attention, and as Anna slowly withered away over the next two years, so also did he. By the time Emily turned eighteen, she had again lost both her parents.

After she graduated from high school, Emily began to search for her real father. When she failed to find him, she had begun her current search to find herself…and to find a place she could call home. Seven years later she found herself here. At Timberline. Could this be it?

⁓

"I'm about out of my mind, Dirk," Jake confessed as they released the mares back into the corral with their foals. The horses hustled past them, looking at the humans as if they considered them entirely irksome. Dirk climbed the fence and sat upon it.

"It's really getting to you, huh?"

"She's so beautiful! All I want to do is reach out to her. It would be one thing if I wanted nothing more than to be friends, but I want more. She makes me ache, you know? And there isn't a thing I can do to ease the pain."

"Jake, man, why did you come to the Elk Horn?"

Jake looked at his friend, puzzled. "You know my reasons—to get away from the city, away from a life that made me feel trapped."

"Away from all that. But to get what?"

He thought for a moment. "To find myself. And to learn more about the things that really matter to me."

"Right. You've had time to think about what you want and how you are going to achieve it. But Rachel tells me this woman's been concentrating on survival for a very long time. Suddenly she has the time to think about where she is and where she wants to go. But first she has to get used to being cared for and feeling comfortable. It seems like that could be a full-time job in itself."

Jake remained silent, looking south, down the valley, listening.

"She might like you, Jake," Dirk encouraged his friend. "Maybe a lot. But love takes a lot, and Emily may not be ready for that yet. Give her time. Let her heal." He kicked his feet over the side of the fence and jumped to the ground with a thud. "You'll get through this, one way or another. Come on. Let's go join the other men and see how the calves are doing."

The fire Emily had started began to drive the cold away, and soon the small chapel was cozy and warm. She snuggled into one huge, overstuffed chair, gazing first at the beautiful, carved cross in the front of the room and then out the giant picture window at the amazing valley beyond.

The mountains were a brilliant deep green, heavily laden with rich forest and still bearing a winter's cap of white at the top. At their feet, verdant spring grass had begun to sprout. The river at the valley's edge wound crazily at times, then rushed forward through the narrows in frantic, white waves toward the call of a distant ocean. The awe-inspiring scene held Emily's attention for almost an hour. Again and again she asked herself, *Is this where I am supposed to be?*

She was unable to answer.

Feeling warmer, she stood to take off Rachel's coat and throw another log on the fire. As she moved to hang up the jacket, she noticed a Bible imprinted with the name DIRK JAMES TANNER sitting on the arm of the second chair. *James.* She remembered Mary telling her that Dirk had worked out his grief over losing his parents by building the chapel.

She understood his grief and the need to act upon it. *I wish I could have done something when my mom died. But what could I do? I felt so lost. I still feel lost.* Emily's heart ached as she thought of her mother, something she had not allowed herself to do for a very long time.

She picked up the Bible and flipped through it randomly. She considered the Tanners deeply religious. She knew that they went to church every Sunday, with the ranch hands in tow, as well as Wednesday evenings for Bible study. They always invited her, but she declined, anxious at the thought of leaving the only safe place she had known in years.

The others noticed her reluctance to leave the house, and they did their best to encourage her to venture out. But the chapel was the farthest she had gone from the main house since her arrival in January. She was glad that Mary had convinced her to go exploring. She enjoyed being out of the house and felt "at home" in the chapel.

It was good to be alone again, yet secure and still. Always before, being alone had meant being on the road, searching for a place she could call her own. She turned her thoughts to the open pages before her. "Grace and peace from God the Father and Christ Jesus our Savior."

Grace. Peace. Father. Savior. The words were pleasing and warmed her heart. As she read from the book called Titus, she thought of one of her early foster homes, a place where the people preached of God yet acted in evil ways. Emily pushed away the ugly memories. Looking again at the text, she noticed that the writer appeared to renounce such people. *That's good.*

She turned to another place in the Bible, not wanting to ponder her past any longer. Isaiah. "Sing about a fruitful vineyard: I, the LORD, watch over it; I water it continually. I guard it day and night so that no one may harm it. I am not angry. If only there were briers and thorns confronting me! I would march against them in battle; I would set them all on fire. Or else let them come to me for refuge; let them make peace with me, yes, let them make peace with me."

These were good words to her heart. *Come to me for refuge.* Emily suddenly felt closer to God than she ever had before. His presence in the room was almost tangible. "Do you even want me?" Emily whispered aloud.

There was no audible response. But a tide of sweet warmth filled Emily's soul, and she knew. She *knew.* She had finally glimpsed true love. And the hint of it made her feel beautiful, wanted, and whole.

"I'm serious! Your stomach is twice as big as when you left," Rachel teased as she handed Beth some herbal tea.

"At least I have an excuse," her friend retorted.

Rachel laughed. "No kidding. With Mary's usual wonderful cooking and Emily's fabulous culinary experiments, I really need to be careful. I've probably gained ten pounds! But enough of *that* fun topic. Tell me more about your folks and the city. Did you go to the office?"

"Oh yes. Susan and I had lunch. She's delirious with joy that you're back on board, even eight hundred miles away. She tried to get me back into it too."

"H'm, *very* interesting. What'd you say?"

"I told her I was perfectly content with the sedate pace of ranch life and that I'd call if I ever got bored. Unlike you, my dear friend, I left more than my job in San Francisco. I left stress."

"You can't tell me feeding and cleaning up after the crew doesn't cause its own stress."

"But it's different. I think ranch life is more tolerable for me than for you. But I will admit that I've toyed with the idea of working with you part-time and hiring on some help."

"Oh, Beth! That'd be so fun! We cowgirls could certainly wow 'em in the city."

"Now, hold on. I told Susan no. I don't want her to get wind of this. If she does, she'll be merciless. I'm just mulling over the idea for when Junior gets into kindergarten."

"Oh, all right. I won't say another word until you bring it up again. And speaking of the baby, how are you feeling?"

"Very well. I won't bore you with motherhood rhetoric about the miracle of bringing another life into the world. But I'll tell you this— it's the biggest thing I've ever experienced. Words can't begin to describe it. And Mary's right. You and Dirk should get on with it. I want Junior here to have a playmate next door."

"Whew! You and Mary. Tick, tick, tick…"

Beth laughed as Rachel looked at her impishly.

"How're your parents?"

"Fearful that all we have for obstetricians and hospitals around here are volunteer nurses at the reservation and a one-room clinic. After we lost our first baby in the accident, they lost faith in

Montana's whole medical system. They can't see that they should be thankful Matthew and I lived through the accident. In fact, they're trying to talk me into coming home the last month to have the baby in one of those plush birthing hospitals."

"Are you considering it?"

"Not a chance. Matthew and I have even talked about having the baby at home. We're checking into the availability of midwives here in the valley."

"You're so gutsy," Rachel said with admiration. "Did you see my folks?"

"I talked to your mom on the phone. She sounded good. And she sent over an adorable outfit for the baby."

"Who else got on your nerves if it wasn't my mother?"

"Eleanor Rierdon. She has decided that if it weren't for me, neither you or Jake would have ever ended up here."

"She's right."

"She insisted on coming over. She was always more your acquaintance than mine, but she wanted to pump as much information out of me as possible."

"Did you tell her about Emily?"

"No way. I'm not touching that subject with a ten-foot pole. It's all yours, honey."

"Thanks a lot."

"How is she doing?" Beth asked quietly, looking over her shoulder toward the kitchen.

Rachel motioned outside with her head, speaking in a normal tone. "She actually left the house today, which is a huge step. She usually skirts around people and talks only when she's forced into it. But she's gained weight and color, smiles a little more often, and seems quite at home. And she works—boy, does she work! It's as if she thinks that if she eases up at all, I'll toss her out of here. She doesn't want any charity."

"Any luck in getting her to church?"

"Not yet."

"How's Jake's courtship going?"

"Slow. The girl is as skittish as a mouse. And you know Jake. He's like a bull in a china shop. It's *painful* to watch him around her. The man looks as if he would faint if she would only bat her eyelashes at him."

Just then Dirk came stomping up the porch, trying to loosen the mud from his boots before entering the house. "Is that Beth's truck I see?" He whooped at the sight of their mutual friend and went in to give her a big hug. He then kissed his wife and moved to sit beside her, ignoring Rachel's exaggerated move away from his sweat-soaked shirt. "You look absolutely gorgeous, Beth. Truly the epitome of glowing motherhood." He looked down at his wife beside him. "What do you think, Rach? Should we get you in the family way?"

"Tick, tick, tick," Rachel whispered to Beth. She turned back to her husband. "You *are* irresistible at the moment. I don't know when I've found you quite so alluring. Maybe last week when you ran into that skunk in the stables."

Beth laughed, her eyes wide. "You're kidding."

"No joke," Rachel said with a smile on her face. "We had to give him a three-hour tomato-juice bath."

Emily hurried down the path, anxious to get back to the house in time to help with supper. She didn't want to give the Tanners any reason to fault her. But as she neared the stables, she noticed a mare alone with her foal and could not resist going closer.

She moved quietly so as not to disturb the horses, speaking softly to the mother in order to gain her trust. The horse nickered in surprising acceptance, apparently deciding that the diminutive woman was no real threat.

Jake stood in the shadows of the barn, unseen, once again observing her. He held his breath as he watched her approach the mare and foal. *Only ten feet away.* Surely she could hear his pounding heart! *What would she think if she caught me spying on her?* White-knuckled, he gripped the pitchfork in his hands as he halfheartedly threw some hay into a trough. His eyes, though, were on her. *Oh, Emily...won't you ever let me nearer than this?*

He watched as she slowly raised her palm for the mare to smell. The mother sniffed, her great nostrils taking in huge amounts of Emily's scent. Jake felt suddenly jealous of the horse and almost laughed at his own reaction. Making a decision, he turned and placed the pitchfork against the stall wall and exited the stable.

As he came out into the open, he acted surprised to see Emily in front of him. "Emily! Hello."

She immediately dropped her hand from the horse, looking as if she wanted to run. The mare raised her head, and her ears rotated forward at the sound of Jake's rumbling voice.

Jake ignored Emily's unease. "Making friends with the gals, are you?"

"I've never really been around horses before," she almost whispered.

Encouraged by her positive, if shy, response, Jake nodded as he moved carefully around her. "I could teach you to ride," he offered.

"Oh no. I couldn't."

"Why not?"

"Lots of reasons."

"Fear?" he ventured.

"Maybe." She turned to go. "I better go in and help Mary with supper."

Jake studied her as she walked away. "Consider my offer a standing one," he called after her.

CHAPTER SIX

*T*hey're for you," Jake held out a handful of wildflowers to Emily as she stood on the porch after cleaning up the breakfast dishes.

At first she hesitated. But then she chanced a look into his eyes and knew she couldn't refuse the gift. In all of her life, she had never encountered a persistent love like Jake's. He was always there for her, ready to help. She was also aware of his continual care in letting her have the space she needed.

Jake was a man of compassion and dreams. He loved his life at Timberline, and Emily had overheard Dirk tell Rachel that their foreman wanted his own ranch someday. Emily was certain he would have it; Jake knew how to put feet to dreams. She thought about how he had given up his prestigious career to start a new life in Montana. *He's so determined, so alive.* Out of all the men she had encountered in her life, Jake was by far the most irresistible.

As she took the flowers, their fingers touched, and she felt the electricity run up her forearm to her chest. "They're beautiful, Jake." She smiled softly.

He grinned from ear to ear. "I can show you where they're growing. They're up in a gorgeous mountain field a few miles southwest of here. The snow's gone, all the way. We could ride."

"You know I can't ride."

"I promised to teach you, remember? I'll choose a gentle mare and pull you along—give you the feel of it. Later you can take the reins. It'll only take me a moment to saddle up Tana and another." He nodded toward the horses, who grazed lazily in the warm sun.

Emily shrank in fear at the idea of being alone for so long with Jake. *How long would it take to ride a few miles and back?* "Don't you have to work?" she hedged.

"I have the morning off. I'll be helping the troops repair some drainage ditches later on, but I'm free for several hours."

Mary came out on the porch, drying her hands on a dishtowel slung over her shoulder. "Now you go on with him, Emily Walker. Here's a perfectly good chance for you to get out of the house and see a little of this beautiful country God's brought you to." She nodded confidently, signaling "that's that."

Emily blushed, realizing that their conversation had been overheard through the open kitchen window. Sheepishly she looked back to Jake, who grinned down at her. "I'll go change."

Emily came out wearing new blue jeans and a chambray shirt, opened to reveal a white turtleneck underneath. Jake knew that Rachel had pestered her for weeks to order a few things from catalogs if she wouldn't go shopping downtown. She must've finally done it.

Both shirts were layered under a blue wool sweater that covered her waist, and new cowboy boots showed off her tiny feet. Jake, sitting astride Tana, let out a long, slow breath at the sight of her. Seeing Emily on the porch, ready to join him, was almost more than he could bear.

He rode alongside the porch so that she could scoot onto the other horse without a huge effort. Considering Emily's tiny frame, he figured it would be better for her to learn how to mount and dismount later, even on the smaller horse.

He gazed up at her. "I see you're ready."

"I guess I *look* the part of a horsewoman anyway."

He grinned at what was, for her, a lengthy comment. "Well, hop aboard. Don't worry. Gracie is as mellow as they come. You could do a handstand on her right now, and she wouldn't move until I pulled her." He resisted the urge to dismount and help her, wanting to give her as much space as possible.

Sucking in her breath, Emily did as Jake directed. She paused for a moment, getting used to the feel of the saddle, and her face burned under Jake's quiet, approving gaze.

"Ready, Emily? Let's just go a few paces." They rode forward, rocking in identical rhythm to their horses'. "Feel it?" Jake asked. "That pace is what will make a good horsewoman out of you. It's the key...that and your relationship with the horse, of course." They walked around the courtyard in front of the house some more. "Ready to head out?" he asked quietly.

Emily squeezed her eyes shut and longed for the peaceful presence she had found in the chapel. With her heart pounding, she fought to trust the man who so obviously wanted to know her better. Rachel trusted him. Dirk trusted him. Mary trusted him. *Trust one more time, Emily. Take one more chance*, she told herself. "Yes, Jake. Let's go see this mountain field of yours."

Jake and Emily rode slowly south toward the Double M and crossed the old wooden bridge over the swirling Kootenai river, swollen from the melting snows. Emily felt dizzy from all that she was seeing and experiencing: the towering mountains, the rush of cool air as they crossed the river, the companionship of the man in front of her. It felt wildly intimate, this ride, and she struggled to ignore the sensation.

As they reached the other side, Jake drew the horses to a stop. "Okay, Emily," he said. "I'm giving you control of Gracie." He tied the two reins in an even knot and showed her how to steer and stop the mare. "Hold the reins lightly. Gracie responds well, so you don't have to exaggerate any movements. Just gently let her know what you want to do, and make her think you've been riding horses for years." She took the reins hesitantly.

Jake squeezed his legs into Tana's flank, urging her forward. Emily let out a quiet gasp when Gracie followed. They edged around the Double M land, catching sight of the ranch hands working on irrigation ditches just as the men at Timberline had been doing.

Jake chuckled as Matt yelled at the sight of them, waving his hat above his head. Enjoying the chance to give Jake a hard time, the other men stopped to yell and whistle as well.

Emily knew she had turned a deep red. She imagined they all could see her bright face from a quarter-mile away and was glad Double M ranch hands had been the ones to see them rather than those from Timberline. As tenderly as they all treated her, she knew Jake's coworkers could be merciless teasers.

The men turned back to their digging, and soon they were out of sight. After fifteen more minutes of riding, Jake pointed to a path ahead. "That's where we'll go, Emily," he said softly. She pulled Gracie's reins to the right, and her head swung over, her body following. The horse grunted as they crested a short, steep hill and then lowered her head as the incline increased.

"Nice job, Emily. I think you have a special touch with horses."

"I didn't think I had a special touch with anything before I came here."

They rode in silence for a few moments.

Jake cleared his throat. "Emily," he said quietly, "do you mind if I ask you a personal question?"

She paused before answering him. "Depends on how personal it is."

"You can just take the fifth if you find it too uncomfortable to answer."

"I suppose."

Jake's voice was gentle. "How did you end up on the highway three months ago?"

Emily said nothing as she considered how to respond.

"I'm sorry. I've asked too much, haven't I?"

"No." She tensed and stared ahead as she prepared to answer him. *Trust one more time, Emily*, she repeated to herself. "My dad left us when I was real little. He knelt down in front of me, promised he'd be home soon, and then never came back again. My mother and I were in an accident shortly after he left. I was seven years old when she died. I only have a few memories of my real family.

"I moved in and out of the county home and foster homes until I was eighteen. Then I set out to find my father. I wanted him to know how much he'd hurt us. But I couldn't find him, and by the time I stopped looking, I was out of money and on the streets. In January, I was hitching my way to the West Coast from the East, trying to make a new start."

Jake stopped and waited for her to pull up alongside. He reached out to touch her hand. She was tense and shaking from the memories but would not allow him to comfort her. Gently she pulled her hand away, not wanting him to feel rejected but also uncomfortable with the gesture.

"I'm sorry, Emily. I shouldn't have…"

"It's okay."

They sat together in silence.

"Not a very happy story, is it?"

"No, it's not," he agreed. "Didn't the county try to help you? Find a home for you?"

"They found homes. I was in three different ones by the time I was twelve years old. After that, I refused to be placed again until I was fourteen. Living in the county home was easier than getting attached to people I knew I would have to leave. Then Arthur came in and spent a month winning me over. He and his wife took me in, but they both died before I graduated from high school." She let out a humorless laugh. "There I was, alone again. I hit the road then, searching for my dad and my place in this world…certain I'd find both."

"How old are you now?"

"Twenty-five."

Emily urged Gracie forward again, and they rode out of the woods and into a sunlit meadow that was filled with flowers like the ones Jake had collected for her. The field was awash with deep red Indian paintbrush, golden glacier lilies, rosy bitterroot, and dainty purple harebells. Higher in the field was a stand of birch trees, and among them, billowing, white bear grass. To their right rushed a deep stream.

Jake got off his sweating horse and raised his arms to help Emily down from hers. As she jumped to the ground, they noticed for the first time a large male elk, lounging in the deep spring grasses and flowers, his antlers spread in an impressive rack. He rose, shook slightly, and stood watching them, regal and undaunted by their intrusion. After staring at them, he turned and disappeared again into the protection of the forest.

Jake gazed at Emily and smiled until she raised her chin to look back at him. For a long moment they stood staring at each other, truly recognizing the heart connection between them for the first time, until Emily looked down at the ground, embarrassed. Gently Jake reached for her hand, and she allowed him to take it.

He tried to contain his excitement and speak in a level tone. "Emily Walker…have you found your place in this world?"

"I think I have."

"Here?"

"Here."

Later they picnicked on fruit and cheese and juice that Mary had packed for them and then lay back among the tall green grasses, enjoying just being together. Propping herself up on one elbow, Emily looked over at Jake. He was handsome in the fading sunlight as he lay peacefully, eyes closed, unmoving. His brown hair glistened, and his eyes twinkled as he opened them to see her.

"Thank you for listening to me, Jake."

"My pleasure. I'm glad you finally let me in a little."

"My past doesn't bother you?"

He sat up and waited for her to do so too. "Your past is past. I'd like to go back and pound those people who knocked you around, Emily. But I want you to heal. I want you to be able to move forward, not be stuck. I'm not saying that I don't want you to deal with the past. I do. It sounds like you have a lot of dealing to do. But I'm looking forward to the future."

She looked into the field of flowers beside them and then to the ground. "The streets have been rough, Jake. I wasn't just knocked around. I was abused in other ways, too. I'm not the kind of person you should waste your time on."

Jake looked down as well, absorbing the ugly news. He seethed with anger at the people who could have hurt the tiny woman in front of him. Closing his eyes, he prayed quickly for help and direction. Then he opened his eyes and looked at her tenderly.

Taking her hand again, he fought the desire to pull her into his arms and kiss away the hurt. Her eyes looked wide and defiant, her shoulders stiff, as if bracing for the possibility that he would walk away from her now that he knew the whole truth. *This is a woman who's been hurt and abandoned too many times*, he thought.

Knowing that she needed words rather than physical action, Jake looked her fully in the eyes and said, "As far as I'm concerned, Emily Walker, when you entered the Elk Horn Valley, you entered as a new person. You've come into my life and completely shaken it up. I want to show you a real love; I want to be someone you can trust. Don't worry about your past on my account. I like who you are and who you are becoming. I'm just glad you've come." He paused. "You have come to me, haven't you, Emily?"

She looked up at him, tears overflowing her lower lids at last. "Yes, Jake. At least a part of me."

"I'll take that part and fight for the rest." He blinked back his own tears.

Without a word Jake rose and grabbed the reins of the horses, who were reluctant to leave the field of delectable greens. He showed Emily how to mount. "I'll give you a leg up since you're new to riding. But you'll be on your own when Dirk and Rachel get you your own horse."

"The Tanners aren't getting me a horse."

"They will when I talk them into it."

"Oh, don't. They've been the most generous people I've ever met, and I never want to take advantage of them."

"I feel the same way about them. They've done a lot for me, too, remember."

"You haven't told me much about *your* past," Emily said.

"I bet Mary and Rachel have."

"Enough to know that anyplace but here, we're in two different leagues."

"You're right. I'm lucky you even looked my way."

They left the cool, forested path and noticed Beth's truck parked near the fields where the ranch hands had been working earlier. The men were no longer in sight, having moved on to another field farther east. As Jake and Emily moved closer, they could see that the truck's motor was running. Jake urged Tana around to the driver's side of the vehicle. At first the truck appeared empty. Then they spotted Beth sprawled across the seat, drenched in sweat and curled up in pain.

"Beth!" Jake jumped off the horse in alarm. Emily, worried by Jake's tone of voice, slid off Gracie without a thought about how high up she was. She immediately moved to the truck.

"Beth, what's wrong?" Jake asked, leaning inside the cab.

The pregnant woman moaned in agony. "My water broke," she said as she panted for air. "Baby's coming fast…I thought Matt was out here. Radio's not working...no one at home." She moaned again as another contraction racked her body.

"Hold on, Beth. I'll get help." Wildly Jake turned around, remembering Emily. "Em? Take care of her." She nodded in quick agreement. "I'll be back with help." He placed his foot in the stirrup and swung onto the mare, at the same time urging the horse into a full gallop. Energized by the opportunity to run at full speed, Tana surged into action.

Beth's scream of pain diverted Emily's attention.

Within a minute it was obvious to both Emily and Beth that the baby would not wait for help. "Oh, dear God, it's coming! I can't wait, Emily. This baby wants to be born now! Please help me." She grabbed Emily's hand.

"I'm here." Emily tried to sound as confident as possible. She ignored Beth's fingernails biting into her hand with each contraction. "How many months along are you?"

Beth laid her head back down on the passenger seat, groaning and not hearing her question. "Pray with me, Emily. God can help us."

As another contraction rolled through her body, Beth cried out and started pushing in earnest.

Emily began to pray.

Beth lay back again, moaning. "Oh no," she said, tears running down her cheeks. "I want this baby, God. Don't let him die too. Please, God. Oh, please, Jesus." She braced herself for the next contraction. Gritting her teeth and holding tight to Emily's hand, she pushed again.

When the contraction was over, Emily asked once more, "How many months along are you, Beth?"

"Eight. Oh, Emily, pray with me! I didn't come this far to lose this child! God can help us."

"How long since you started contractions?"

"Twenty-five...thirty...minutes. Pray, Em, pray. I want this baby!"

"Please God, help us. Protect...protect Beth and her baby," Emily whispered awkwardly but urgently as she watched Beth push again and again. A cold, late spring wind came off the mountain and gently drifted through the driver-side door.

The next contraction came even harder than the last, and Emily could tell that the baby would arrive in short order. *Please, God, no more sadness. Don't let me let this baby die. They would never forgive me.* "Are you okay, Beth?" she asked urgently.

"You mean," she panted, "aside from giving birth in a truck?"

"Yes," Emily said, ignoring her attempt at a joke.

"Think so. Never gave birth before."

"Well, by the looks of things, you're about to have one, and we're on our own," Emily said softly.

Beth gritted her teeth and bore down on her next contraction. When it was over, she leaned back on the seat, moaning. "We're not alone, Em. We're not alone."

Jake rode at full speed into the gathering of men that had paused to watch his urgent arrival. He pulled Tana to a quick stop, mud splattering around her hooves. Matt wiped sweat from his brow. "What—"

"Matt! It's Beth. She's having the baby! Two miles west, where you were working! Come on! Jeff, radio Timberline. They can call for the Life Flight chopper. The Double M house radio isn't working.

Remember, two miles south of the Double M's northwestern corner. Got it?"

Matt was already in his truck and bouncing off toward his wife over the uneven field road.

"Got it." Jeff grabbed for the radio as Jake reined his tiring horse around for the ride back.

"Come be with us, Jesus," Beth prayed urgently. "You can do all things, let us—" A contraction interrupted her prayer, and she clenched her teeth. Sweat drenched her bangs and ran down her cheeks and scalp.

"You can do all things," Emily repeated after her. She took off her sweater and chambray shirt in preparation for the baby, leaving only her turtleneck. "Be with us. Keep Beth and her baby s-s-safe!" Her sentence rose in pitch as she spotted the baby's head. "He's coming, Beth! I see his head!"

"Oh, thank you, God," Beth moaned and continued pushing. The baby emerged, screwing up its tiny face at the feel of mountain breezes on wet skin.

"He's moving, Beth! He's moving," Emily yelled excitedly. "Come on! You'll hold him soon!"

With one more huge push from Beth, the baby's shoulders emerged, and the body quickly followed. Wrapping the baby in her chambray shirt, Emily smiled down at the child, laughing as the baby took in the first clear breath and squalled in anger at the frigid air.

"Is he okay?" Beth asked in anguish.

"*She* is perfect," Emily said as she handed Beth her baby. Both cried as they looked first at the baby and then each other.

"Thank you, God!" Beth exclaimed through her tears, and Emily silently echoed her thanks. Looking over the dashboard, Emily saw an oncoming car and presumed the speeding madman at the wheel must be Matt.

"Your husband's on his way, Beth. You and the baby will be okay."

"I know. Thank you, Emily. Thank you for being with me. I couldn't have done it without you."

Emily hesitated and then ventured, "It felt like we weren't the only ones here, you know?"

Beth raised her head and looked at Emily. "I know."

Matt brought the truck to a screeching halt, the back sliding a bit in the mud. As he rushed toward them, his face a mask of concern, Emily smiled at him broadly. "Bet you want to meet your new daughter."

He let out a joyful yell and ran around to the passenger-side door.

Opening the door carefully, he found his wife cradling their swaddled daughter. He covered both their faces with kisses. "Beth, sweetheart...you okay?"

"I'm fine. Wish you could've been with me, but Emily was wonderful as a stand-in."

Emily turned away to give them a moment alone with their daughter and cut the cord.

"Is the baby okay?" Matt asked worriedly.

"She looks fine to me. I think Doc Harmon must have miscalculated my due date. She's so big she can't be four weeks premature."

"She has my genes, remember," Matthew said, humorously puffing out his chest to make it appear bigger.

"What should we name her, Matt?" Beth asked, smiling up at her husband.

"Well, she's been surrounded with an awful lot of prayer and hope." Then to his infant daughter, "We weren't sure you were possible, little one." He cradled the baby's head in his big, rough palm and stroked her forehead with his thumb. She appeared to be on the verge of crying.

With Matt's help, Beth sat up and looked out to the valley in front of them. She watched as Emily greeted Jake and talked animatedly of her efforts as a midwife. Then she gazed back at her daughter, watching her scrunch up her face in preparation for another full wail. In the sky, the blades of a Life Flight helicopter chopped the air.

"Hope. We'll call her Hope."

Matt smiled at his wife and daughter and then greeted Jake and Emily as they approached the vehicle. "Jake and Emily, I'd like to introduce you to my daughter, Hope." He looked first at Emily, and then to his wife, who nodded in understanding. "Hope *Emily* Morgan." All four of the adults grinned.

Awestruck and overwhelmed by the honor, Emily took the baby's tiny hand and yelled over the roar of the landing helicopter, "It's nice to meet you, Hope!"

CHAPTER SEVEN

FRIDAY, MAY 12

*E*mily, will you come out for a ride with me after supper?" Jake asked, trying to be patient. He stood by the kitchen door as she rolled out biscuit dough, cut out perfect rounds with a glass, and set them on a cookie sheet.

"I don't think so. Thanks for asking though."

"Why not? You've been avoiding me for weeks! I thought we were just starting a relationship, not ending one."

"I need some space, Jake. A lot went on that day."

"You want space? I'll give you space." He turned and started to storm out in frustration but stopped, not wanting her to feel that she was being abandoned as she had been so many times before. "Keep in mind, I'm not leaving you, Em; you're sending me away."

Que caught him as he stomped out of the kitchen. "Hello there, Jake. Any word on the Morgan child?"

"How should I know?" Jake said irritably. "I'd ask Emily what she's heard, but she isn't having anything to do with me."

"Ah. Woman trouble. I know what that feels like, unfortunately. Byron once said, 'Alas! The love of women! It is known to be a lovely and a fearful thing!'"

Jake looked at the middle-aged man. He was tall and good-looking, with thick, graying hair and warm eyes that melted into perpetual smile lines. "When have you had woman trouble, Que?"

The two men walked at an easy pace, side by side. "There was a young lady named Joanna whom I deeply loved when I was a lad. We studied at school together, and then she set off to travel." He lifted a booted foot to the porch step and set his chin on his hand, lost in reverie.

"She apparently found foreign men to be much more charming than she found me—as hard as that is to believe—and we parted ways. She continued to travel, while I came to America and took up ranch work. I've cared for other women since Joanna…but none has been quite the same. Yet, in each relationship, I learn something new." He looked over to Jake, who was stepping down to the ground.

"When you are fifty-five years old, Jake, I expect you'll know a lot about women too."

Jake came to a stop. "I don't think I'll ever figure this woman out."

"You know better than I how much Emily has been hurt. Let her sort it all out so she *can* care. She'll get to it." He patted Jake on the shoulder. "Don't try to understand *all* of Emily all at once. Let her come to you willingly and share each part of her life as she is ready to do so."

Que walked back toward the porch steps, leaving Jake to look out on the valley and ponder his words and entered the kitchen with a singular goal: to sweet-talk Mary, with verse and prose, out of one of her freshly baked apple fritters.

As soon as Que entered the kitchen, Emily untied her apron and took the opportunity to flee the room. Her brief conversation with Jake was upsetting to her. *I'm just so scared,* she acknowledged inwardly. *I've put myself out too far. I've trusted too much. I'm just going to get hurt again.*

She grabbed a jacket from a nail by the mud room's side door and looked back toward the kitchen to tell Mary where she was going. She saw Mary shooing Que out the door, his hands full of fritters. The woman was obviously flustered and happy, but she was maintaining control of her own kitchen. "Ah, Mary, you're baking your way into my heart," Que teased.

Emily could hear Rachel in her office, typing furiously at her computer. With a shrug of her shoulders, Emily decided to duck out without letting anyone know where she was going for once.

Climbing the path behind the house, she headed toward the chapel. Gray skies obscured the tops of the mountains and threatened the valley with rain.

Emily pulled up the collar on her jacket and walked faster. The forest was quiet, as if anticipating the rain. Emily stumbled in her haste, taking the brunt of her fall with one knee. Groaning, she brushed off the damp earth that clung to her jeans and hurried on.

Emily didn't pause at the chapel door; she simply walked in. Dirk was at the altar, on his knees, praying. She stood awkwardly in the doorway, embarrassed. After a tense moment, Dirk turned and smiled at her. She shifted her weight uneasily from one leg to the other.

"Well, hello. I didn't know you were coming here regularly," he said.

"Uh...I wouldn't call it regular. This is my second time."

Dirk rose, continuing to smile. "I'm glad. I want this to be a place where people can come and go freely. Make yourself comfortable," he said, indicating a chair as he returned to his knees. "I'll be through in a few minutes."

Emily sat down, watching Dirk's back as he returned to deep prayer. *How can I get out of here without hurting his feelings?*

She looked outside and studied the gray sky until Dirk's voice, low and soothing, interrupted her thoughts. He sat on the kneeling bench, studying her. She blushed and looked down at her hands.

"You make me think of Ruth," he said.

"Who?"

"Ruth. A tremendous woman. She's in the Bible; you can look her up sometime. She was young and incredibly loyal and humble, like you. She had pain in her life, but God used her to accomplish great things."

"Oh," Emily muttered, flushing at Dirk's indirect compliment.

His face became serious. "You, too, know about pain, don't you, Emily?"

"I…I suppose so."

"Me too. You know my parents were killed in an auto accident."

"Yes," she said, raising her eyes to meet his.

"The pain was suffocating. I hurt so bad I thought there was no way I could continue to live. They had so much to teach me, so much more to share with me, so much more *life*…you know? But there I was, alone. I had to do something with my pain. So I built this chapel. I worked like a madman until it was finished, never letting anyone else lend a hand.

"And yet, when it was done, I still felt empty inside, and my body felt like I'd been run over by a truck. I'd supposedly built this chapel to honor God. But when I finally sat down inside it, I was mad at him…furious, in fact. I was so angry I was unable to express anything. I wanted to be left alone. I never wanted to care about anyone again."

He moved to sit beside her in the second chair. "I'm sure you've had a harder time than I have, Emily. But I do know the emptiness your heart feels, the fear that makes you edge away from anyone who tries to get near you. You don't want to hurt again.

"I know you have to come to God on your own terms, in your own time. But as your brother in this thirst for God"—Dirk paused and pointed with his other hand at the cross behind him—"I want to tell you that he can help you heal. He can touch your wounds where no one else can reach you." She could feel his kind eyes studying her.

"I think you want to let him in, Emily. But you have to tell him how angry and hurt you are first. It's okay to talk with him about it. He already knows."

Emily sat still, gripping the arm of the chair as she listened to his words. Tears flowed down her face unchecked. She sensed Dirk's protective, brotherly love and felt closer to him than ever before. Beside her was an orphan who had somehow been able to come to peace with his loss and his God. She wanted that too.

"Do you want me to stay with you while you pray?"

"Okay," she said, her voice shaking. They moved to the kneeling bench, and Dirk placed his arm around her shoulders. Haltingly, one by one, Emily recounted the horrors that life had dealt her and begged God for understanding and peace. Sensing the Lord's presence in the little chapel, Dirk remained silent, letting God work his healing within Emily.

CHAPTER EIGHT

A month later, sitting beside Jake on the porch swing, Emily talked excitedly about the book of Ruth and how she could identify with the Moabite. Jake was entranced by the new light that danced in Emily's eyes. Although she still kept him at arm's length, she had opened up enough to sit with him in the evenings and talk under the cool skies of early summer.

Time had flown for Emily. But to Jake, their relationship moved forward at an agonizing crawl. Six months after they had first met, and more than a month after their ride to the meadows, Jake still hadn't found the right opportunity and moment to kiss her. He prayed for patience, as Dirk had been coaching him. Jake respected his friend's advice but couldn't fathom waiting much longer.

Jake's desire for Emily was strong; he wanted to hold her close, to make her feel utterly safe and protected. But he was confused by the woman who was emerging before him. She grew stronger and more independent every day. She had taken to an early morning ritual of rising and walking to the chapel before breakfast. Her relationship with God was growing, and Jake found himself feeling left behind. Jake hated his impatience. Hated feeling in competition with the Lord instead of rejoicing in her newfound relationship with the heavenly Father. And as he gazed from Emily's deep blue eyes to her adorable little nose and full lips, he knew he would spend another sleepless night thinking about her.

Jake stood abruptly and jumped off the porch. His action surprised Emily. They had been meeting every night for two weeks, and she had always been the one to cut off their time together. "I have to go," Jake mumbled, giving her a half smile.

"Okay," she said. "Are you all right?"

"Yes. Just getting used to the new Emily Walker." Jake kicked the dirt with the toe of his boot, then looked back up at her. "Don't get me wrong, Em. I like what I see. Too much. Your new confidence and independence just makes me want you more. But that desire's a dangerous thing. And I want you to come to me when you're ready to dance."

"Dance?"

"Ah, nothing unscrupulous. It's just that all I want to do is kiss you. But I want you to finish finding out just who Emily Walker is before you begin to discover us. We'll be better at the dance for it." He sighed heavily and looked toward the barn. "There are going to be times when I have to walk off the tension. Waiting doesn't come easily for me. Okay?"

"Okay. Thanks for giving me space, Jake."

Her sweet response made Jake want to jump back on the porch, forget everything he had just said, take her in his arms, and kiss her until dawn. He took a deep breath. "Good night, Emily. I'll see you in the morning."

"Good night."

Emily watched as he walked away toward the lodge, wondering at the man who had taken to her so strongly and who exercised such self-control out of devotion.

THURSDAY, JUNE 29

Rachel and Dirk returned just as Jake bid Emily good night. Dirk caught Jake as he left the main house, and the men walked away, deep in conversation about a ranch project. Rachel joined Emily on the porch swing, and Emily smiled at the friend she so deeply admired.

Mary ducked her head out the kitchen door. "Can I get you two some tea?"

"No, that's all right."

"Oh, Emily, stay a minute! Talk to me. We haven't had any time together for weeks."

"Well, okay."

"Hot lemon tea would be fabulous, Mary," Rachel said. "And why don't you join us?"

Mary grinned. "I'll have it ready in a jiffy. But I'll leave you two to chat. I think I'll go read." The door slammed shut behind her.

"Is everything okay? Have I done anything wrong?"

"Of course not, woman! You are practically an angel. I thank God every night for bringing you here."

Emily kicked her feet evenly to the rhythm of the swing, absorbing Rachel's words. It was still difficult for Emily to believe that anyone wanted her around or that she was able to accomplish things that were actually appreciated.

"Emily, are you happy?"

"Happier than I've ever been." Emily smiled, and her gaze drifted to Jake, walking in the distance with Dirk.

"Do you enjoy your work?"

"Oh yes!"

"Would you like to be doing anything else?"

"I'm pretty happy."

"Well, as I said, you are doing a great job. But I want to make sure you're doing things that please you. Mary can cook for hours on end, but that drives me bonkers. What I'm getting at is this: I want you to be content, Em." She grabbed Emily's hand and smiled down into her eyes. "We're getting quite attached to you here, and we want you to stay."

Emily smiled back at her shyly, not knowing what to say.

Rachel was silent for a moment, then asked, "How much education do you have?"

"I got my high-school diploma."

"Well, I know you like to read. I notice a different book missing from my shelves every two weeks."

"Oh, I put them back! You have such wonderful books that I thought I might—"

"I know. It's perfectly fine. They're there for people to enjoy. And I think reading is one of the best ways to get an education." She paused, thinking to herself. "You know, Montana State offers some extension classes by mail and video. Would you be interested in trying one out?"

Emily raised her eyebrows at the suggestion. She had never considered college. "Oh, I don't know... Do you think I'm smart enough to get through it?"

"Absolutely! And what's the risk? The only people who will know are you, me, and anyone else you decide to tell. I wish I could've taken my college chemistry class by mail. Then ol' Dr. Peabody wouldn't have had the chance to glare at me every time I failed an experiment."

"*You* failed a course?"

Rachel laughed at Emily's shocked expression. "Oh yes! And that wasn't the only one. I was about as good at biology as I am at cooking," she whispered conspiratorially.

Emily tried to absorb the fact that her friend was capable of failure. *This is the woman who was a topnotch ad exec and now leads a successful career from a remote ranch, the woman who risked everything to marry Dirk.*

"Emily Walker, you're going to give me a complex," Rachel complained, seeing the look on her face.

"I'm sorry. I guess I thought you were perfect."

"Nearly so," Mary said, as she walked out onto the porch with the tea and a plate of gingersnaps.

"Nearly?" Rachel mimicked as if shocked by the estimation. "I'm not?"

Mary pursed her lips as she bustled back toward the sanctity of her kitchen. "If you were perfect, my Dirk would not have had to follow you all the way to San Francisco to woo you back here."

Rachel smiled as the door banged shut. She looked at Emily beside her, who appeared worried at their exchange. "She was just kidding! Emily, you've got to learn that you can give people you love a bad time. If Mary thinks I failed by not swallowing the first hook Dirk threw me, who cares? I know she loves me to death. That's all that's really important. You have to keep it all in perspective."

Emily smiled over her china teacup. "I'm learning a lot these days."

"Isn't that a good thing?"

"Yes, it is."

"Well, let's see. What sort of classes would interest you? What did you like in high school?"

"I liked most of it. I was best at history and English."

"Me too! I'll get a catalog from Montana State, and maybe you can try out one of those courses this fall. If you like it, we can talk about what comes next." Seeing Emily's alarmed face, she said hurriedly, "But we'll take it one step at a time. *Your* time," she finished reassuringly.

"But what if I can't do it, Rachel?"

"Nonsense! You can do anything, Emily Walker. You're extremely bright…and a hard worker. That's the key."

Emily studied her hands shyly, then looked directly at Rachel, feeling strong and encouraged by her friend's confidence in her. "Say, Rachel, what's this Sweet Pea Festival Mary keeps mentioning?"

"Ah…the Sweet Pea. It's a beautiful county festival that supposedly celebrates those flowers that are starting to bloom all over the western trellis. But mostly it's a chance for the people from all around Elk Horn to gather and throw a party. The dance is the biggest shindig of the year…" Rachel looked off to the mountains, suddenly lost in thought.

Emily studied her. "Rachel," she ventured, "what're you thinking about?"

"Oh," she said, embarrassed. "You've probably heard about last year's dance from Mary."

"Some. Is that when that crazy guy made his first move on you?"

"Not his first, and definitely not his last. Even worse than what Alex did to me was what he did to the Morgans on the highway. I was so scared Beth would never have another baby. She was born to be a mom. I would never have said that five years ago, but when I see her cradling Hope in her arms and the tender look in her eyes, she makes me want to have a baby too—for half an hour a day," she laughed.

"Rachel," Emily whispered softly, "how did you get over what Alex did to you?"

Rachel pondered her question. "Loss of control is a big thing to me. I never gave up the fight, you understand. I had to relinquish control a few times in order to survive. When somebody forces you into that—into submission—it's hard to get over it. He never raped me, but I still felt violated."

Emily nodded, looking out to the horizon and the sun that was setting later and later in the northern valley.

"You weren't so lucky, were you, Em?"

Emily paused. "No, I wasn't so lucky. The streets…are not a safe place."

Rachel put her arm around Emily and pulled her close. "I'm sorry, Emily. I'm so sorry. You should have been protected and warm and safe always."

For the first time, Emily leaned on a friend's shoulder and let a tear slowly slide down her cheek. "Well, it's not a safe world, is it?"

"Not safe. But always, always worthy of hope."

CHAPTER NINE

*A*fter a wearisome day of scrubbing wood floors—making preparations for their guests, Jake's parents, due to arrive in a couple of weeks—Rachel sat down to page through mail-order catalogs. When she turned the page, she called Emily in from the porch swing. "Emily! You have to see this! It's so you!"

Emily came in the door, carefully catching it before it banged shut behind her. Frustrated by the interruption, but curious, Jake followed. "Uh-uh, Jake Rierdon. This is for Emily's eyes only. It could be the Sweet Pea dress of the century. Now get out! I'll only borrow her for a minute."

Jake backed out the door, pretending to be genuinely frightened. "Okay, Rachel. I'm goin', I'm goin'." He returned to the swing that was not yet still.

Dirk rose from the couch. "You take my seat, Emily. I'm going to make some decaf. You'll make a better shopping partner than I'll ever be anyway."

Rachel patted the cushion next to her. "Sit, sit, sit! Isn't it adorable?"

Emily smoothed the page and studied the photo. "Oh, Rachel. It's gorgeous! But I can't. Look how much it is! It would take me"— she counted in her mind—"three days' salary to pay for it."

"It'll be your spring bonus! You have to have it! Look at that blue-green—perfect for your eyes. And the cut…you'll be the Sweet Pea princess for sure."

Emily looked horrified. "They don't do that sort of thing, do they?"

"Of course not. I'm kidding! But didn't you ever want to be the princess, the queen, just once in your life? Dresses are a funny phenomenon. Slip the right one on, and you feel ten pounds lighter, a hundred times more attractive…" She looked at the young woman beside her. Beautiful blond hair and dark eyebrows perfectly framed Emily's blue eyes.

"Em, have you ever had a new dress in your life?"

"When I was little. And when Anna was alive… But not for some time."

"That settles it."

Thursday, July 13

"So you're getting the dress," Jake said a week later, as he lifted bales of hay from the truck and threw them into the stable doorway. Emily observed him from her seat on the side of the truck's bed. The thought that Jake cared so much and took such an interest amused her.

"What's it to you?" she challenged with a grin.

Her sass obviously surprised and delighted him. It seemed that at every turn Emily was growing and becoming more confident. He straightened and then sat down on another bale. "Maybe I'm just curious about how the gal I'm escorting to the Sweet Pea is going to look."

"I'd say she'll look okay." They exchanged smiles, and Jake resumed working.

After a while he paused again to catch his breath.

"Jake?"

"Yeah?"

"Do you know how to dance?"

"When I was a boy, my mother made me attend every cotillion lesson for three years."

"Oh."

"I take it you don't." He wiped the sweat from his brow.

"Didn't say that."

"Didn't say you did."

Emily was quiet for several long minutes. Jake tried to cheer her. "What do you say we go for a ride tonight?"

"You're on!" She hopped off the truck and walked away with a spring in her step.

Jake watched her every step of the way.

Jake rode up to the house promptly at seven o'clock with Rachel's mare in tow. As he helped Emily on, Rachel and Dirk drove away in the Jeep, en route to the Morgans' for an evening of cards.

Emily waved and felt happier than she ever had before. *This is a life worth living. This is happiness. This is peace.*

As she and Jake rode, the steady rhythm of the horses lulled her into relaxing. Jake deferred to her. "Lead on. You're the trailblazer tonight, Kemo Sabe."

Surprised, she nonetheless took the lead, looking both directions as they exited the courtyard. During her many riding lessons, she had not returned to the meadow where she and Jake had first gone together. She headed that direction now.

From behind her, Jake smiled, recognizing her decision and silently celebrating her choice.

The evening was still warm but had a touch of dampness to it. Looking ahead, Jake noticed that clouds were beginning to engulf the mountainside. He frowned. "Emily," Jake began, motioning toward the mountains with a nod of his head. "Do you think we should go on up? That storm is coming in faster that I thought."

She followed his line of vision. "Oh, it will hold, Jake. And if it doesn't? We get a little wet. Besides, look over east. It's clear as day."

"Yeah, but we get our weather from the west."

She said nothing but continued to direct Rachel's mare forward. Jake followed her without another word, admiring her gumption.

"This poor thing doesn't get much riding," she remarked as she patted the horse's neck.

"Rachel seems to favor Cyrano, even though I think Dirk would be happier to see her on Tana there. I've heard she's thinking of giving Tana or Gracie to you."

Emily liked the strong, stalwart mare and had come to believe that she would flourish if someone would give her more attention. The thought of being given the horse thrilled and horrified her at the same time. "I couldn't take a gift like that!"

"Now, we've been over this before. Everybody on the ranch has a horse, except Mary…and that's because she doesn't like to ride." He leaned down and affectionately patted his own new palomino, delivered the week before. "It's only right for you to have one too. Take it as a perk of the job."

"But they've given me so much already."

"You earn your keep."

The acknowledgment that she did, indeed, earn her keep made Emily smile. "Come on, slowpoke," she taunted the man behind her. "Try and keep up!"

By the time they arrived at the meadow, gray clouds had swallowed the mountainside. The meadow grasses were wet, and Emily thought twice about jumping down, afraid that she would spatter herself with mud. She rode Tana in a circle, looking for the best place to dismount, as they crested the meadow's central hill.

Jake solved her dilemma. "If you'll hold on for a minute, I'll spread this old barn blanket for us." He jumped down and untied an old plaid blanket from the palomino's back. He had packed several other items beneath it, including a small portable CD player. He grinned up at her. "I thought I'd take advantage of our privacy for a dance lesson—if you'll accept one from a humble cotillion veteran."

Emily ducked her head shyly. "It sounds great. I don't know how well your feet will do though."

He walked over to help her down. "I think my boots will keep my toes safe."

She took her right foot out of the stirrup and swung her leg over the horse to face him. As Jake reached for her waist, she slid off Tana's back. Jake brought her down slowly, watching her face the entire time but feeling her body close to his own.

Reluctantly he released her and turned to his horse again. "Dirk suggested I bring a radio, but I one-upped him on quality." Jake untied the CD player and placed it on the corner of the broad blanket.

Jake knelt by the CD player and pressed Play. "Unforgettable" sounded softly on the portable stereo.

Emily turned her eyes down.

"Bad choice?" Jake asked with concern, not wanting anything to ruin the moment.

She looked up at him with tears in her eyes and shook her head. "No, the best. I remember my mother playing Nat King Cole on the record player and pretending I was her dance partner. We used to swing around our tiny living room for hours."

Jake drew close to Emily and gently raised her chin with his hand. "I bet if your mom had lived longer, she would have taught you to be a terrific dancer."

"I bet my mother would have really liked you, Jake."

"What makes you think so?"

"Because I haven't met a better man in my life."

Jake pulled her into his arms and held her as Cole's honey-smooth voice lilted through the hush of the rainy evening.

"She gets more gorgeous every time I see her!" Rachel said, peering into Hope's crib.

The baby looked up at the four adults around her and waved her arms, struggling to focus her big blue eyes.

Rachel looked over at Beth, whose eyes shone as she, too, admired her little miracle.

"I think she looks like her mother," Dirk put in.

"Hold on there," Matt protested. "I think she has my good looks. Look at that nose! Does that look like it's going to turn into Beth's perky little nose? No, I'd say that one will definitely take on the more aristocratic Morgan slope."

"I think you've been doing too much creative visualization in the middle of the night, Matt," Rachel teased. "I bet you can see anything you want to when you're awakened at four in the morning."

Matt nodded gravely. "Could be, could be. But we'll see in a few years who was right, won't we?"

"Ten bucks says she's the spitting image of our Beth," Dirk baited him.

"You're on, my friend." Matt clapped Dirk on the shoulder as the two walked out of the nursery. "Easiest money I ever made."

"I can't stand it any longer," Rachel said, as she scooped up the irresistible infant. The tiny body felt warm and soft in her arms.

"You look pretty natural holding a baby," Beth said.

"I'm content coming over to hold yours."

"You're not getting any younger…"

"Dirk and I'll make that decision for ourselves when we're both good and ready, thank you very much."

"Just wondering, just wondering," Beth said, putting up her hands in surrender. "Don't want Hope to grow up without any play-mates next door, you know?"

"So you've said."

"Who's holding out? You or Dirk?"

"Me. I'm just getting settled into working from the ranch, telecommuting. It's hard for me to change that routine so soon."

"Having a baby gives me a bigger high than winning a big account or coming up with the perfect campaign ever did."

Rachel laughed and crossed her eyes at her friend. "You've made your point, Beth. And Hope is the best advertisement for mother-hood you could have ever cooked up."

Jake and Emily swayed to song after song.

"You have a great sense of rhythm, Emily Walker," he said, his voice low. She stepped on his toes for the second time, but he ignored it, too intoxicated by the woman in front of him to care. Nothing could distract him.

Jake taught her some basic steps but concentrated mostly on showing her how to follow his lead. He expertly turned Emily in a circle, admiring her natural grace and poise even in a situation where she was not practiced. Her eyes met his own, and he pulled her close, singing softly into her ear.

Cool mountain rain began to fall, but neither minded. Jake pulled her closer, feeling her body melt against his own.

As the rain dripped from their hair and their clothing, Jake and Emily danced on. The winds began to gust, and the horses raised their heads at the thunder and lightning that was closing in. Emily looked up at him and then closed her eyes, raising her face softly for a kiss.

With the greatest intensity and desire he had ever felt in his life, Jake complied.

It was the peal of thunder and a nearby flash of lightning that finally roused them from their private sanctuary. With a moan, Nat King Cole's voice groaned to a stop as the water finally entered one crevice too many and shut down the CD player. The horses moved nervously, with ears twitching and eyes widening by the minute. Emily reached for their reins, and Jake quickly gathered up their soaked belongings.

Emily smiled at Jake through chattering teeth as he gave her another quick kiss. "I'll tie Tana to my horse!" Jake almost yelled above the roaring wind. She nodded, pulling Tana close so he could tie her to his palomino's saddle. Jake lifted her up into her saddle, then mounted his own horse and quickly directed them out of the meadow.

Emily pushed her face under the collar of the coat Jake had loaned her, breathing in the comforting smells of leather and rain, the horse...and Jake. She giggled. Even in the midst of the storm, she felt safe, happy, and loved.

CHAPTER TEN

The following Sunday Emily rose and dressed in time for church. Rachel and Dirk forced themselves to remain silent when they saw her come into the kitchen for a quick breakfast. Rachel and Dirk had consistently invited Emily to church but never pushed her. They wanted her to come and worship of her own accord, just as God wanted. Emily had begun her faith journey in the chapel on the hill above them, and Rachel hoped that she might find a special affinity for the church and the fellowship it would offer her.

Mary, however, could not hold still. "It's about time you went to worship with the rest of us, Emily Walker! Pastor Lear will be delighted to see you!"

"I hope so," she said quietly.

"For goodness sake, why on earth wouldn't he be happy to have you?"

"I didn't exactly grow up in a churchgoing family."

"People come from all walks of life."

Rachel smiled at Emily and thought of her first visit to the little white church in town. For her, it had been a profound experience, one in which she first learned about God, faith, and fellowship.

Jake walked into the kitchen, and his face broke into a broad grin. "Why, Emily Walker, are you finally coming to church with me?"

She did not match his smile. "If you make a big deal about this,

I won't go. I don't want any pressure, and I don't want to feel bad if I decide I don't want to go again."

He backed off immediately, holding up his hands. "Okay, okay. We'll do it any way you feel comfortable. I'm just glad you're coming."

"I know." She dropped the matter and moved to the stove to pour herself a cup of Mary's dark brew. "Anyone else want some coffee?"

Jake nodded, somber faced, but a smile lit his eyes.

As they drove to the small sanctuary, Emily's heart pounded. Any excursion outside Timberline made her feel panicky. But she had been working on getting out more often, running to the market, post office, and stationery store to do errands for the Tanners and Mary. She didn't want her feeling of safety at the ranch to make her homebound.

Dirk brought the truck to a stop in the church parking lot, and everyone got out. Emily and Jake followed the Tanners up the steps. As they neared the door, Jake gently took Emily's hand and grinned down at her. He introduced her to Pastor Lear, who welcomed her warmly, and then Jake pulled her away with ease before she had a chance to feel uncomfortable. She squeezed his hand in silent thanks. Altogether, with the Tanners and the other ranch hands who attended that day, their group took up three of the long wooden pews.

Emily looked around, trying not to be obvious in her curiosity. The old sanctuary was straight out of an episode of *Little House on the Prairie,* and that sensation of familiarity from her childhood days gave her a feeling of calm. A lay minister, one of their neighbors, got up with his guitar and led the congregation in singing. Although

Emily had the words in front of her, she did not join in, choosing instead to sit back and take everything in.

As the service progressed, Emily appreciated what she saw and heard, but she was a bit disappointed. She had expected the spiritual high she had experienced in the chapel to happen here as well. Instead she felt the commonality of coming together for one purpose, which she enjoyed. And the pastor's sermon made her think deeply about the gospel they read aloud together. All in all, it wasn't what she had anticipated.

Afterward, Jake eagerly asked her, "Well, what did you think?"

"It was…nice."

"Nice?"

"Nice."

He paused, thinking. "I don't get it. For me, it was mind blowing to come to a congregation like this. I grew up in a church where it was more important to wear the right clothes than to be right with God. This little church and the Tanners have revolutionized my faith. And all you think is that it's 'nice'?"

"Jake, I have to find my own way in this."

He took a moment to mull over her words. "That's true. I was just hoping you'd be as excited over this place as I was when I first came here."

Catching Jake's last statement as they approached the truck, Dirk and Rachel elected to say nothing. They simply smiled and got into the truck, leaving the door open behind them. Emily looked up at Jake's saddened face and whispered, "I didn't say I wouldn't be back."

Emily and Jake joined the Tanners for their evening ride that night. The foursome laughed and talked as they skirted Timberline's eastern edge, enjoying the sight of the mountains silhouetted against the summer's brilliant sunset. They paused, silent, to simply gaze in awe. "People can't look at that and tell me that God doesn't exist," Dirk said quietly.

His comment stirred Emily's thoughts, and she considered for the first time the Elk Horn Valley as the result of the Creator's hand. The setting sun cast deep shadows in the valleys where each mountain met its neighbor, bringing out the deep green of the forests. The peaks above them appeared dark purple against a tapestry of gold and orange and pale green fields.

"He's an artist," she said finally.

"You should see what he does with dawn," Jake remarked.

They moved on after a while, talking about a number of subjects. Emily noticed that when faith was the topic, the others made it clear that they accepted her exactly where she stood and always would. She felt a growing sense of security that deepened her appreciation for them all.

As they rode through a forested section, Jake came alongside her, reached over, and pulled Tana to a stop. The Tanners rode on, perhaps consciously ignoring the couple behind them, Emily thought.

Jake looked over at Emily, sitting tall and serene in the saddle. "I just needed to look at you," he said. "Do you know how impossibly beautiful you are?"

Emily ducked her head and blushed. "No, Jake. Not me. I'm decent looking. But Rachel…she's beautiful."

"You've got it all wrong, Em." He leaned closer to her. "You're the most gorgeous woman I've ever laid eyes on. You look at me with those eyes of yours, and I think I'm sinking. You touch me with your hand, and it sends a thousand volts through me." He paused, inches away from her face, his eyes clearly serious, even in the growing dark. "What I'm trying to say, Emily, is that I'm deeply, madly, and completely in love with you."

He leaned over and kissed her softly. "You don't have to say anything. I just wanted you to know that."

She smiled at him tenderly, wanting to say something in return, but was mute, overcome, strangled by all that was in her heart.

The next day both Emily's dress and the university extension catalog arrived. Rachel had been right. The dress looked perfect on Emily.

She admired herself in the full-length mirror, conscious that it made her look great. The short, capped sleeves fed into a soft scoop neck and fitted bodice that showed off her tiny waist and gentle curves. The skirt flared and dropped to just above her ankles.

Rachel surprised Emily by giving her a pair of perfect sandals to finish the ensemble, then oohed and aahed from the bed as she watched Emily try it all on. The deep teal of the ensemble highlighted her dark skin, bronzed from hours of work in Mary's summer garden, and made her eyes appear an even deeper sea-blue.

"You'll be the belle of the ball," Rachel said.

"I don't think so," Emily protested.

"I do." Rachel looked at Emily thoughtfully as she continued to stare in the mirror. "Do you ever wear makeup, Em?"

"No."

"Would you let me try my hand at a touch of it the night of the Sweet Pea? Nothing heavy. I'll just bring out your natural beauty." She jumped off the bed.

"You'll have your work cut out for you."

Rachel paused at the door as she was leaving. "That, I will not.

As I'm sure Jake has told you by now, you are a very attractive woman. And if you know what's good for you both, don't let him see you in that dress unless you're in public," she teased.

Eleanor and Jacob Rierdon Sr. arrived at Elk Horn International Airport two days later, four days before the Sweet Pea Festival. Eleanor frowned as she deplaned, perturbed with the pilot, their turbulent ride into the valley due to high winds, and the wrinkles in her white linen suit. At fifty-five, Eleanor was svelte and carried herself like a fashion model. Tall and dashing with graying hair, Jacob Sr. was her perfect counterpart.

Spying Rachel, Eleanor smiled and kissed her on both cheeks, then turned to embrace Jake. "Well, you do hide yourselves away in this remote valley, I must say." Eleanor's voice held a distinct note of distaste.

"Keeps out the Californians," Jake remarked dryly.

Eleanor ignored his comment and turned to Rachel. "You certainly look the part, dear."

"Part?"

"Montana ranch wife. Very…what is the word? *Natural.*"

"I live in a different world now, Eleanor. I don't have access to shopping where I can get an outfit like yours." She gave the woman's white suit an admiring glance. "Nor do I want to take the time to iron it. I'll leave the clotheshorse world to you."

Rachel's statement did not appear to affect Eleanor. "Perhaps you could help me find an authentic western outfit to take home. The ladies at home would simply die; western's just the thing these days."

"Lucky for us," Rachel said, looking down at her jeans, boots, and shirt. She turned to the man standing beside Eleanor and shook his hand warmly. "Jacob, I never thought you'd get Eleanor out of the city."

"Well, you know my dear wife. Country is not her thing. But she figures it's her only chance to talk Jake into coming back home."

Rachel smiled at her former associate. "She has her work cut out for her if that's her agenda."

"That's what I told her," he said resignedly. "I'm just glad we can get together and see what Jake has been raving about all year. It certainly is beautiful so far." The day was hot, clear, and windy, and several dust devils rose in the nearly empty parking lot. Eleanor struggled to keep her jacket from flying in the breeze while she maneuvered through the dirt in high heels.

Jake threw his parents' bags into the back of the truck and grinned at Rachel when Eleanor realized the truck was their mode of transportation. "How thoroughly *western*," she muttered and daintily climbed into the large truck's tiny backseat.

Rachel let out a long breath as she got in beside her. The Rierdons' visit was already beginning to feel like a long one.

They arrived at the house just before supper. The wind had died down, making the temperature seem even hotter than it had been at midday. As they walked up the porch steps, Jake could hear Mary and Emily in the kitchen preparing the meal. His heart pounded, as it often did when he thought of the woman he loved. He carried the bags down the hall and then quietly slipped back.

Rachel gave Eleanor and Jacob a tour of the house. Eleanor was obviously pleasantly surprised. "Oh my dear, it's straight out of a Ralph Lauren catalog. Beautiful. Perfect for this setting."

They descended the sweeping front staircase and went within earshot of the kitchen, where Mary was scolding Jake for snitching food. Emily's musical laughter rang out as they drew near, and then it turned to playful shrieking. Anticipating a scene, Rachel tried to steer Jake's father and mother away, but Eleanor pushed her way past Rachel into the kitchen, where she stopped in her tracks.

Jake had picked up Emily and was using her to shield him from Mary, who was threatening him with a wooden spoon. Emily's hair was held back from her damp forehead with a handkerchief, and she was fairly drenched in sweat from working in the hot kitchen. The look on Eleanor's face silenced their laughter.

Emily patted Jake's chest without looking away from the woman's white face. "Put me down, Jake," she whispered.

He complied. Realizing he had created an awkward situation, he forced his voice to be cheerful. "Mother, Dad, I'd like you to meet Mary." He nodded toward the woman with rosy cheeks and a dirty apron. "And this…this is the most wonderful woman I've ever met. Emily Walker."

Emily shored herself up and extended a hand to Eleanor. "It's a pleasure, Mrs. Rierdon." She smiled sweetly, fighting to gain composure.

Eleanor did not take her hand.

"I'm sure," she said to Emily, smiling a bit too broadly. "I'm afraid my son neglected to tell me he had a new…friend. But then, he doesn't always keep us informed about his latest." She turned away with a look of disgust, and Emily's face fell.

"Mother," Jake said angrily, "I'd like to speak to you outside."

"Certainly, darling." Eleanor's eyes flashed as she followed her son out of the hot kitchen.

"Emily," Jacob greeted the young woman warmly. He shook her hand gently, with a genuine smile in his eyes. "Please pardon Eleanor's manners. It's tough for her to see Jake make decisions that lead him away from her. Leaving the firm, adopting ranch life, falling for a new girl. We had no idea. I know there's no excuse for her behavior. But please understand that the situation would be an adjustment for any mother." He paused awkwardly, as if he wanted to say something more, then with a rueful smile toward Emily, followed his family outside.

Rachel put her arm around Emily's shoulders, seeking to comfort her. "He's right, Em. She'll soften up over time. I'm sorry for what happened though. She had no right to treat you that way."

Tears welled up in Emily's eyes and then flowed down her cheeks. "I was just hoping that we'd get along…that maybe she would like me."

Rachel smiled back at her, her own eyes filling with tears of compassion. "Give her time, Em. If she has any sense at all, she'll come to adore you. And if she doesn't…believe me, the loss is hers."

At the side of the house, Jake seethed, struggling to keep his temper. "You had no right to be so rude to Emily."

"You could have done the decent thing and warned me that you were dating the hired help."

"I *am* the hired help. I don't hold a better social station than Emily. Besides, it's different here in Elk Horn Valley than in San Francisco. That kind of thing doesn't matter. And I like it that way."

"My dear, wherever you go, social station matters. And the truth is, you come from a wealthy city family whose name has graced the very best social circles for decades. You might not like that fact, but it will always be there, between the two of you. Eventually your little...*Emily* will end up hurt."

"How can you say that? You don't know anything about what I believe. And you certainly don't know Emily. She is wise and poised and gracious. And I'm learning a lot from her—things you don't learn at the university."

"I bet you are," she said sarcastically.

Furious, he turned his back to her. He saw his father approach, concern etched into his face. "Mother, I suggest you learn to accept Emily. I plan to have her in my life for a long time. Otherwise"—he turned back to face her, his eyes afire—"if you make me pick between you and Emily, I'll have to choose the woman I want to be my wife." He walked away.

Eleanor stood mute. When Jake disappeared around the corner of the house, she looked out at the mountains, hating all that she saw. "This place," she said to Jacob, "and that *woman* have stolen my son from me."

Supper was a quiet affair. The ranch hands were uncomfortable with the Rierdons at the table, and Jake was still angry. Everyone finished eating quickly and then escaped from the table.

Rachel sighed into her napkin as Dirk leaned to whisper in her ear, "Ten more days of this?"

While they prepared for bed that night, Dirk asked Rachel about Eleanor. "How did you ever become friends with that woman?"

"We were never what I would call friends. Her husband is such a sweetie. When I was working on his account, he was nothing but wonderful. Obviously that's where Jake got most of his character. I got together with Eleanor once in a while purely for the sake of business. You know…schmoozing the clients."

Dirk quietly thought over the situation. "Must have been fun to do lunch with that woman."

"She seems different somehow. Either I've forgotten how snobbish people can be, or she's gotten worse." Rachel slipped on a lacy nightgown.

She climbed into bed, and Dirk pulled her into his arms. "Maybe we'll just have to retire to the bedroom early each evening to escape her," he whispered into her ear. "You know—claim ranchers' hours."

CHAPTER ELEVEN

*I*n the days that followed, Eleanor seemed to make an effort to be polite to Emily. Occasionally she complained about the wind, the pollen, the dust, the cold nights, or the hot days. But most of the time she gave the appearance of being deeply involved in reading a novel, using it as an excuse to avoid the trouble that threatened her at every step.

One afternoon she rode along with Jake to the north fields where the men were working on the Timberline irrigation ditches. She planned to read and "get a change of scenery."

As she fanned herself in the truck cab, Eleanor watched her son, bronzed and bare chested, working along with the others. He stood a head taller than the rest and easily outweighed the strongest. *What he could do in the business world! His leadership...his determination. Success could be his!*

Jake rose from his work to wipe his forehead and looked over at his mother. Seeing her watching, he waved and walked over to her. He hung his tall body through the open truck window and asked, "Finished your book?"

"No. Taking a break."

"I see. You were looking at me like you wanted something. You okay?"

"I just was sitting here contemplating how I've lost my son. What have I done wrong? Was it something I said? Something your father did?"

Jake ran a hand through his sweat-soaked hair. "Mother, you haven't lost me. I'm simply following my own path. I love this life. I want my own ranch someday."

"Your own? But if you had one, you'd never move back to the city."

"I don't want to move back. I'm a thousand times more content here than I was in a downtown office. I was stifled all those years as an architect. Miserable. This is what makes me happy." Jake stepped back and gestured toward the valley. "This is what makes me"—he pounded his chest for emphasis—"alive! I know you wanted me to follow in Dad's footsteps, but that wasn't my choice, Mother. He seems to have accepted it. I wish you could too."

"You stand there, only twenty-eight years old, and tell me what you want, but I know it's a tragic error in judgment."

"Twenty-eight. When you were twenty-eight, Mother, you'd been married for seven years and had two children. You can't tell me you didn't feel like an adult by then, fully capable of making your own decisions."

"It was different then," she sniffed, caught off guard.

"How?" Jake smiled.

He had her in a corner. "It simply was."

"I see." His grin clearly told her she had lost that round.

In the stables, Jake sneaked up on Emily from behind while she fed the baby calf that had taken ill. She let out a cry of delight as he picked her up in his arms, swung her around, and then set her down gently for a long kiss. After a moment, he pulled away and looked into her eyes.

"I've missed those lips, Ms. Walker," he said.

"And I've missed yours," she said shyly. "I've also missed our evening walks and conversations on the swing."

"You know you're always welcome to join my parents and me. I've invited you often enough."

"I know, Jake. She just scares me to death. And she's brought up a question that I can't answer. We do come from two different worlds. How are we supposed to meet in the middle? It's okay here in the Elk Horn, but what happens when you want to go home for Christmas and you have to introduce me to all your society friends? I don't belong there."

"You'll do fine. You are a wonderful human being, and anyone with any sense will be able to see that. Besides, what do I care what people think? I just care about you. You are the most important person in my life. If Mother won't accept you, then she won't be a part of our lives. I've already made that clear to her."

Emily's face turned white. "How could you say that, Jake? You'd allow your parents to walk out of your life? Do you know how much I miss my folks? What I would give to have them back? And you'd *choose* to never see them again? Maybe your mother is impossible, but I know how you feel about your dad. How would you feel about your decision in ten years?"

Jake's jaw was set firmly. "They'd come around. Dad would make Mother see the light."

"You can't make her see something she doesn't want to see."

Jake turned away from her to look out the window toward the house.

Emily grabbed his arm and searched his face, her own eyes overflowing with tears. "Don't you see, Jake? I'd give anything to be with my folks again. How could I get between you and yours?"

He turned and held her tightly in his arms. "It will be okay, Emily. You'll see."

But deep inside he knew it might not.

SATURDAY, JULY 22

Excitement filled the air as work on the ranch was finished early in anticipation of the Sweet Pea dance. The town council had voted to begin the festival with a supper of barbecued ribs from the valley's prize swine. The idea made Eleanor ill, so she and her husband excused themselves from the event, much to the others' great relief.

Jake waited at the bottom of the stairs for Emily. He hoped he looked dashing in black jeans, a crisp, cream-colored shirt, black boots shined up for the occasion, and a bolo tie. His mother passed him en route to the kitchen and smiled sweetly but said nothing.

At long last, Dirk and Rachel's door opened, and Emily emerged. She looked beautiful and ethereal in her new dress, and the sight of her left Jake speechless.

With artfully applied eyeliner and mascara on her blond lashes, Emily's eyes looked like huge, sea blue pools, and Jake wanted to stare into them forever. But he could not, for his eyes were too busy taking in the rest of the vision she created. Her hair was bobbed in a stylish new cut. Dainty greenish blue stone droplets that matched her dress dangled from her lobes. And the dress...he tore his eyes away.

Rachel followed Emily down the stairs, and Dirk let out a long, low whistle. "Even more incredible than last year," he said, taking her hand. "Em, that's an amazing dress—you look gorgeous. But I must say Rachel will always be the belle of the ball to me." Emily smiled at her friend.

Rachel did look stunning in a new white dress that fit her hips snugly, highlighting her own great curves. Her hair was styled in large curls that bounced as she walked and, like Emily's, shone brilliantly in the soft light.

"It's a Kodak moment," Rachel said, grabbing a nearby camera and grouping people for pictures. Smoothly she moved Emily and Jake together for a photo, whistling at the handsome couple.

The evening was magical, and the weather cooperated perfectly, just as it had the year before. Outside the grange hall, Emily noticed men surrounding the three huge pits, removing steel covers to pull out the huge racks of ribs and roasts from underground barbecues. The meat, perfectly cooked, was delicious, and everyone wore plastic bibs to protect their dance attire. The noise in the tent was almost deafening, as laughter and loud conversation rang out from every table. When Jake smiled down at her, Emily was almost able to forget their disagreement from the previous afternoon.

Each table sported a big bouquet of sweet peas in hues of pale lavender and pink and yellow, collected from around the valley by those attending the dance. Rachel had not contributed any, preferring to leave the gorgeous flowers alone on the trellis in order to enjoy the longer-lasting blooms. Instead, she had coerced Dirk into donating one of their prize sows for the roast.

Emily smiled to herself. *The pork was a more expensive donation than flowers, but I guess value varies from beholder to beholder.*

"Just like last year," Rachel admired the grange hall as they entered after eating. Japanese lanterns softly lit the room, and bales of hay lined the wall. Two older women from their church waved from across the room where they were loading the punch table with clean glass cups and large bowls of lemonade.

"Hope this year you're not carried off by a madman. I can avoid the headache, and the Morgans should fare better," Dirk answered her ruefully.

Matt and Beth entered just then, having opted to skip the supper. They found it was easier to stay home with the baby for as long as possible rather than to try to last through a long evening, only to be called home by a desperate baby-sitter unable to stop the child from crying. This night Beth had decided the dance was far more important than ribs, even if some of those ribs came from Timberline.

"Get her to sleep?" Rachel asked as Dirk and Matt edged away to talk.

"Just barely. Matt thinks we should leave her with a sitter more often so she'll get used to someone else putting her down, but I can hardly stand it. I think it's my favorite time of day when her little eyes start to droop and she looks at me so dreamily."

"It will be easier when you stop breast-feeding her. You're becoming so bonded you're almost fused into one," Rachel teased.

Beth smiled at her. "You just wait. You'll be worse by a mile."

"No way. I'll have the kid on a bottle within a month."

"Ha!"

"Well, I don't want anything to interfere with Dirk taking me out on the town to one of the French restaurants or ballet," she said with a wry smile.

"That's true. There is *so* much here in Elk Horn that pulls a mother away from her child."

"Yes. Look at you! Tonight you had two very attractive options: luscious pork ribs or the dance of the year. The social options are endless."

"You notice I've chosen the calorie-burning dance over the meal."

"Yes, you did," Rachel agreed. "I'm very proud of you. But I'll bet Dirk and Matt aren't so disciplined. Ten bucks says they slip out the side door to sneak a few leftover ribs."

"And leave their beautiful wives? No way. You're on."

As the band warmed up, the two women sat down on a hay bale and watched the people file in, alone and in pairs.

"Remind you of unpleasant things?" Beth asked gently.

"Not really. The dance last year was wonderful. It was the after-hours events that proved to be a nightmare. How about for you?"

"No. It's amazing the healing a year brings. I still think about my first baby. But Hope is such a gift, there isn't much room for sadness."

Rachel nodded at her friend's words. She looked over to Dirk and Matthew, who were in deep conversation over by the punch bowl. "It's hard to worry about the past with Eleanor Rierdon to worry about in the present."

"I'm sure this whole thing with Emily is putting her over the edge."

"Do you think anybody would have been good enough for her son in her eyes?"

"A daughter of one of her friends might have been more palatable, but even she would have fallen short."

"How did we ever stand her back home?" Beth asked.

"Business demanded it."

"I guess so."

Both turned as Jake and Emily walked into the room, glowing with smiles. Beth gasped. "What in the world did you do with that girl?"

Rachel smiled. "A little makeup, a haircut, and that dress from the catalog I've been telling you about. Doesn't she look stunning?"

The band began playing, and Jake swept Emily out on the dance floor. Her dress skirt flared, exposing lean, tan legs above her dainty sandals. Although she was at a country dance, she carried herself as if she were a princess at a ball. And Jake, smiling down at her, was perfect as her handsome prince.

Rachel and Beth looked around for their husbands so they could join the couple on the dance floor. On a hunch, they opened the side door and found their men laughing and devouring leftover ribs out of a tinfoil container as if they would never be fed again. The women broke out into hysterical giggles as their husbands looked at them guiltily.

"What's so funny?" Matt asked. "I was hungry."

"I guess *so*," Beth said.

"I'm not trying to lose twenty pounds."

"No, you're not. But for commenting on that, *you* owe Rachel ten bucks."

Rachel put her hand out expectantly. Looking from one woman to the other, Matt reached for his wallet. "I don't know what I'm paying for, but I hope you two think it's worthwhile."

The women grinned and walked to the door without explana-

tion. "You guys had better report to the dance floor within ten minutes, or you'll be in hot water," Rachel said.

"We'll be there in a minute," Dirk replied, returning her smile.
He gazed at her with a look that still had the ability to make her
knees a bit shaky. "We'll be there," he repeated.

Emily and Jake danced the night away, twirling to the fast-paced
country tunes and swaying to the slower ballads. Emily could not
remember ever enjoying herself more.

Late in the evening, Jake steered Emily out a side door as if per-
forming the tango, leading her through the supper tent and out into
an empty field. He held Emily close, and they gazed upward, overwhelmed by the bright galaxies in the night sky.

"There's no place I'd rather be, Emily Walker, than right here
with you in my arms. I'm just so thankful to God for bringing you
into my life." He cradled her to his chest and gently kissed the top
of her head.

Emily leaned against his shoulder, her eyes filled with tears. In
her heart she knew she couldn't stay. Timberline had been a dream,
a dream worth chasing. But she could already feel it fading away.

The next day passed uneventfully. After church Jake spent most of
the day in the fields, helping the ranch hands round up part of the
herd to begin vaccinations. Emily worked in the kitchen with Mary,
more quiet and reflective than usual.

That evening after supper, Jacob and Eleanor went to find their
son in the stables, hoping for an opportunity to speak with him
alone. Unaware that they were looking for Jake, Emily went out to

find him as well. When she reached the stable windows, she could hear voices rising in anger.

"Son, I think you should hear your mother out. She mistreated Emily at first and has apologized for that. But she has some valid concerns."

"Now, darling, listen," Eleanor said. "I don't like the life you've chosen, but I am working to accept it, just as I'm trying to accept the fact that your sister Julia is moving to the East. However, your home is not the real problem here, nor is your job. The problem is Emily."

He clenched his jaw. "Be careful, Mother. You're on thin ice."

"Don't be so stubborn, Jake! Obviously I am not thrilled that you have chosen the girl. And I admit that I have not handled my objections well. But I am concerned about you. I don't want you to do something you will regret." Jake turned away, shaking his head. He ran a hand through his hair.

"You two are from different worlds," Eleanor continued, "and you know it. She can't really come into yours, nor can you go into hers. What if, for some unforeseen reason, you have to go back to San Francisco? What happens to Emily then?"

"That won't happen."

"Son," Jacob said, "you clearly have a talent for this sort of thing. But financially, ranches *are* going under all the time these days. What if you had no choice but to return to the city in order to make a living?"

Jake was silent.

"There's just too much going against the two of you," Eleanor insisted. "You may not see it now. But when the blush of young love wears off, you'll find things aren't as perfect as they once seemed.

You'll wind up tearing each other apart. If Emily really loved you, Jake, she wouldn't put you through the pain."

Emily's brow furrowed as she fought back tears. *She's right. What was I thinking? How could we ever make it long-term?* Unable to control her fear any longer, she slipped away silently and ran back to the house. It was the only coping skill she possessed.

Inside the stables, Jake ran his hand through his hair once more in frustration and agitation.

"I know you care," he said. "And you've said your piece. But now it's done. I love Emily. I believe God can help us work through any challenge we might face." He walked to the door, then turned and said forcefully, "Emily is a part of my life, and she always will be. Never again say a word against the woman I love." He waved a finger at the two of them. "Never again."

Emily crumpled up in the corner of her bedroom, sobbing in fear, frustration, and agony.

After a while, someone knocked softly at her door. "Wh-who is it?" she asked, choking back the tears.

"Emily, it's Rachel. Jake's downstairs, and he wants you to come down for a walk."

"Oh, Rachel, I have an awful headache, and I'm already in bed. Could you tell him I'll just see him tomorrow?"

"Sure," Rachel responded. "Is there anything I can bring you?"

"No, thanks. I just need to sleep."

Emily listened to Rachel's footsteps fade away, then stood and wiped the tears from her eyes. She had to decide on her next move.

CHAPTER TWELVE

$\mathcal{M}$ ary turned the bacon and mixed batter for pancakes, becoming more frustrated by the minute. *Where is that girl this morning? She could have told me if she was going to be late.* She paused, remembering that Rachel had mentioned Emily had turned in early, complaining of a headache. *Maybe she's really sick.*

After ten more minutes she could stand it no longer. Placing her bowl and spoon on the counter and taking the bacon off the heat, she walked down the hall to Emily's bedroom and knocked on the door. There was no response.

She knocked one more time, then poked her head in. The form on the bed lay still and quiet. Mary knew it was unlike Emily to over-sleep, and her irritation fully gave way to concern. She walked over to the bed to wake the young woman but discovered only a pile of pillows under the blanket and sheet.

Mary rushed upstairs to inform the Tanners. Alarmed, Rachel dressed quickly and ran to search the barn and stables, while Dirk went out to the bunkhouse to see if any of the ranch hands had seen her. Neither found Emily, but Dirk did turn up a rather agitated Jake.

"What do you mean she's not here? Where could she be?"

Hoping she might be in the chapel, Jake sprinted up the hill and through the forest to the tiny stone building. He opened the door quietly, not wanting to disturb her if she was praying. The room was empty. Jake tried to imagine where else she could be.

But he knew. There could be no other reason for her deception in making it look as though she were in bed. Emily was gone.

***

"Let me out!" Emily demanded. The truck driver's hand had rested on the seat behind her head for an hour or more. Now he had begun stroking her hair.

"All right, all right. No need to scream, little lady. I just thought you might be lonely, in need of some com-pan-ion-ship." He drawled out the word, trying to sound seductive.

"Now!" she insisted.

The truck driver dropped her off around noon, just east of Coeur d'Alene, Idaho. Emily walked the remaining distance to town and then set out in search of a place to sleep for the night, determined not to spend her meager savings too fast. She wondered where to go, what to do.

As she walked along a lake on the outskirts of town, she discovered what appeared to be a family weekend cabin, left empty during the week. Hoping that she was right and that the residents would not return for a couple of days, she located a hammock in the backyard trees where she could hide among the branches.

Jake, I miss you already. Was I wrong to leave? She had to write to him and explain. Emily walked to a small diner off the main highway, where she purchased several postcards and stamps. After ordering hot coffee and a bowl of soup from a kindly looking woman behind the counter, she settled herself at the counter and began to write. The waitress filled her cup as Emily tried to find the words to make Jake understand.

Dear Jake,

How I miss you already! Please do not worry about me. I needed to leave. As much as we care about each other, we both know we were never meant to be together.

You must forget me and move on. Find someone who is more worthy of your love.

I will always treasure our days together and carry you in my heart.

Yours always,
Emily

The waitress brought a box of tissues from behind the counter while Emily completed her message. Drying her tears for a moment, she began to write the next card.

Dear Dirk and Rachel,

Words can't express what I owe you, but I will try.

Thank you for nursing me back to health—for taking me into your home and giving me work. Never before have I known people so loving and trusting.

Please forgive me for leaving my job without notice and for not telling you in person. I could not bear to see you again and still leave.

Gratefully,
Your friend, Emily

She spent the rest of the afternoon in Coeur d'Alene, walking the main streets and peeking in windows, trying to pretend she was on a shopping spree with Rachel. Emily noticed that she did not blend in with the other tourists, however. In her flight from Timberline, she had left most of her belongings behind. She had brought along only two changes of clothing, and those she wore were in need of a good washing.

Emily headed back toward the cabin, stopping reluctantly to mail her postcards. She wanted to relieve Jake's worry. She wanted to explain. But she also knew that the postcards would reveal her location to him within a day or two. That meant she would have to move on quickly, and she hated to leave Idaho. It reminded her so much of her home in Montana.

She collected her roll of clothing and set off toward the lakeshore to wash and dry her clothes in the sun. Hoping to avoid the crowded boat launch and public beaches, she turned down a narrow road that looked as if it were seldom traveled. Soon she found herself on an isolated, abandoned stretch of beach. *Perfect.* Emily was pleased that her old survival instincts had returned. *I'll be okay. I'll never let it get as bad as before.*

As she sat staring into the water, Emily's thoughts turned again to Jake and Timberline, and the tears began to flow. She felt the anguish of losing her home once again, and her heart ached when she thought about how she had left without saying good-bye.

Needing to escape her sad thoughts, Emily took off her dirty jeans and threw them into the lake. She waded into the water and then slipped off her shirt, leaving on only her underwear. She rubbed her clothes together in an effort to clean them and then spread them out on the bushes to dry in the hot sun.

Dipping back into the icy mountain water, Emily took a deep breath and dove farther out from the shore. The water grew significantly colder when she dove beneath the top twelve inches warmed by the sun and sent goose bumps across her bare skin.

Refreshed by her swim, Emily climbed out of the water, slipped on a change of dry clothes, and sat looking out over the lake. *What will I do next? How am I going to make it without Jake? Without anyone who loves me?* She realized that in her heart she was directing her words toward the God she had just begun to know. *Please help me, God. I don't want to go back to the way things were. I don't even want to go on.*

Suddenly her heart was filled with peace, as it had been during her first visit to Dirk's chapel. Comforting thoughts filled her mind. *There will be a way out of your pain. I will give you peace. I am with you always.*

Dirk, Jake, and Rachel spent the day searching the cafés, truck stops, bus stations, and parks that bordered the highway for twenty miles, north and south. But Emily was nowhere to be found. *She must have been picked up on the highway.* Jake's heart pounded at the thought of her hitchhiking with strangers. *Please, God, protect Emily. Help me find her before she gets hurt. Let her know that I love her and that nothing else matters.* He stopped the truck and rested his head on the steering wheel, giving in to deep sobs.

Emily rose from the hammock the next morning at daybreak, awakened by the dull thud of swollen pine cones dropping to the ground. As much as she hated moving farther away from Jake, she knew she had to move on. *There's no going back.*

She returned to the café with the kindly waitress, where she was the first customer of the morning. Starving, she ordered the early-bird special—eggs, bacon, pancakes, and coffee for two dollars—and ate it all quickly. The waitress refilled her coffee cup, remarking on her appetite. "Never saw a bitty thing like you eat like that."

"Didn't eat much yesterday," Emily allowed.

The waitress's eyes narrowed. "Sufferin' over some deadbeat, no doubt. I saw you writin' those letters the other day. Ain't a man alive worth that kind of grief." She walked away.

"I disagree," Emily whispered, thinking of Jake. She longed for his strong arms and easy smile. Steeling herself, she took a last sip of coffee and counted out money for the bill and tip. She figured she had two hundred and thirty-four dollars left.

Her funds would last her awhile if she handled them right. At the door she looked at the tattered United States map pinned to the wall with a large red U ARE HERE arrow posted at the tip of the lake.

Where do I go? She looked at San Francisco on the map and for one crazy moment longed to see where Jake had grown up. Then it hit her. San Francisco would be the last place they'd look for her. *Too near his parents. Too risky for a runaway. And a place big enough to disappear in.*

"Where you headin'?" the waitress asked with friendly interest.

"West," she declared. "I'm heading west."

CHAPTER THIRTEEN

*A*s the Rierdons left Elk Horn, Jake Sr. expressed genuine sympathy for his son, and even Eleanor seemed somewhat remorseful. When Jake stiffly hugged her good-bye, she said, "Look, if you're so devoted to Emily, we'll support you. We just want you to think things through."

Jake only half heard her. His thoughts were focused on finding Emily.

Within fifteen hours of her disappearance, he had handbills posted all over the valley asking in red letters, HAVE YOU SEEN THIS WOMAN? The fliers bore a picture of Emily, taken on the night of the dance. Every time Jake looked at her image, his heart lurched in agony.

As soon as the mail arrived, Dirk called Jake in from the porch, where he was pacing. The postmark on the cards told them where she had been, at least the day before. Jake read them three times, looking for further clues. He was relieved to know that Emily had been safe when she wrote them, and yet he was alarmed by the finality of their tone.

Within minutes he was speeding down the highway toward Coeur d'Alene. He drove seventy miles an hour all the way to Idaho, but he felt as if he were going only twenty.

As he pulled into town late that afternoon, Jake scanned the sidewalks with hungry eyes, willing Emily to appear in the fading summer sunlight.

He found an empty parking space and began to canvass the town, distributing fliers in every store and stopping pedestrians on the street. After several hours of searching without success, he decided to check one last café by the waterfront. The place was filled with loud, sunburned boaters who were tired and anxious for a late dinner. Jake made his way around the people waiting in line for a seat, ignoring the angry looks they gave him as they assumed he was trying to cut in line.

He intercepted the hostess and held Emily's picture in front of her face. "Have you seen this woman in the last few days?"

She took the handbill, then looked back at him, frowning. "Are you the jerk who had that little girl crying?"

Startled, Jake tried to gather his thoughts. "You've seen her? She was here?"

"Well, I don't know just how much I ought to tell ya. You're the man who upset her, aren't you?"

"Look, it's a long story. I just know Emily is on the road alone, maybe in danger. She doesn't have a car. She's hitchhiking. Did she say where she was going?"

The woman looked at him skeptically.

"Please! I love her."

The waitress paused a moment longer. "West. That's all she said."

As Jake searched Coeur d'Alene, Emily traveled west with a group of sorority girls who were on a summer road trip. It had taken her all day to find a ride with people she could risk trusting. The girls were friendly and asked her lots of questions about why she was on the road. Emily limited her answers to two or three words, and soon the girls elected to ignore her.

They giggled and talked loudly all the way to the outskirts of Seattle. Emily did not say another word until they let her out on an off-ramp near nightfall.

"Thank you," she mumbled.

Tires spun, rocks flew, and the girls were out on the highway once more. Together they postulated what Emily's real story was: lost job, lost money, or lost man.

"Lost man," they agreed, judging from her manner. Then they moved on to other topics. Emily was out of their thoughts almost before she was out of sight.

Emily was pleased to find that the girls had dropped her off near a state park. She stopped at a corner market for a carton of milk, an apple, and a bar of soap. Then she sneaked into the park by skirting the front entrance and slipping in through the woods.

Blessed with clear skies and an unusually warm evening, she curled up on a bed of pine needles and covered herself with the rest of her clothes. Hidden from the world, she slept fitfully, dreaming that Jake had come for her.

In her dream she could not even remember why they had parted.

THURSDAY, JULY 27

West. She's headed west. Jake sped through the night, arriving in Seattle just after five o'clock the next morning. He checked into a cheap motel and called the Tanners from his room. Jake told them about the café waitress, his subsequent night drive, and his present location. "I'll be searching the greater Seattle area today."

"Hey, Jake, we'll let every police station in the area know she might be in their jurisdiction. I'll fax her picture. It's a huge area, but with their patrols on the streets, we just might find her."

"I don't have much hope."

"Jake," Rachel said, "remember that I once left Dirk to go home. I didn't think I could handle ranch life, and I wasn't sure we knew what we were doing after our crazy courtship. But there was nothing I longed for more than for him to come after me.

"I was just about to go back to Montana when he showed up. Emily loves you the same way, Jake. She's running because she's scared, scared to death she'll be hurt again. And right now she's lonely, sad, and wishing you were with her. Find her."

It was the encouragement he needed. "I plan on it. It might not be today or even the next day. But I *will* find her. She'll have to tell me to my face that she doesn't want me."

At dawn Emily rose and washed her face at the park's bathhouse. At the front of the park, she found a map of the area and noted her proximity to the nearest highway south. Unfortunately, she had over-shot it by four miles with the sorority girls. The streets were nearly empty at that hour, making it difficult to find a ride, so Emily walked to the freeway's entrance. There, feeling the sun's warm rays, she stuck out her thumb and was picked up within five minutes.

Jake slept fitfully for a few hours, dreaming that he saw Emily in a seedy downtown alley but that she was pulled away from him every time he came near her. Her face implored him to help her, but the alley got longer and longer, and her outstretched hand was always beyond his grasp.

He awoke in a sweat. Walking over to the sink, he splashed his face with water and looked at himself in the peeling mirror. *What could have driven her away? What could I have said to make her run?* He went over those last days with her in his mind, while his parents— His parents! That day in the barn. Had she overheard? It would've been enough to push her away. She would've left, believing it was for his sake as much as hers. He had to find her, tell her nothing could change the way he felt. Nothing. He had to find her.

Emily watched the truck driver carefully, but this one did not make any moves on her. He was an older man, apparently interested only in passing the time with different people. "What has you on the road, miss?" he asked with concern.

"I guess I'm running away, in a manner of speaking," she said, looking out at the green mountains.

"Why are you running?"

"I'd rather not say."

"Oh, come now. You've got me intrigued, and I spend a lot of hours on the road by myself. You probably have a story worth three or four hundred miles. Tell me your story, and I'll take you as far south as you want to go."

"Sorry. If you're serious about my having to tell you, you can pull off right up here and I'll get out."

The driver looked at her determined face.

"Aw, now, I was just curious. You don't have to tell me nothing you don't want to. I'll even give you part of my lunch. If you feel like talking, though…"

Emily slept soon after getting in the truck, napping all the way through southern Oregon and across the state line. At four o'clock they bypassed Sacramento and turned off onto I-505. Emily watched as the road signs and houses increased along the freeway. *Suburbia.* By six o'clock they were in Oakland, and Emily asked to be dropped off. Without complaint, the driver pulled off the highway and into a gas station. He was obviously reluctant to see her go, worried about her safety.

She opened her door and climbed down the steps. "Thanks, Henry. I appreciate the ride."

"Wait. Where are you going to stay tonight?"

"I'll find a place. I can take care of myself."

"I know. Still…here." He dug into his back pocket, pulled out a wad of cash, and stretched out his hand.

"No, Henry, I can't."

"Go on, take it. I have a daughter not too much younger than you. I know I'd want someone to help her."

"Well…can I take down your address and repay you someday?"

"Whatever. I just want to know you'll have a roof, bed, and locked door tonight. This isn't the safest place in the world for a pretty girl like you."

"Thank you, Henry," she said gratefully, "for everything. I will pay you back someday."

"I don't doubt it." He scribbled down his address for her and handed over the cash. "Take care of yourself now."

She shut the door and he drove off, his exhaust pipe letting out a long stream of black smoke. Emily walked into the gas station, picked out a Coke and half-sandwich from the refrigerated display, and purchased them from an attendant standing behind what she assumed to be bulletproof glass. She was careful not to display her cash.

Before leaving she entered the women's bathroom. Behind the locked door, she stopped to count the money Henry had left her. *Sixty-three dollars.* "Thank you, God," she whispered. "You're taking care of me, aren't you?"

⟳

Jake spent day and night searching the streets of Seattle. Tired and discouraged, he called the Tanners after midnight to inform them of his progress.

Rachel picked up the phone on the first ring. "Jake?" her voice was filled with excitement. "We're getting closer! A truck driver named Henry called the highway patrol. He thought he had given a ride to a runaway and was worried about her. They checked with police in Seattle. The girl's name was Emily. And, Jake, you won't believe this. It looks like she's headed for San Francisco!"

CHAPTER FOURTEEN

*A*t the YWCA the next morning, Emily arose early, gingerly walking around the sleeping form of a woman with an obvious hangover. During the night Emily had watched as the woman rolled off the cot next to her, hit the ground with a grunt, and then resumed her snoring.

Emily grabbed her clothing bundle from beneath her flat pillow and headed toward the showers. For twenty-five cents, she rented a clean towel and soaped up underneath the hot water that was metered out of a drought-sensitive showerhead. The warmth was good after her last bath in a mountain lake. She was the first one out of the shelter.

She headed toward the city center, picked up a paper at a newsstand, and then stopped at a corner café for a pastry and coffee. "Can I borrow a pen?" she asked the waitress.

"Sure," the woman handed her a blue Bic, chewed at the tip.

Emily bypassed all the other sections of the *San Francisco Chronicle* and turned straight to the employment ads. Most of the listings were for executives, nurses, and other hospital staff. But Emily felt she might have a chance at the handful of house-cleaning and kitchen positions. She circled them and then returned to the newsstand, where she bought a city map. She took a deep breath, willing hope into her heart. She was ready to begin her new life.

Jake plastered handbills on every available post and wall he passed. *She has to be here. She couldn't afford to go any farther.* It was merely a simple matter of flushing her out of the forty million other inhabitants. Wearily, he posted another flier.

He walked into a small deli on the corner, ordered a sandwich from the man behind the counter, and then asked to borrow the phone book. The owner handed it to him reluctantly.

Jake seated himself at a table and began to look through the book. "Excuse me," he asked the deli man loudly. "Where do the homeless sleep at night?"

"On the streets!" The man's jowls jiggled as he laughed at the obvious answer.

"No. There must be some shelters or some place."

"Yeah, sure." The man handed over the sandwich, sobering at Jake's stern look. "There's Sister Mary's, up the street here. The Catholic church takes in a few people every night in their spare room. Other than that, it's pretty much up to the Y for those people who have a few bucks." He watched Jake write the information down. "You lookin' for someone?"

"Yes." He pulled a flier from the top of his stack. "You seen this woman?"

The man took it from him and shook his head no. "Pretty gal. Your girlfriend?"

"Yes."

"You better hope she's made it to one of them shelters I told you about. These streets are no place for a girl at night."

Jake said nothing. He paid for his sandwich and carried it to a table, no longer hungry. Staring at the food before him, he fought his rising panic that Emily was gone forever, that she would disappear into the dark city streets, never to be found again.

Help me, Father. His eyes filled with tears. *I can't do it alone. Please, help me.*

He left the sandwich on the table, tore the listing of shelters out of the yellow pages, and laid ten dollars on the counter to pay for the book. Then he walked back out into the San Francisco streets, determined to find her.

SATURDAY, JULY 29

"Two hundred dollar a month. Four hundred now, and a fifty-dollar deposit."

"You want four hundred and fifty dollars for this?" Emily asked incredulously. She was having no luck finding work. All the nice establishments wanted references, and she certainly did not want anyone calling Timberline. She was desperate.

Even more frightening was the prospect of not being able to get an apartment. The YWCA would only house her for one more night. Her search for something in her price range and near the most job opportunities had brought her to this: a dirty, tiny apartment in Chinatown. As awful as it was, it was the first place she had found that she had the cash to cover.

Miserable, she said, "I'll take it. But I can only give you two hundred and fifty now. I'm looking for work."

"I hear that one before."

"Please, Mr. Chan. I'll be able to pay you next week."

The scrawny, sleazy man sighed and then stuck out his hand

expectantly. "You don't have next week. You get out. I keep all money. Deal?"

She turned away and counted out the bills. He grabbed at the wad of cash greedily and handed her the key, leaving his hand on hers in a suggestive manner.

She recoiled, and he smiled a toothless grin, shrugging his shoulders in apology. "You not have job?"

"Not yet."

"You not look long. I have job for you." Mr. Chan nodded his head up and down in excitement.

"You do?" Her eyes narrowed.

"My cousin have hotel for boys who want girlfriends. Lotsa money. Good times."

"Get out."

Again the toothless smile and the shrug. "You could be my girlfriend. You could pay hundred dollar 'stead of two."

"Out!"

"Okay, okay." He turned to go and then stopped at the door. "One more idea. I have restaurant. Need someone wash dish."

"How much?" Working in his restaurant was the last thing she wanted to do, but it meant fast cash.

"Four dollar an hour. Under table."

"Where?"

"That way. Few blocks."

"I'll take it."

Smiling, Mr. Chan turned to go. "Two tomorrow afternoon. You walk with me. I show you."

"Okay." She sat on the sagging bed with its dirty mattress and watched him go. He didn't really threaten her. He was just annoying.

In any case, she now had a place to live and a job, at least until she could find something better.

Mr. Chan spoke in what Emily guessed to be Mandarin Chinese all the way to the restaurant. Storekeepers swept front steps and innkeepers brought out loads of linens to hang as the city streets bustled with midday activity. He seemed to know everyone.

Emily had barely slept the night before. The bed in her room squeaked each time she moved, and in the blinking light of the neon sign outside her uncovered window, she could see rats darting about her room. Emily shivered at the thought. Still, it was better than being on the streets. Rodents she could handle. Rapists and robbers she could not.

Mr. Chan's restaurant consisted of six tables. At the back was a large aquarium with exotic fish. The carpeting was a bright red, and the lights were garish, gold-foil creations. Mr. Chan headed into the kitchen, flipping on lights. As he and Emily walked in, a portly Chinese man dressed in white entered from the back. The cook, Emily decided. The two men bantered back and forth, and the cook took a moment to look her over carefully.

Out of the blue he began yelling in Chinese and waving his arms, emphatically trying to tell her something. She simply nodded, hoping his tirade would end soon.

"He want you wear white," Mr. Chan explained with a smile.

"Oh. Yes," Emily agreed, looking directly back at the big man. She would need to purchase kitchen whites.

Her response launched him into another tirade.

"He don't like you lookin' him in eyes," Mr. Chan warned, a little more sharply.

Emily lowered her gaze. *You need this job,* she told herself. "Yes sir," she replied, looking at the floor.

The cook stared at her for a moment and then grunted his approval.

Swallowing his pride, Jake picked up the receiver and began to dial.

"Rierdon Architecture," a cheery voice answered.

"Jacob Rierdon, please. It's his son."

Jacob Sr. was on the phone in less than a minute. "Son? How's the search going?"

"Not so good. I need a name, Dad."

"A name?"

"The private investigator you've told me about. The one your firm has used in the past. You said he was the best, and I need him. Emily may be in San Francisco."

The senior Rierdon went to his filing cabinet and pulled out the information. "Steve Nadam. He's a real professional, Jake. He'll find her if she's within the city limits."

"I hope so, Dad. I really hope so."

Emily finished her shift at ten-thirty that night, after the last customer had left and the last dish was washed, clean, and dried. Exhausted, she untied her filthy apron and wiped her forehead to keep the sweat from her eyes. Throughout the evening the kitchen had become increasingly hot and the cook increasingly agitated with her.

She could not keep up with the dishes pouring in, and too many had passed imperfectly cleansed. The cook strode up to her several times and yelled in Chinese in her face, gesturing wildly and pointing out bits of rice stuck to the dishes.

Emily fought the urge to cry or to quit. She would not allow herself either. She needed the job, and with long days and the wage her landlord had promised, she knew she would be able to live and eat. *I'll find something else next week. Right now, this is the only thing that stands between me and the streets.*

Never did she allow herself to think of how much more pleasant cleaning up the kitchen at Timberline had been. Emily drew herself up to her full height and smiled the sweetest smile she could muster. The cook glowered and walked away, past the huge iron stoves and cooktops and out the door, mumbling to himself unhappily.

"Be with me, Father. I need you," she whispered. The door closed with a bang. She was alone again in the back of a strange restaurant in an unfamiliar town.

"Jake, I'd like you to meet Steve Nadam, a private investigator I've come to prize."

The three men stood in Jacob Rierdon's plush office, a room that smelled of rich leather, polishing oil, and coffee. Two walls were filled with windows that looked out onto the lights of the city and the bay.

"Thanks for meeting us so late," Jake said, shaking Steve's hand. Steve Nadam had wise eyes, outlined by dark circles, and a belly shaped by too many stakeouts with doughnuts for companions. His cheeks were unshaven, but Jake instantly trusted the light in his eye.

"It's actually early for me. Investigator's hours aren't normally eight to five."

"Right," Jake said. "I don't want to seem rude, but if you don't mind, let's get down to business."

⌒

Emily walked out of the restaurant's kitchen door five minutes behind the cook and found herself in a dark alley that smelled of rotten garbage and urine. She turned to go back inside, but the door had automatically locked behind her. She was drenched from her work in the sweltering kitchen, and steam rose from her arms as the cool night air embraced her. She saw a faint light from the street up ahead and walked toward it, eager to get out of the alley and into a place with people.

She walked right into the gang.

Surprised, one member whirled, drawing his knife at the same time. The young man smiled as he looked Emily up and down.

"Ah, hello." He waved for the others to continue spray-painting a challenge to a rival gang.

"Hello," Emily said, not looking at him. She brushed by his shoulder as she walked past him.

He ran around in front of her, whispering to her suggestively.

She stopped. "Knock it off or I'll scream."

"Ooh," he mocked, obviously not threatened. The other gang members stopped their vandalism and surrounded her. He reached out and grabbed a handful of hair. The others laughed as he drew her closer to him and kissed her on the neck.

With a quick and forceful movement, Emily pushed him away despite his hold on her hair. The boy moved toward her again as she tried to back away. Closer and closer he came, until her back hit the brick of a three-story building and she could go no farther. *Please, God, help me.*

Emily closed her eyes, and suddenly the laughing stopped. The only sounds she heard were switchblades clicking open.

"Vic," one of the young men near them whispered, seeing the rival gang approach. "It was a trap. The girl…bait."

Vic looked back.

"Bait," he snorted. "Get out of here." He glared at Emily before turning to face the enemy gang.

Emily ran as fast as she could toward her apartment building. Gasping for breath and with shaking hands, she managed to get her key into the lock and let herself into her apartment. She ignored the scattering rats, climbed onto her bed, and gave way to the sobs that racked her body.

That night Jake stopped at a phone booth and called the Tanners.

Rachel answered on the second ring, her voice hopeful.

"I've had no luck so far," Jake said. "But we've got a private investigator on it now, and he has several men looking. He's supposed to be the best." He leaned his head wearily against the grimy glass of the phone booth.

"You'll find her soon. You'll see."

"Oh, Rachel! How can you be sure? You know how big this city is. It's not like being lost in Elk Horn. This is San Francisco." His tone was biting, angry.

Jake heard a click on the line as Dirk picked up the other extension. "Jake? Jake, listen to me, man. I have some verses for you. Que and I were looking at these this afternoon. Listen to this: 'Do you not know? Have you not heard? The LORD is the everlasting God, the Creator of the ends of the earth. He will not grow tired or weary, and his understanding no one can fathom. He gives strength to the weary and increases the power of the weak. Even youths grow tired and weary, and young men stumble and fall; but those who hope in the LORD will renew their strength. They will soar on wings like eagles; they will run and not grow weary, they will walk and not be faint.'"

As Dirk spoke, Jake felt his spirits lift and his confidence grow.

"Do you have your Bible with you, Jake?"

"Yes."

"Read it. This thing is bigger than we are, and we need the Lord's strength more than ever. And Jake?"

"Yeah?"

"It won't be the last time."

CHAPTER FIFTEEN

*E*mily awoke late the next morning, lacking the energy even to get out of bed. She lay still, listening to the few sounds out on the street and staring at the cobwebs that filled the corners of her room. *What have I done? How have I come to this?* She was miserable. She missed the ranch. Most of all, she missed Jake.

The worst thing was that she felt as if she had shut out Jake forever. *I ran away. He could never trust me again. I'm probably fading from his mind already. Oh, Jake, what have I done?* She rose and walked to the sink and took a quick sponge bath, washing away the tears on her face. *No more tears,* she told herself angrily. *No more tears! You have to push on.* She stood and squared her shoulders and took several deep breaths. She dressed and joined her landlord shortly thereafter for their walk to the restaurant.

Jake's first order of the day was to meet Steve Nadam. As planned, they rendezvoused three blocks away from Rierdon Architecture. Eleven o'clock.

"Hey there, Jake." The investigator held out a crumpled white bag filled with doughnuts. Jake shook his head.

"I'm not hungry. Just tell me the latest. Any news?"

Steve laid out the city map in front of Jake. He pointed as he spoke, his mouth half full of pastry. "I've covered here and here. I've spoken to my lookouts in twelve separate sections of the city. If she's in the city, man, we'll know within twelve hours."

"You've got to be kidding. I've been all over the city posting handbills and talking to people, and you think you can just put the word out to twelve people and find her?" Jake's frustration level was increasing rapidly.

"Trust me. I've been doing this for years. I've got the contacts. Let me handle it."

"Okay, but I have to do something. I'm going to go post more handbills."

"I'd advise against that," Nadam said.

"Why?"

"Because she might see one and run. It's best if we find her first. Just give me twelve more hours, and try to get some rest."

Jake stared out into the street. "Twelve more hours."

~

Emily perspired as the dinner rush peaked and evened out, then dropped off altogether. She reflected on her trouble from the night before and frantically tried to think of a safe way to get home. *Dear God,* she prayed. *You've been with me through a lot these last six months. Please help me get home tonight.* If she could survive just a few more days, she could collect her first paycheck and search for a safer workplace.

At first she tried to finish cleaning up before the cook could leave, hoping she could tag along as he walked out. But it became clear that there was no physical way for her to finish when he did. Miserably, Emily watched as the older man put away his last knife and hung up his apron. He grunted a good-bye in her direction and then exited through the alley, leaving the door ajar.

Emily's heart pounded. She eased toward the door, pulling the butcher knife from its hook as she went. From six inches away she reached out and pushed the door shut, her hands shaking as she heard the lock slide into place. *Safe for a little while anyway.*

She returned to her dishes.

Eleven hours after their morning meeting, the phone rang in Rierdon's plush office where Jake waited with his father and Steve Nadam. All three men jumped up at once. The private investigator reached the phone first. "You're sure? When? If you're right, you'll be paid well for your work."

He turned to the others. "I have a man who swears he saw her last night. The bad news is that she seems to be drawing some unwanted attention on the streets."

Jake's heart, already pounding, skipped a beat as he looked back out the window to the setting sun. "Where is she?" he demanded.

"Chinatown."

Finished. Not a spot left to clean. Not a drop left to dry. There was no way around it. Emily had to make a break for it or sleep there all night. She did not feel much safer in the restaurant than she did on the street. One brick through the windows, and her fortress would come crashing down.

She made her decision. Grabbing the knife again from its hook, she walked out into the night.

The alley was empty.

"Are we close?"

"We're in the right district. She has to be within three blocks of here. My man said he saw her going back to her building on foot around eleven last night."

"But he didn't tell you which one it was?" Jake asked in exasperation.

"He didn't know," Nadam answered, his voice level.

"Great."

For the fifth time, Jake pulled the car around again to repeat their search pattern of the three blocks. *Maybe we missed her.*

Maybe they're not in the neighborhood tonight, she told herself. *Maybe I won't have any trouble at all.* Making a decision, she turned left instead of right, hoping to avoid the gang members. She walked fast, never looking back.

From an alley behind her, they emerged out of the shadows and into the foggy moonlight.

She heard the metallic click on the sidewalk behind her and whirled. The sound came from Vic's black leather boots as he walked toward her, followed by six other young men. She backed away slowly, then turned to walk faster. The others matched her stride.

A block away from the restaurant, she broke into a run, desperately hoping that she might escape them. They caught her within a minute.

"Why do you run? We haven't even said hello." Again Vic backed her up against a brick wall. He stood a few feet away, taking his time with her. "Why are you working in this district? You don't look Chinese to me."

"I-I needed a job."

A few of the toughs laughed at her response. Vic's white teeth flashed in the moonlight.

"No one brought you here?"

"No, I came here myself. I didn't know I couldn't work anywhere I wanted to." She clutched the knife behind her back. Whipping it out, she jabbed toward the gang leader.

Vic didn't flinch. He calmly took a step away and smiled back at his friends. "Well, well, well. The girl's got herself a knife." He turned back to her and advanced menacingly. "Where are the others? Did they set you up as bait again and then leave you all alone?"

"I don't know what you're talking about! I act alone. I don't hang with gangs. To me, you're all a bunch of losers."

Vic clutched his stomach, pretending to laugh. "Such a little woman with such a big attitude!" The smile fell from his face, his voice becoming deadly serious. "We lost two of our brothers last night on account of you." He took a step toward Emily, and she swung the knife wildly in his direction. Expertly he struck her arm as it passed, causing her to flinch and drop the knife. "What will protect you now?"

"Come on, Victor," one of the gang members spoke up. "Maybe she's telling the truth. Let's get outta here. I got a bad feeling."

"You challengin' me?"

Vic turned to face his companion, and Emily took advantage of the opportunity. She broke into a run, but Victor was quickly after her. Closing the distance between them, he grabbed the back of her shirt, pulling her to a stop. He swung her against the building wall.

Emily's head struck the bricks, and she sank to her knees. Victor leaned over her, catching his breath as the others ran up behind them.

They rounded another corner and spotted the group in their headlights. With a screech, Jake brought the car to a stop.

"Emily!" Jake yelled. He was out of the car in seconds, ignoring the other men's pleas for him to stop. Jake saw only Emily and that she was hurt.

He spanned the twenty feet between the car and the gang members without stopping and pushed them aside. Stunned, they watched as he walked directly over to the woman, picked her up in his arms, and began walking away.

"Hey!" a young man yelled, enraged. He was obviously the leader.

Jake turned to look at him, his eyes steely flat.

"You can't just walk off with her, man. You have me to face first." He pointed proudly to his chest.

Jake looked at him straight on, his eyes filled with fire. "I've crossed four states looking for this woman. I haven't slept in days. Now I'm taking her home. I've been through too much to lose her now." His father and Steve Nadam moved to stand with him. "If you're the one who did this to Emily," Jake continued, "you *definitely* do not want to take me on."

The guy stood still, sizing up the situation.

"Come on, Vic. They probably called the cops anyway," urged one of his friends.

Angrily the gang leader spit in their direction and then turned to face his cohorts. Without a word, he walked away. The group faded into the dim light of the streets and quickly disappeared.

Jake turned and walked to the car with Emily still in his arms.

Emily roused. "Jake? Jake, is it really you?"

"It's me, Em."

"I'm so sorry, Jake. So sorry."

"Promise me you won't ever run away again."

"Let's go home, Jake. Take me home."

Chapter Sixteen

*C*ome with me," Jake whispered into Emily's ear with a sparkle in his eye. "I'm taking you out to dinner."

She smiled at him and then looked at Mary from across the kitchen counter. The older woman nodded in approval.

Emily took off her apron, and Jake put his arm around her and led her onto the porch.

"Wait here," he said. She stood on the steps and closed her eyes, filling her lungs with the crisp autumn air. When she opened them again a few seconds later, she saw Jake trotting up on Cyrano, with Tana at his side. Emily smiled as Jake pulled up beside her.

"So, where are you taking me to dinner by horseback?"

"You'll see."

They rode for two miles and then turned off into a field of grain. There, in the midst of the golden wheat, stood a table with a white linen cloth, silver candlesticks, and two place settings. Emily looked at Jake in bewilderment.

He dismounted and looked at her tenderly. "Mademoiselle." Jake took her hand and helped her down and then seated her at the table with a deep bow.

As if on cue, Dirk's Jeep appeared on the horizon and turned into the field, kicking up dust as its wheels disappeared among the wheat

305

stalks. Emily watched in amazement as the vehicle pulled up beside them and Rachel and Dirk hopped out, each clad in a white apron. With napkins draped over their arms, they quickly served the couple and then were gone, smiling broadly as they drove away.

Emily laughed. "I guess I'm not dressed for the occasion," she said as she looked down at her jeans, T-shirt, and denim jacket.

"You look perfect," Jake said. He lit the candles just as the sun dipped behind mountains colored by deep rust, orange, and gold foliage. He and Emily looked at their plates and surveyed the wonderful meal the Tanners had picked up at a new café in town: sautéed chicken and vegetables, rice pilaf, and pumpkin soup.

"Pretty racy food for these parts," Emily said appreciatively.

"I thought you'd like it," Jake said.

They bowed their heads, and Jake offered up a blessing for the food and for God's answer to their prayers. As they ate, they smiled at each other between bites, rarely talking but feeling utterly happy.

After they finished, Emily leaned back and sighed deeply. "Thank you, Jake." Her eyes were bright as she gazed at the man she loved. "I feel so blessed to have you in my life." She looked at the valley, the mountains, and the sunset that surrounded them. "I'm so thankful to be home."

"And I'm so thankful to have you home."

She paused, hating to ruin the moment, but needing to know the truth. "What about your parents, Jake?"

"They'll come around. Eventually Mother will see you as I do. Until then, we'll be family. Dad already likes you. My sister will love you too. We'll go visit her in Maine. You'll see."

Emily looked across the table to her romantic, handsome, perfect love. She reached out to take his hand. "I'm glad to hear it, Jake, because I'm never leaving you again. I can't. I love you too much. It hurts too much to be away from you."

"I know the feeling," he said, then paused. "Emily, could this be your home forever?"

She squeezed his hand, taking a chance. "If you're by my side."

"Forever, Emily Walker," Jake said, relishing the words. "Forever."

Dear Reader,

Thank you for picking up the re-release of the first book I ever wrote! Eight years ago I got a job with a Christian publisher and an offer on this novel in the same day (it was a banner afternoon!). *Refuge* began with a story related to me by a friend. Sandra had a girlfriend who actually answered an ad in Wyoming's *Rancher's Journal* and became a Rachel-type bride. Spawned by my love of Montana, my enjoyment of romance, and my desire to point women back to the Ultimate Source of comfort, *Refuge* was born.

Ten novels later, with more than 700,000 books in print, I'm still at it. It's taken awhile to consider myself a real writer rather than a hobbyist, but I'm getting there, I think. God is so good to me! I'm spending this year concentrating on my family, my fiction, and my faith—hoping to really take time and be with the Savior.

I hope you enjoy these light retreats from real life in the Full Circle series. The others that follow are all connected in some way, showing how we are all one big body of believers, regardless of how spread out we are. It is for that reason that I so enjoy hearing from readers. If you would care to find out more about me or my books, check out my Web site: www.lisatawnbergren.com or write me a snail-mail letter in care of WaterBrook Press and let me know what you thought of this book. I consider you all dear friends in my own full circle—who knows how many ways we are connected?—and appreciate each one of you.

I would be remiss if I didn't mention my friend Ginia Hairston and tell you how she gently broke it to me (after *Refuge* was in print) that Cyrano, Dirk's stallion, should be gelded and that there's no way, no matter how skinny one is nor how romantic, two people could fit in one saddle. Hopefully I got some horse sense kicked into me in this rewritten draft of *Refuge*. Thanks, Ginia.

Every blessing,

Lisa Tawn Bergren

Write to Lisa Tawn Bergren
c/o WaterBrook Press
2375 Telstar Drive, Suite 160
Colorado Springs, CO 80920

or e-mail her through her Web site:
www.LisaTawnBergren.com

TREASURE (Book 4) • Ever since she roomed with Bryn Bailey *(Pathways)* at Harvard, nautical archaeologist Dr. Christina Alvarez has been obsessed with finding her ancestor's sunken treasure ship. Only one man—Caribbean treasure hunter Mitch Crawford—can help her, and he refuses to do so. But Christina's fight to win Mitch over may lead them both to a treasure more valuable than either of them ever dreamed.

CHOSEN (Book 5) • As supervisor of the Solomon's Stables dig in Jerusalem, archaeologist Alexana Roarke—grad-school friend of Christina Alvarez *(Treasure)*—knows she is in significant danger. Yet she will let nothing impede her excavation, not even the concern of handsome, world-renowned news correspondent Ridge McIntyre. Her stubbornness, however, could cost Alexana her life—and a future with the man she loves.

FIRESTORM (Book 6) • As a forest-fire-fighting crew boss, Montanan Reyne Oldre—friend to Rachel Tanner and Beth Morgan *(Refuge)*—once led a team of courageous firefighters into a blaze that ended in tragedy. Now that the flames of love have begun to flicker between her and smokejumper Logan McCabe, Reyne must face the fears from her past and battle the raging firestorm that burns in her soul.